Miranda Blue Calling

Miranda Blue Calling

MICHELLE CURRY WRIGHT

AVON
TRADE

An Imprint of HarperCollins*Publishers*

HarperCollins books may be purchased for education, business, or sales promotional use. For information please write: Special Markets Department, HarperCollins Publishers Inc., 10 East 53rd Street, New York, NY 10022.

FIRST EDITION

Designed by Elizabeth M. Glover

Library of Congress Cataloging-in-Publication Data

Wright, Michelle Curry.
  Miranda Blue calling / Michelle Curry Wright.—1st ed.
    p. cm.
ISBN 0-06-056143-2
1. Women—Colorado—Fiction. 2. Aged—Services for—Fiction. 3. Greenhouse gardening—Fiction. 4. Loneliness—Fiction. 5. Colorado—Fiction. I. Title.

PS3573.R5372M57 2004
813'.6—dc21   2003051836

04 05 06 07 08 JTC/RRD 10 9 8 7 6 5 4 3 2 1

In memory of my parents,
Jeannine and Jim

ACKNOWLEDGMENTS

Thanks again and again to Liv (and Bill) at the Blumer Literary Agency, for their loyalty and diligence through the years. I am very much indebted to Lyssa Keusch, my editor at Avon Books, for her interest, savvy, and care. Thanks also to Sara Schwager, my copyeditor, who said just the right things at just the right time.

# PROLOGUE

One sweltering summer day, a day hot enough to melt butter, wax, or even brainwaves, Miranda Blue was sitting in an air-conditioned tearoom off Lexington Avenue—up one of those tree-lined side streets perpetually choked with traffic—when a truck rolled by, the word HARKEN painted in inky black six foot script on the side.

Harken? Miranda tipped her head with interest to see who might be steering an itinerant billboard through city gridlock, hauling a word around as if asking onlookers to listen, to take note. For her part, Miranda had taken note not only of taking note but also of the driver's rakish good looks.

"Are you listening to what I'm saying?" Miranda's sister Vivianne, who sat opposite her, rapped an insistent spoon sharply on Miranda's teacup and then put the utensil down. She had just returned from another business engagement—in Delhi, India, this time—and was brimming with narrative, as usual. She followed Miranda's gaze to the truck before Miranda could pretend to be looking someplace else.

"I'm listening," Miranda said. But she had already noted the driver's five o'clock shadow and jet-black hair. His rolled-up shirtsleeves. And the fact that rather than cursing traffic, he was thrumming his Popsicle lazily to the beat of music Miranda could not hear. Jazz, she wagered. Something cool but sizzling hot.

"I heard everything you said. You don't think your trip could technically be called a success," she recapped, "because instead of focusing on Garuda, the winged messenger of Vishnu, and doing research after your presentation like you promised yourself, you got all caught up in the winged elephants of India, which led you to Dumbo, which irritated you because Walt Disney isn't someone you necessarily want to research let alone quote. Even if Dumbo's ears have popped up—so to speak—several times in your research, sometimes even angled scientifically. Someday the Dumbo paper, you daresay, will have to be written." Miranda had a knack for recapitulation but really only liked flaunting it around her sister.

Vivianne, draped in a recently purchased sari of crimson and gold, fussed with the bunching material at her shoulder. "Your parroting," she began, "should be put to better use. Don't think that I didn't notice you gawking at Al Pacino in that truck." She closed her eyes as if willing the tediousness to be gone. "Of *all* the eligible men in New York . . . a city rife with suitors." She opened her eyes again and stared, unblinking, at her sister. "Can't Lydia arrange a meeting with one of her ilk? She hobnobs with income-producing offbeat types—" Again, the eyes closed, this time to beseech the patron saint of impossible wishes.

Lydia, Miranda's roommate on and off since their NYU

days, worked on Madison Avenue. "She hobnobs with opportunities not people," Miranda said. "She'll suffer the suits—I prefer my ilk in jeans. So unless I bumped into an income producer on casual Friday or on the weekend . . ." She let the words trail off. "Well, you see my quandary."

"Your quandary is you slaver over truck drivers."

"I'm not slavering. I was just laying my eyes on what was directly in front of me."

"Yes, well, next you'll be laying more than your eyes on what becomes yet another ill-suited, ill-fated liaison. It pains me to utter such tiring words."

This exchange typified Vivianne's brief and regular layovers in the city. After recapping her most recent engagement, she would criticize Miranda's directionless life and hopelessly predictable taste in men, implore her to move back to San Francisco, where they'd grown up, or to Colorado where they'd vacationed as children, then finally bring the reunion to a close with a gift—something beautiful, costly, and meant to assuage her own guilt while tempering the critical blows she'd delivered to her sister.

Not that she wasn't right about Miranda's undistinguished six-year city girl stint, or that Miranda didn't need to hear, one more time, how incomprehensible it was that the daughter of an ethnodendrologist and a renowned costume jeweler—and "clever in her own right"—had not been able to come up with anything more original than a string of glorified receptionist jobs. Then there was all that wasted free time: Why didn't she join book groups, go to lectures and plays, frequent the halls of some of the finest museums in the world? Where was self-improvement, Vivianne wanted to know, Miranda's *engagement* in the changing, thronging world?

Miranda frequented Village bookshops, vintage clothing stores, dusty antique warehouses, and Eastern European delis. She liked old movies, old vinyl music, even old magazines, all of which Vivianne viewed, when coupled with the blatant lack of a career trajectory, as "mildewy and depressing."

Vivianne, after all, had managed to spin herself into an authority on mythical winged creatures (a double major in biology and classics and, Miranda liked to add, a doctorate in self-promotion). In Delhi, she had spoken on "Air as a Medium for Creatures of Legend, Myth and Fantasy." Her skills ran the gamut, however, from organizing Hollywood theme parties to judging airbrush logos for the Fantasy Readers of America bookclub.

But then Vivianne had ten critical years on Miranda. She was already thirty-one when an icy interstate had taken the lives of their parents. Vivianne was old enough to have set a life in forward motion while Miranda, in the middle of her senior year in college, suddenly found herself riding trains all day, then city buses, and finally the Staten Island ferry whose smooth ride over the dark and churning water seemed somehow to say everything there was to say about life.

She returned to school eager for more order in her life. "Why not dentistry?" she asked Lydia. "What's more straightforward than a finite number of enamel pegs all huddled together in a manageably-sized orifice?" That's when Lydia staged an intervention, counselors and professors working together to get Miranda graduated in her default major, Urban Studies. "It doesn't matter if you can memorize all twelve cranial nerves and their functions in two minutes flat," Lydia said. "You weren't meant to fix teeth."

Once officially graduated, it took Lydia half a week to find an entry-level job as an assistant to a junior copy-writer's assistant. Miranda was offered her first receptionist job by a woman in Chinatown who had mistakenly gotten Miranda's whole fish with scallions instead of her extra spicy lo mein.

And here, half a dozen jobs later, Lydia was still success-fully clawing her way to the top of her chosen field, while Miranda was still flailing, still suffering Vivianne's self-imposed roles of surrogate parent and advice-giving thera-pist. Sometimes—at the present moment, for instance—it irked Miranda to the point of her doing something just for the sake of irking Vivianne back. She glanced at the truck's driver—who just happened to be looking her way, orange Popsicle tipped and dripping suggestively in the heat—and sent a lip curl his way. This had the surprising effect of cat-apulting Vivianne, who had seen it, out the door and toward the truck window, the entire bolt of red fabric wafting under the spiked heels of her sling back pumps.

Half hidden behind her water glass, Miranda watched him listen, smile (cruelly revealing the suggestion of dimples), and take out a business card, which he handed Vivianne.

"Here," Vivianne said, thrusting the card at her sister upon her return. "Here's all the information you need to make yet another go of yet another frittering waste of a re-lationship."

Miranda, letting the comment slide, fingered the card. "John Franco Costa, President. Sound systems for wed-dings, wakes, fiestas, galas, fêtes, and other events. *Harken.*" What was the message here? To harken to him personally, or to Vivianne's melodramatic little object lesson?

John Costa, meanwhile, was mouthing something to her. Me? She crooked her index finger to her chest. He nodded. Cars had begun to honk. He made a phone sign with his thumb and little finger. Then the sign of a cup, pinkie up. Drinking tea. You and me? Another *Call me* sign. Traffic continued to honk, more insistently she thought, and she shrugged at him, then nodded a *Maybe*.

After tying off a portion of her insubordinate yardage, Vivianne whipped the card from Miranda's hands. "I wager he's first and foremost a musician," she said. "Had the look. And we don't have to go over what *they're* like. Just the type you like, and this is just the way you meet them, right? Although now that he might be interested, you're probably not. Oh, the predictability of it all—"

"Spare me, *please*," Miranda said, refusing to acknowledge the truth in her words. "First of all, I do sometimes meet guys the regular way. There was Julius, that messenger from work—you actually *liked* him."

"I'd wager that one has his own company by now. He only held your attention in his temporary Bohemian trappings and too-busy-for-you manner—the most enticing of Miranda lures."

"You think that your way—meeting men at conferences or men who come to listen to you speak—is better? You just want to be worshipped."

"And you want to worship, Miranda. Yes, which *is* more advantageous?"

A petite, middle-aged woman in a straw-hat had approached the table, and plopped her purse down as if about to start unpacking it. "I couldn't help but overhear," she said, cool but courteous. "You're not exactly speaking in hushed tones."

"Sorry." Miranda's apology and heightened color were genuine. Only with Vivianne did this sort of thing happen, this calling attention to herself, getting everyone involved, making a scene. Vivianne had already taken her tea water back twice to ask them to boil it *fully*. And that *sari*. Miranda's flowered pedal pushers and '50s bowling shirt were positively subdued compared to her sister's getup.

"But," the woman continued, hands gripping the clasp on the alligator bag, "I wouldn't call that man. If it were *me*." She looked at Miranda and smiled, pained, as if forced by some code of honor to speak up. She wore tiny cameos in her ears. "I was dizzied by that demeanor once myself. You never end up getting what you need from that kind of man."

Fearing Vivianne would reach into her purse for the obligatory tip she gave everyone from counter help to theater ushers, Miranda thanked the woman, and, indicating her sister with a sideways toss of her head, said, "And just for the record, *her* boyfriends aren't exactly lessons in humility either. Even if they are uglier than mine." Their mother would have been about this woman's age. "Won't you join us?" she asked. It seemed like the right thing to do.

So a stranger named Janet sat down and politely listened as Vivianne waxed on about Bollywood and Indian heat, and Miranda pitched in with recent developments at *Scribbler, The Magazine of Personal Graffiti and Journaling* where she worked. To give her credit, Janet never once mentioned Miranda's eye color (pale gray, and the source of much commentary) or hair (very short, prematurely flecked with white, and another tired out topic).

"If you can't listen to me, listen to her," Vivianne said the minute they were alone again. Then she pulled out a tissue-wrapped gift from her shopping bag and put it in front of Miranda. Four inches of silver Indian bangles, hammered with images of women with wings. "You never told me about submitting an article to your magazine," Vivianne said. "Anyway, short layover. I'm leaving today. These are to remind you to find your wings, Mimi. Sounds like you might have already started doing that. I should stop being so hard on you."

Miranda slipped the bangles on, the cool weight tugging pleasantly at her left wrist. "I will find my wings," she said, momentarily under her sister's spell and resolved to do better, *be* better.

But it wasn't wings Miranda needed at that point, it was grounding, more weight, something gluing her to the terra firma beneath her feet. She'd lied about that article just to sound like a productive person, someone going somewhere. And the echo of Janet's warning lasted a mere seventy-two hours before being sucked irretrievably into the black hole of good advice never taken.

Yes, she called the number on the card.

Not to spite Vivianne or Janet, she told herself, but to take responsibility for her own actions. If he was a bad boy—"a Lothario, a rebel, a user, a taker, a Mr. Aloof, a mama's boy or a Peter Pan," she revisited Viv's list in her head—she wanted to be able to read the signs, take control, and turn on her heel. But that didn't happen either.

After meeting for Turkish coffee in the Village, John took

her to the Strand where, from acres and acres of books, he began selecting random spines, cracking them open, and then reading whatever serendipitous wisdom was meant to be revealed. Bibliomancy, he called it. For a grand finale, he unwedged a leather-bound and tattered copy of *Moby Dick*, the yellowed pages of which fell open in his hands like the parting Red Sea. "Dig this," he said, scanning the text before launching into a sermon on harpoons and sperm whales.

Well, if literary giant Herman Melville was going to give her the go-ahead from the great beyond for whatever activities *harpooning* and *sperm whales* brought to mind, Miranda reasoned, she was going to take it.

She never questioned John's wanting to meet only during lunch at her apartment when Lydia wasn't home. His apartment in Hoboken was too far, he said, and nearly always overrun with either roommates or musicians.

Something else might have tipped her off though. The fact that he still used his roach clip from the eleventh grade. Or how cute he thought it was to leave the shoelaces of his black-and-white Converse sneakers untied. She might have realized that all it really took for a man to make practical use of great literature was a pre-arranged turned-down page and someone gullible enough to fall for it.

Eventually it was Lydia, both suspicious and loyal, who found him listed not in Hoboken but Newark and called his home number pretending to need a karaoke system. She was the one who reached his wife Valerie, once a singer, who had become an elementary school music teacher in order to take some of the strain off John. "He has roommates all right, a wife and child," Lydia snorted, adding that he was good in bed because a man cheating on his wife was always good in bed, at least for as long as it still felt dangerous.

"You're making this up," Miranda said feebly, "because you never liked him to begin with."

"Uh-uh." Lydia had strategically taken her to a well-known men's lifestyle magazine party to tell her this—where not only the men were abundant but the flow of champagne and obscene piles of caviar. "No, I didn't even have to meet him not to like him, but I didn't have to make it up, either. This," she gave the grand gesture towards all the men in the room, "is how we celebrate getting rid of someone like John fucking Franco fucking Costa. This is what we do." She picked up a pale cracker and gave it four loads of fish eggs with the tiny spoon.

Miranda attempted a brave laugh but shriveled up inside, felt all of New York shrivel up, too, as if the city, a giant helium balloon of illusion, had begun to leak its hot air and would soon set her down with a thud. Maybe it was time to leave.

A few short months later, Lydia actually had occasion to order up that karaoke system for Miranda's surprise going away party. She made sure Miranda arrived drunk enough to sing all the Doris Day tunes she sang so regularly at home. And when Miranda received a standing ovation for "Everybody Loves a Lover," Lydia pointed to John Costa, fumbling with his shoelaces in the back, and said, "You can do better than that." *Yes*, Miranda thought, *you would think so*.

In early October, right before moving out, Miranda took the Number 6 train uptown and made her way to that same tearoom where she sat at the window, sipping and watching leaves fall on the ever-present pile-up of vehicles. She thought about Janet and her purse full of advice, and, needing someone older and wiser in her own life, imagined the woman with her now.

"I tried to warn you," Janet might have said. "But really didn't expect you to listen."

"You didn't?"

"No. People only listen when they're ready; and even then, it's not someone's advice that ends up being instructional, it's life itself, whether you follow the advice or not. You had to learn about that pretty-boy by calling him."

"You're judging him solely on the basis of his looks—"

"No, I didn't like his deplorable table manners, either—the way he licked his knife. Didn't like the Virgin Mary he wore like a lure around his neck. And no matter how handsome he was, I didn't like the way he didn't kiss you enough, neither in bed nor out of it. But I still say you had to find these things out for yourself."

No truer imaginary words had ever been uttered.

So *much* had depended on Miranda's not listening to Vivianne and Janet about John. Had she not been involved with him, she would not have even considered moving away. There would have been no caretaking one of Lydia's client's second homes in Aspen, which had eventually translated into a business of her own.

Had Miranda not started her own answering service, she would not have had any reason to listen to Lydia and advertise it in the local paper, which is how she met Keith Muckler. And without Keith—well, lots of things. She would not have reclaimed ownership of the two puppies she had given him, or sold her business, or left Aspen after just two and a half years. She would have had no reason to seek out new frontiers with one thing in mind: to eliminate men from her life, and to do so by eliminating people. Without losing herself, she could never have hoped to be found. Or something like that.

To the general public (including her sister and her best friend) she announced she was going on a man fast and that she'd found a place in the middle of nowhere to do it.

But she never really told them or anyone else the whole story until much later.

That wind! Miranda's foot tapped restlessly on her hardwood floor as window casings rattled and trees lashed the roof.

That wind, snaking around, then slamming into things, as if spring were the Pandora's box of seasons. Could the fickle airstream be anyone's friend? Miranda didn't know. A breeze could become a whirling dervish. Any number of things might reel up and blow, corkscrewing past the window and out of sight, then just as suddenly as it had heaved and huffed at everything in its way, stop—leaving nothing of itself but bits and pieces of airborne matter drifting slowly out of the sky like fallout after a parade.

She glanced up from her desk at long-lived scraps of trash skipping and sailing fitfully along. She had been known to run outside and grab at the flying papers, catch them, and hold them up greedily, as if hoping to read what someone had sent her on the wind. Forget the dull and lumbering delivery of regular mail: This was immediate, magical, surprising! Besides, she rarely got regular mail.

Another violent gust, and dirt flew up in eddies. Down the road, a dust devil wound itself up, tilting and coiling, until it disappeared. Everything attached to the trembling earth—including the brittle box of sticks Miranda called her home—seemed fragile, ready to pull free and fly off into the nether world of the Southwest, a world of gales, breezes, breaths, and currents, of whipping winds, trees that bent in all directions at once, plains that waved and parted, and a powdery grit that swirled about like a specter.

Otnip was just the kind of place where a person—or even a house—might be dropped from the sky. Perched on the far eastern edge of a massive geologic zone spanning four states called the Colorado Plateau, Otnip teetered precariously on the brink of several worlds. To the west and parts arid stood soaring mesas, desert arches, spires, cliffs, chasms, and canyons, all red and purple and rust. To the east the jagged and towering San Juan Mountains rose up, a dozen fourteen-thousand-foot peaks among them.

A sleepy town of bean fields and tin gray silos, Otnip was the uneasy place of truce, a neutral zone where mountain and desert collided, winds commingling in every which way at the crossroads. Though nothing ever seemed to change, nothing, either, seemed destined to settle, this uncomfortable transience being the thing that had struck Miranda at the beginning. Now? Well, having become acquainted with the power and relentlessness of the wind, half of her struggled against it still while the rest of her succumbed. Disconcerting as it was, this was the allure of Otnip.

Adjusting her headset, Miranda fingered through her box of filed index cards for Evalina Peguy's and dialed the

Trinidad, Colorado, number, her fifth number of the morning. It was ten-thirty.

"It's me, Evalina. Got your cup of tea ready?"

"Oh, hi, Miranda," came the voice of an old but eager woman. "I'm ready for you, dear. I'm drinking oolong this morning with lots of milk and honey." Miranda's heart leapt at the pleasure in the shaky voice even though she would hear the same kind of gratitude somewhere between fifteen and forty times a day.

"Is there a cat on your lap?" Miranda inquired.

"Both of them actually. Rheumatism's fierce this morning. Someone really should invent a lubricant for bones." She cleared her throat. "Anyway, dear, I've been reviewing my I Ching for this morning." She had always pronounced it "eye ching."

"What does March 27 have in store?" Miranda pictured the ninety-two-year-old, frail as a dried-flower arrangement, sitting in her rocker with two armfuls of vibrating fur. Not everyone sent a photo, but Evalina had seen to it after her first or second week with Miranda. A professional had taken this one, one who'd made a house call to do the job. Studying it again, Miranda smiled at the puckered portrait of self-reliance topped off by a San Francisco Giants baseball cap. The lipstick was perfect, as was the eyebrow pencil. She loved this woman.

"Well, I was meditating on Herb's divorce—break's my heart so every time I think of it. Why, those two have been together twenty-eight years. Had my dear grandchildren together! *It's okay, Tick-tock. Talulah, be nice to your brother.*" She shuffled, rearranging the cats.

"The marriage is over, they both declare. Well, what can

15

you *say* to that, Miranda? The world can be a lonely place, let me tell you. Well, you probably know that, out there in the middle of godforsa—"

"Maybe they're lonelier *with* each other," Miranda interrupted. Lately, Evalina had been asking lots of questions about Otnip, swearing to Miranda that she could not find it on her map of Colorado. Just how small was it, anyway? That's what she wanted to know.

Miranda had explained that yes, it was quite a bit smaller than Aspen. That in Aspen you could buy good chocolate and go to a different restaurant every night for nearly a month. Not that she ever did, she'd told Evalina, all that had been wasted on her. It was meant to make Otnip seem like the right place for Miranda to end up, but Evalina had said, "Well, what *did* you do there, dear?" When Miranda had answered, *Caretaking—not a person but a house*, Evalina was quick. "Oh. That sounds lonely, too. Didn't you have a boyfriend?" That was when she'd had to mention Keith just for the sake of explaining where her dogs had come from. There were other men, she'd said, but she'd gotten pickier. Besides, she had added with feeling, in Aspen she'd rediscovered skiing and hiking and the deep blue Colorado sky.

"You can even be lonely surrounded by people, you know," she said now.

There was a long pause, and then a slurp of tea. "This morning I tossed the pennies and got Khan, The Deep Above, The Deep Below. Which is all about learning from and living with crisis—" Another pause and another amplified slurp.

Miranda meanwhile had opened her own I Ching book

to No. 29, called The Abysmal in her translation. She had had no prior experience with the ancient Chinese *Book of Changes*, but it had certainly seemed the perfect choice for her client. Ancestral. Dignified. Complex and obscure. Evalina had expressed an interest in things esoteric but had also stated categorically, "Nothing flaky." Now, she had come to depend on the ritual of throwing three pennies six times.

"Does yours say anything to clarify what I've said?"

"Pretty much the same," Miranda read. "Misfortune if the first line is a moving line. The danger is in habitual danger."

Evalina sighed. "Well," she said, "there it is—"

"Really?" Miranda admired Evalina's instant synthesis, her clear insight into the messages.

"You can't live in a permanent state of crisis. Something's got to give, as they say. Poor Jippy. I've always loved that woman. And I know what it's like to be a woman *alone*."

Evalina rang off before her minutes were up, just as she always did. Miranda never once had had to say, "I've got to be going."

"Call me tomorrow, Miranda, dear. I need a check-in. And be good to yourself."

After Miranda heard the click at the other end, she absentmindedly scribbled in *Jippy* on Evalina's card, and then *Look up Herbert in Menlo Park?* What would she say though? She had no business interfering in family matters. She could ask about the real status of Evalina's health, ask for the name of her doctor. She might be better off asking Jippy, it sounded like.

No. She was supposed to be a professional—compassionate, giving, and helpful, but not a member of the family. Sometimes, with Evalina for instance, it was tempting. Fortunately, not all of her clients had nestled so close to her heart. Of course, they needed her, which is why she'd started the business in the first place. Just as she had predicted, there were plenty of old folks who needed company in the state of Colorado. The business was thriving.

Only as her fingers were punching the number for Agatha Colgate of Leadville did she realize that Evalina had requested a call the next day, a check-in. Why so soon? And why the repeated mention of being alone?

"Hi, Mrs. Colgate, it's me Miranda!" She upped the volume on professional cheerfulness for this client.

"Miranda," the irritated voice replied. "I couldn't remember whether we decided on Luke 14, *Jesus Heals a Sick Man*, or 15, *The Lost Sheep*. Well, I read them both, but I probably could have done better with only one. Concentrated on it better. Which one was it, Luke 14 or 15? Which one did you read?"

Agatha fretted and argued over nearly everything, made admirable mountains of puny molehills. Only then could she ring off feeling newly fortified, frisky enough to work her word searches and crossword puzzles.

Miranda countered with steely brightness. "Hang on, Mrs. Colgate, I need to adjust my chair for a sec—" The windy trance had interrupted her state of preparedness. Normally the index card would have been out, the reading material open in front of her. Flipping quickly through *Good News for Modern Man, The New Testament in Today's English Version*, she stopped at Luke 15 and scanned quickly.

"It was Luke 15, *The Lost Sheep, The Lost Coin and The Lost Son.*

"Well, I read 14 more carefully, because it was first. But I guess I could discuss 15 if that's what you read—"

"Chapter 14 would be fine, too—"

"I'll bet you just opened the Good Book right before dialing my number anyway . . . I've always said 'An ounce of preparation is worth—' " She stopped, stuck in the scramble of proverbs. "A pound of intelligence," she finished.

This patter would go on for several minutes as the retired schoolteacher continued to scold Miranda and make excuses for herself. Miranda had some time ago suggested they reverse roles and let Agatha be the teacher again.

"What would be the good in that?" she had snapped. "I'm supposed to be the one gaining spiritual insight here!"

Meanwhile, Miranda scribbled *Luke 15* on the daily notation while entertaining thoughts of different conversations, even the least bit more spontaneous.

A crumpled wrapper flew by on the wind, the quick evocation of a Baby Ruth bar, something Miranda had not eaten in a very long time. "Can I ask you something, Mrs. Colgate?" In grade school she'd particularly favored both O Henrys and Baby Ruths.

Her silence was followed by guarded apprehension. "Ask me what."

"Well. I was just wondering what you yourself remembered most about being in school—"

Another pause. "What does that have to do with anything?" Suspicion listed toward paranoia. It was almost funny, the idea that Miranda's prying was anything but friendly.

"I'm just interested. You're off the clock, by the way; this

19

part of the call is on me. But somehow you got me thinking about my school years. Reminiscing."

More silence. "I'm not sure what you're getting at. I was
a normal child, not particularly smart. Had to work hard
for each and every good grade I got." She paused, and Miranda remained quiet. Finally, carefully, as if daring to recall the past, she said, "I did fail one class in high school.
Art." The word had a dirty sound the way she said it. "I
couldn't understand perspective to save my life. I bet you
never even had to take it, did you?"

"Actually, we spent a few days on it in geometry," Miranda answered. "It was hard," she added. "But then I
passed too many notes in math class to begin with."

"*That* doesn't surprise me," Agatha lunged. "I was always
very hard on note-passers. Their shenanigans were read
aloud to the rest of the class." Victory gilding her words,
she was able to sign off having won the upper hand.

Perspective, Miranda scribbled on the card after hanging
up, then *Shenanigans.* It pleased her that Agatha might be
reminiscing right now, allowing herself to float on the
blow-up raft of memory rather than jamming round letters
into the square boxes of her crosswords.

When the wind kicked up again, its wheeze was joined
by the shrill cry of a hawk piercing the air from high
above. Sometimes the loneliness of her clients—their at-
tempts at connection—touched Miranda so sharply, tenderness would sprout in her raw and pink like new skin
under a burn. She took off her headset and grabbed her
canvas coat at the door before stepping outside. With a
hand to her brow, she looked far into the distance, both

content to be standing where she was and longing to be somewhere else.

Eventually, her eyes fell to the ground and she began to walk the property, intermittently stooping to pick up the accumulated trash. There was that wrapper, sure enough a Baby Ruth. An empty windowed envelope postmarked February 12 of this year. A crumpled pink napkin. An entire page from the Pigeon newspaper, dated October 2, 1998 (where had it been all those months?). A plastic bag with handles containing the receipt for a twenty-ounce Coke and a bag of Bugles from Go-Mart. A fairly large piece of trash had blown up against the old toolshed, and Miranda made her way over to pick it up. Another receipt, this one for six bags of plant nutrient, signed by her closest neighbor (her only neighbor, in fact) who lived directly across the street in a house very much like hers. Identical, people liked to say, though she wouldn't know, she had never gotten close enough to his house to pit her doorknob, dormer, or floor plan against his.

"So now I'm picking up his trash, too?" she muttered, scanning the handwriting. The name at the top of the receipt above the address was *William Wordsworth Steadman, Try a Little Tenderness*. She had not known his full name before or the name of his company. For a moment, as she stared at the neat, vertical cursive, she thought this might be a different man than the one who lived across from her, a person who had paid attention in school, perhaps even pleased teachers. An upstanding, caring person. Just exactly the type of person she needed in her life.

Crumpling the paper, she recalled their last encounter just a few days ago. He had marched over in rubber

Wellington boots and a suede shirt, the kind of shirt any-one would want to stroke, just to test its nap, its velvet soft-ness, and he had brought her something, something equally soft—a pair of deerskin work gloves, the ones she was wearing now. "Here you go," he'd said. "If you're going to clean up your yard this spring and actually learn something about Otnip soil, you'll need the proper gloves. These are the only choice."

"Proper sounds like something my grandfather would have said." Instantly she had regretted the allusion to a family member, to her own grandpa whose name was also Billy and who had also been a gardener.

He, however, had picked up on it. "And your grandfather—I gather he's no longer with us—would have been right. I'm not leaving until you try them on."

"I'm busy." She had never told him her parents were no longer alive, either, that they'd died even before Grandpa Billy. She didn't want his sympathy, of all things—why had she ever mentioned her family?

"You don't look busy."

"In my head, I'm very busy. That's impossible to see, for obvious reasons."

"Well, I'm not busy. My head's empty. My body is idle. So I'll just wait here, until you relent and I know they fit and that you love them."

Pressing her lips together into the flat line of long-endured suffering, she had slipped her fingers into leather so soft it translated immediately into an extension of her own skin. In putting the other glove on it had felt—she dis-tinctly remembered—as though she were undressing for the man. The softness? The idea of fingers?

22

Billy had taken one of her hands in his then, studying the fit with satisfaction as he squeezed her fingers like newly cased sausages. "I went through all the men's extra-smalls to find the smallest. This pair had a good quarter inch on the others." He pulled out his own identical gloves and jammed them on. "You ever shook gloved hands before?"

No, she'd told him, convinced now that a hand was a private part that did in fact require covering.

He had taken her hand in his and given it a regular shake, then had grabbed her thumb and rotated their wrists, and, finally, had hooked their fingers, all quickly and deftly. And then he'd laughed. "Can't you feel the heat, babe? Even through the deerskin?"

"No," she had shaken her head again, "I feel no heat." But that had been a lie. She had felt the shock of heat, yes, and beyond that, when their eyes had met just for the briefest of moments, pale-sky gray colluding with his dusky amber, she'd felt something else that startled her—something that felt like simple affection.

She'd yanked her hand away too fast, she thought now, because he'd laughed again and shook his head.

While reorganizing the trash in her arms, with gloves she had slipped on as naturally as if she had done it her whole life, the plastic bag pulled free and did a couple somersaults on the ground before being sucked up into the wind again. Casually hypnotized, she watched as it flew up and over her head and into the stronger currents. Ducking phone lines, the bag traversed the street and, after negotiating several trees, landed up against the small window of Billy Steadman's foyer.

Miranda continued to stare at the bag. Much to her dismay, her consuming hope—the only thought she seemed to have in her head at all—was that her neighbor would not erroneously conclude, based on his examination of a vagrant piece of trash haphazardly clinging to his house, that she was the one snacking on Bugles and Coke. Like a person who didn't know how to take better care of herself or something.

 2

Back at her desk, Miranda fiddled briefly with a blank index card before writing a fresh name at the top. Then she dialed the number for a Mr. Gregory Gilliam Vogt in Denver.

A deep but singsongy voice answered after five rings. "Yes?"

She pictured him a bent and big-boned man, wearing a heavy wool cardigan and the kind of watch you still had to wind. "Hello, Mr. Vogt?" She took a stab and pronounced it "vote." "This is Miranda Blue, of Respect for Your Elders Companion Service—"

"Oh, yes—"

She liked his liveliness. "Mr. Vogt—"

"You can call me Gregory," he interrupted. "Everybody does, even m'own children. When they call me, that is. And they're Baptists. I saw your advertisement," he continued. "I don't generally do this sort of thing, but, well, something drew me to it."

The same ad—one she placed regularly in several retirement magazines—had snagged 95 percent of her clientele.

It read, "Respect for Your Elders Phone Service—A Little Talking Goes a Long Way. Daily Reminders, Meditations, and Reading Assignments. Let someone who cares care!" Of course, Lydia had come up with the copy. Underneath was her logo, the black silhouette of a raven with a piece of paper in its mouth, which she felt somehow nicely countered the enfeebling notion of a nursemaid. Though Vivianne had been the one to suggest the raven, Miranda had come to appreciate the smart, sly, and independent birds, which outnumbered people in Otnip by about thirty to one.

"There's no obligation, by the way, if this isn't what you had in mind. I bet Denver has its share of—"

"Where do you live, Ms. Blue?"

"Me?" She liked his cutting her off. "I live in the southwest corner of the state in a slip of a town called Otnip—"

"Pinto backwards," he said, laughing. "I know where it is, right there on the shoulders of Disappointment Valley."

"Yes!" Miranda couldn't hide her surprise. "I can't believe you know it. The fact that it's not on most maps drives the general population crazy. Not to mention my friends and family." Aunt Raye, who had called her once a month like clockwork from Carmel ever since the accident, said she'd had to special order a map in order to make sure Miranda hadn't invented the place.

"Well sure I know it," he answered. "Third-generation Coloradan. Used to have kin over there near Pigeon as a matter of fact. Ranchers. Mostly sheep, a few cattle. That was before reservation gambling, recreationists, and all the archeological fuss." He cleared his throat, coughing the cough of a smoker. "Anyway, sorry to interrupt."

"Not at all," answered Miranda, pleased someone could actually picture where she lived. After explaining the different calling options as well as her service for matching up seniors with similar inclinations, she asked if he had any specific hobbies or areas of interest.

"I whittle," he offered with some hesitation. "But I don't necessarily want to talk about that." She heard him cough even though his hand had covered the receiver, a cough that turned into a wheezing laugh. "I mean what's there to say?"

"True," Miranda wrote down *Whittles*. Then *What shapes?* "You kind of do that to get away from talking."

"Yes. But I don't whittle too much nowadays. I read though. I do read."

"Okay," she penciled in a few bullets, ready to fill them in. Her old cronies from *Scribbler* would have chided her for her lack of inspiration. Each of these cards should have had more character, more artistic definition. "Any particular subjects?" She added a flourish to the W of whittles.

"Oh, lately it's been about gardening. Sustainability, greenhousing, all that. I get magazines to keep up on it. Interesting stuff."

"So, you're a gardener?"

"No, no, dear. I don't garden, not anymore. I'm pretty much confined to a wheelchair now. Broke m'hip a couple months back, damn thing. No, I'm strictly an armchair gardener. A wheelchair gardener, that is. Except for the terrarium." He paused. "And my container tomatoes."

Miranda had learned never to offer sympathy for a condition that wasn't likely to change. She waited for him to continue.

"You know, if I had to do it today, I'd raise hothouse tomatoes. Everybody likes a good tomato. And they seem to be fast disappearing from the world as we know it . . . But do go on."

"That's okay," she said. "My closest neighbor happens to run a greenhouse. I believe hydroponics are involved." She was mentioning Billy strictly for the sake of the conversation. She had never brought him up before with any client. But no one had ever mentioned hydroponics before, either.

"Hydro farmer in Otnip? Na-a-a-ah," he countered. "But I know I'm taking up your time. I think you should tell me about your phone services."

"Yes," Miranda replied, glancing at her watch. "Good."

She was about to stretch out one leg and lift it onto the Formica slab of her desk when she caught a glimpse of a sheriff's vehicle flying toward her house at about eighty miles an hour. She straightened just as the vehicle slowed and pulled into Billy Steadman's driveway.

Oh God. What she had predicted, feared, been sure would happen, was happening right before her eyes. *They're coming to get him.*

"Ms. Blue?" the voice at the other end called her back.

"I'm sorry," she said, panicked, wondering what might have given him away. "A police car just went zooming by. Don't get a lot of that around here."

"Lights on?" Gregory's interest was immediate.

"Flashing away," she answered, thinking, *at about the same rate as my heartbeat.* "No siren though."

"Hmm." Miranda could hear him taking a drag on something, a pipe, possibly unlit. "Let me know what's gone down."

"I will," she said, forcing herself—as two officers got out of the car and ambled to Billy's door—to concentrate on her new client. "Now in terms of phone services, it's kind of a personalized thing. If you like routine, for instance, I call and I ask you if you've taken your pills, and what's going on in your favorite TV shows. When I get to know you, I talk to you about the things you need to talk about. One woman has me inquire about each of her four cats, same order, every time I call." She heard Gregory grunt in pleasure.

"Beatrice, Martha, Saint Augustine, and Doodle. Seriously." She'd also discovered it was good for seniors to glimpse the full spectrum of others out there, in all their splendid character finery, for, like hothouse flowers, they had no other blooms to compare themselves to. Shut-ins just became more and more exotic, for better or worse, with each passing day.

"Then," she continued, "the other kind of service is more cerebral. You tell me what kind of inspirational reading you like, and I sort of hold you to it, give you assignments. For instance, I read Norman Vincent Peale to one client, every day for five minutes. Lots of folks read the Bible or have it read to them, but just as many others have different tastes. Interesting things, too." No activity across the street. "I can order books and send them to you if you need them, and I can also send you a list of things others have chosen, just to give you some idea." Miranda paused to give the man a chance to speak.

"I'm not much on religion," he started off. "M'wife, she raised our children in her own faith and that was fine by me. Baptists, you know."

Miranda didn't know too much about Baptists, but they were beginning to sound interesting. "A lot of seniors aren't that religious, per se," she noted. "Do you have any idea what inspires you?"

"Well," he mused, "the poetry of both Walt Whitman and Ralph Waldo Emerson used to speak deeply to me. If I recall."

Her first poetry lover! "Good," she said. "Great! Now you understand," she felt the need to caution, "that I don't claim to be an expert on any of these subjects—not on the Old Testament, Chinese medicine, or Walt Whitman. I just create a program for you to follow, and we both follow it. With a little luck, we both come out ahead. Personally, however, I'm thrilled someone has finally indicated an interest in poetry, and I'd be happy to read it with you."

"Well, then, I think that's what I'd like to do. I don't have the materials though, not anymore, not since I moved."

"So I should order some Whitman and Emerson then?"

"If you would, Ms. Blue."

"Call me Miranda, please," she said. "If you feel comfortable doing that."

Having anticipated the mental and emotional drain of a new phone client, Miranda had given herself an hour until the next call, for lunch and for dog walking. Now, however, she could think only of what the police were doing at her neighbor's house.

She stood up and gazed across the street/road/highway, the only blacktopped surface in Otnip, whose faded yellow line divided Billy Steadman's world from hers. There was his pickup in its usual place and a squad car right next to it. What were they doing in there? Miranda wondered if the police wouldn't come knocking on her door next, the only door in the vicinity, to contact her, the only neighbor in the vicinity.

In a brief moment of projected melodrama she saw them boarding up her house and confiscating it. It would become a trash-attracting wind block again, a magnet for errant plastic bags.

Miranda had first seen her small, white, sweetly dilapidated house this way: abandoned, boarded up, lonely, and crooked.

In fact, it still appeared to lean and look precarious—given the lay of the land around it, the tilted metal T-shaped poles holding four laundry lines between them, and the unequivocally slanted stone steps leading to the bungalow-style porch.

But according to people who knew—Parker Pivey, her Realtor from Pigeon, Rocky Torez, her closest neighbor a mile to the west, and Vivianne, who'd been out to visit only once but knew everything about everything—the house couldn't be faulted.

"It looks crooked," Miranda had said to Vivianne, "like the wind has truly taken its toll."

"Optical illusion," her sister had corrected her. "It's standing up straight but everything around it is crooked." The statement was more a reflection on Vivianne than the house.

But, sure enough, when Rocky had carted over his five-foot antique level it measured out plumb. "It *looks* crooked," he'd said finally, beautifully dumbfounded in a way Vivianne could never be, "but the fucker is upright as can be. My compliments on your naked eye, Ms. Blue." He'd looked at Vivianne shrewdly then, as if in this one character trait everything could be summed up.

Miranda ended up buying the place along with twenty acres, the down payment for which constituted ten years of savings plus the sale of her Aspen business. Most normal middle-class children would have had inheritance money, or insurance money from the death of both parents, but Miranda's father had not been a believer in life insurance, or health insurance, or even retirement plans; he'd been a believer in trees. Every cent had gone to an undisclosed group in Indonesia for reforestation purposes. "You can take care of yourselves," he'd always said. "Trees cannot." Could she take care of herself? She didn't know the answer, but it had become one of her sister's favorite topics of deliberation.

"The original meaning of the word 'sequester' was *to give up for safekeeping,*" Vivianne had stated shortly after Miranda moved in. "I know you're doing it strictly to prevent yourself from making more bad decisions in the relationship department."

"What's the matter with that? Isn't that what you've wanted all along? For me to look inward? Give myself some time?"

"I didn't suggest you fall off the face of the earth and regret if I ever gave that impression. The only way to learn about yourself in relationships is to have them. Bad ones teach as much as good. Maybe you need to rebel against dad a little longer—even if he is dead—before you get over it. You'd need people for that though."

"What about your rich-men addiction? You haven't gotten over *that*." Vivianne's beau of two years, Ivo, an entomologist from a wealthy Czech family, had given her a Volkswagen Beetle for her fortieth birthday, a vintage specimen painted opalescent white, which had induced in Miranda the kind of envy reserved especially for recipients of first-class gifts.

"But I don't want to get over it. That's where we're different."

Yes, they were different all right. Keith, by way of contrast to Ivo, had missed Miranda's last Aspen birthday entirely on account of a friend's two-day-long bachelor party. No card, no late present, no remorse, no awareness of any kind, even after she had given him puppies for his birthday, little hound-dog mutts she'd instantly wanted to keep for herself. When he couldn't reciprocate—not even give it a thought—something in her had snapped.

Instead of haranguing him with the gifts issue, she told him calmly that she'd had an affair with an entomologist who had given her herpes. She figured the entomologist part would mystify him, and that the herpes part would hit home. Besides, she liked the way the words "entomologist" and "herpes" had sounded together, perhaps because harpies—which sounded like herpes—were rapacious winged creatures. Vivianne's vocabulary, as usual, had infiltrated Miranda's life. Evidently, so had Lydia's theatrical sense of just rewards.

How was she to know what effect the mere mention of contagious blistering on a man's organ was to have on Keith? That he was not a man to be tampered with in that way? How was she to know that in a fit of blind rage, he would haul off and punch her in the face, 180 pounds of force behind his fist, then leave the premises while she lay unconscious on the floor?

No one had ever laid a hand on Miranda before. She didn't come from a physically violent family, did not have violent dreams, did not like to be dominated, and certainly had never considered herself to be an inducer of violent acts. With two black eyes and a broken nose, however, she had had to revisit her way of thinking. Confining herself to her Aspen caretaker's apartment long enough to perfect the application of heavy makeup, she acknowledged that she'd screwed up. She *was* screwed up. Somehow she had chosen a hitter.

Later, Miranda concluded that Keith's knuckled come-back had had absolutely nothing to do with jealousy or with being cheated on, which would have been one thing, the more normal thing. This had been a gut reaction, more to do with the safeguard of his most cherished body part. Everyone is entitled to a gut reaction every once in a while. Only in Keith's case, it was obvious he was no stranger to the use of his fist.

Miranda was too ashamed and too embarrassed to mention the episode to anyone or to seek the medical attention she needed—not for the initial blow, and not for the vicious headaches that materialized shortly thereafter. She read up on battered women and placed herself in a far more pathetic—if vague—category. She thought about calling one of those hotline numbers pasted up in the stalls of public bathrooms but was afraid they would tell her what she already knew: that she had brought it all upon herself.

Every once in a while, later on, she would imagine Keith

checking his penis earnestly—looking at it in a way he probably had never looked at a woman—and she would feel two things: stupid and relieved. Stupid for having pursued him, then pressed his rock-'em-sock-'em button. Relieved for having gotten away and for having managed to take the dogs with her.

Oddly, she knew Keith wouldn't come after her, not to beat on her again and certainly not to check up on her. She just knew. He'd made his point. Besides, it wasn't Keith Miranda feared the most after the incident but herself. This had led her to the idea of a cleansing fast, something to shock her system into rebooting itself, setting its appetites aright. And for this to happen, she knew she needed complete physical seclusion.

Once the swelling in her face went down, Miranda lost no time initiating her quest. Focusing on the southwest corner of the Colorado map (where populations were scarce), she blindly circled her finger in the air, stuck it down, and opened her eyes. North of Cortez and just east of a town called Pigeon. Not that far from Mesa Verde. She marked the spot with an X, then drove to it three days later. By her calculations, she had pointed to a miniscule western zip code called Otnip. Pinto backwards.

Tending already to romanticize seclusion, especially under the spell of that oblique late-afternoon light, Miranda was instantly won over. A handful of houses, all spread out along the highway. A ramshackle post office. A different view in every direction. Two miles east of the PO she pulled into the driveway of a faded and boarded-up house with a FOR SALE sign nailed to the front porch rails. After the dogs spilled out, Miranda wandered around a bit, then stopped when she came to the overgrown rosebushes on the east side of the house. Pale pink beauties, thriving there all alone. Domesticated once, and yet left to grow wild. Miranda took heart.

She peered in through the thickly glassed window of the side door and saw black-and-white linoleum on the kitchen floor and just the kind of table she was crazy about: metal-lipped Formica (which would eventually become her desk). The dogs jumped up and scratched at the window, wagging their tails.

Now, looking back, it was hard to imagine not (at the very least) remarking upon the identical homestead across the street, the fairly new pickup, or the greenhouse behind it. Taken with the idea of a cute little homestead waiting to be inhabited, she could recall only having had a passing thought about Billy's—that it was probably some old-timer's place, someone with a gimpy dog and a regular seat at the nearest café. Someone she would probably end up checking in on from time to time.

Even the dogs had to be bribed to get back into the car, and once they'd driven back to Pigeon, Miranda indulged herself by stopping at the only real estate office on the main street, a cubbyhole operating out of Dirty's Garage. Parker and Cherise Pivey, the Realtors (and local car mechanics), happened to own the house in question. They took one look at Miranda and told her the house had been waiting for just the right person, and they knew she was the one. Cherise had a twinkle in her eye, and Parker kept staring at her. Cherise convinced Miranda to let them take her to the local burger joint, a tightly packed and bustling diner known for its beefalo burgers. And there, as Miranda finished the best milk shake she'd ever had, Cherise convinced her to buy the house.

The actual move had occurred fifteen months ago, in the dead center of January—probably the worst possible time of the year for an introduction to Otnip. Miranda had had to struggle through those first hard months. A new home, a new business, a life alone. While others might have been satisfied with a new chapter, Miranda started a new book, and not exactly a page-turner.

She told herself she had done the right thing, of course, even believed it; but that didn't make the loneliness any easier. And even though she cataloged her legitimate complaints against New York, then against Aspen, happy memories of those places seeped through anyway like ink through a blotter. Lydia dragging her out for pedicures or hot chocolate or a drink at the Carlyle. Faces on ferries, and trains, and buses. Her neighborhood deli guy and newspaper guy and dry-cleaning woman. As to Aspen, she most missed her one indulgence there: voice lessons with Majesta Fein, a fixture who knew more Dinah Shore, Debbie Reynolds, and Doris Day—more Ella Fitzgerald and Dinah Washington and Mabel Mercer—more tunes!—than anyone Miranda had ever met. In fact, she was the one who had inspired Miranda to want to take care of older people, to give them the time of day: so why hadn't she been able, when Majesta turned eighty, to write a card? Fear of sounding sad to someone who'd told her she was too young and too untrained to sing "It Was Just One of Those Things" so well?

Fortunately, Miranda's dogs, her opinionated sister, and her even more opinionated best friend saved her. Though she would not admit it, she also grew to depend on the regular visits from that neighbor she had never bothered to research, the one directly across the street who was neither old, nor infirm, nor prone to sitting on stools. The one the Piveys never mentioned because she'd never asked; the one she'd never mentioned to Viv and Lydia because they'd never asked. The one who was finally being hauled off to jail for what she presumed was large-quantity cultivation of marijuana.

After all, Billy had admitted as much to her very shortly after she'd moved in. In addition to herbs, flowers, heirloom vegetables and tomatoes, he'd said, he had a more lucrative cash crop.

Countless times she had asked herself why he had told her. Why? Shock value? Because as his only neighbor she needed to know? Because she had inadvertently given off signs of her weakness for rebels? Because she appeared trustworthy and capable of keeping a secret? Because her pale eyes were prone to getting red at the drop of a hat, and from that certain assumptions could be made?

Whatever his reasons, from the minute he told her, Miranda clammed up. It was a test—that much was obvious—to see if she would hold to her convictions and stay away from the wrong kind of man. And for over a year, she had. Occasionally, yes, she admitted to having accepted a particularly useful gift or offering or having indulged in a limited amount of casual repartee—but never without keeping it brief and then shooing him away.

Miranda had gone back outside in the hopes of rallying her hounds, Artie and Wayne (Arthur and Gawaine, unalterably named by Keith), and, more significantly, to sneak a look across the street. The dogs, who had run themselves silly earlier, could not be budged from their quiet but vigilant post on the front porch. Miranda joined them, sat down in her wooden rocker, and gazed out onto the landscape. A stingy layer of wind-raked snow covered the ground like the thinnest of blankets. The flat range, from its brick-colored fields to its desert sage and pinon, took on a bleak appearance. Perhaps Miranda was projecting her own feelings onto it.

Eventually, she got up and made her way toward the white picket fence at the front edge of the property. Wrapping her coat around her tightly, she tried to remember that as haughty, blustery, and sharp as the weather was now, in just a few weeks, perhaps even days, it would all begin to change. The sun on her shoulders would feel like Rocky Torez's fresh honey, and the ripening breeze would caress her, its breath warm, sweet, and full of promises.

Finally, the officers emerged with Billy.

He was chewing gum (probably Juicy Fruit, which she had smelled on his breath several times before). They were not belligerent, and he did not seem shocked or confused; but still, it appeared he was being taken into custody.

I will not panic, Miranda thought. *Because this is not my problem. It never has been, and it never will be.* In order not to give any indication of either interest or involvement, she turned quickly around and called to the dogs (who remained completely unresponsive and still). Out of the corner of her eye, she saw Billy's head turn in her direction.

Good, she thought. *Let him see me turning my back. That*

could have been me in that squad car had I allowed myself one more involvement with one more leather jacket.

But heading back toward her side door, she nevertheless flashed on the face of William Wordsworth Steadman—a strikingly handsome face if one were to be honest about it—and she could not help feeling sick to her stomach.

 3

"Steadman, you've got to give your mother your phone number. The boss says we can't be coming out to get you anymore. Taxpayer money and all that." Two deputies wearing blue uniforms and cowboy boots hovered over the pea plants, trying to pick off pods before being told to stop.

"After all I've done for you, LeFevre?" Billy was grinning. He had a hose in his right hand and a pair of clippers in the other. He was chewing two relatively fresh pieces of Juicy Fruit and took one last swallow of sugar before shoving the wad of gum to the side of his mouth. He turned serious. "There's nothing wrong with her though, is there?"

"No, Bill. Nothing wrong, as usual. But if there ever was, wouldn't you feel bad about it? Your own mother or father not being able to get in touch?" LeFevre, an excitable man with a feline face, sounded so earnest it surprised Billy.

"Yeah, whatever happened to honoring your parents?" The other one, Scupper, had pulled up a carrot. "I talked to your mother this time, Billy. She sounded real nice. And worried."

"She's always worried, nothing new there. Sheriff Sawhill's just mad because you tell him I give you tomatoes for your trouble."

LeFevre remained unsatisfied. "Why can't you just give the woman your number? What's the worst she could do? Call you every day? I mean what's really going on, what's the real story here?"

Billy turned around to face them squarely. "My mother would be sending me new tube socks every week. Dad would be enlisting my brother to extol the virtues of selling wine, trying to drag me back into the family business. No. For their own protection, this system must stand."

"Well, Sawhill is about to give them your number unless you do a little compensatory work," LeFevre said, scratching his nose.

"If it's about tomatoes"—Billy had put the hose away and was tucking in his tee shirt—"I'm not giving him a deal. They take too much time, and he can't blackmail me that way. People pay maximum buck for my tomatoes this time of—"

"It's not tomatoes," LeFevre cut in with a tiny smile. "He wants you to give another meditation seminar."

Billy stared at them both.

"His wife found a book about calming the mind at the bookstore, and there aren't any teachers around. So, he wants you to coach some of our intrepid detainees like you did before, and she's going to pretend she's doing an article on it. That way, she gets what she wants without him looking like a fool with a Hare Krishna for a wife."

Billy focused on a pimple on the side of Scupper's neck. Meditation seminar. Another opportunity to be the imposter he truly was. He had learned to meditate with Elena years ago when she had first gotten sick. Even then, he'd never been very good at it, and now he was virtually hopeless. "Sawhill thought it was stupid the first time around."

"Yeah, well now Mrs. Sawhill's involved, Steadman. And it looks like our boss sees you as harmless enough to be her guru. If you want your number to remain confidential, that is."

Billy was already walking toward the door, ready to do whatever it took to retain his privacy. He'd always had an unlisted number, and his first instinct was to protect it. "I have carrots and radishes to thin, and their time is imminent," he said distractedly. "So let's get this over with. Do I look anything like a guru, LeFevre?"

"No, Steadman, you don't. You look like a white man of Irish descent with enough bad taste to sport not only a mustache but a little gold earring. Your smug expression is saved only by the fact that a certain amount of fear and discomfort is visible to the discerning eye. Definitely not guru material. But hey, what will Sharon Sawhill ever know?"

Billy, irritated by LeFevre's quick rendering, was careful not to show it. "You trying to make detective or something, LeFevre? Hone your pathetic powers of pop psychology?"

"Peter Piper picked a peck of pickled peppers," LeFevre said, checking the time on his watch.

Scupper had uprooted a radish, which he dangled, stiff-fingered, like a dead goldfish. "No one eats radishes, Steadman. I've never seen one served. Peppers yes, not radishes. Now peppers, there's a gold mine."

"Yeah, well." Billy grabbed the radish out of Scupper's hand. "Peppers are old news. It's about time radishes were revived. I eat them with butter and salt. I take them across the street to my neighbor, and she likes them—even if she would never admit it."

As they exited the greenhouse and came around to the front, he caught a glimpse of Miranda looking his way. A split second later she was calling to those goofy dogs and heading back in, like a meddlesome neighbor caught red-handed.

Startled with delight, it occurred to him then that Miranda would think he was being dragged to jail for breaking the law, for growing with intent to sell. Oh joy, oh great and wonderful kismet! He crouched into the back of the squad car, sneaking his hands behind his back as if handcuffs were involved, and asked them to turn on the lights again.

"What for, Steadman?"

"To add a little spice to my neighbor's otherwise boring life. Just like you did it the first time to add spice to your own."

Scupper turned on the lights and, without being asked, hit eighty in about four seconds. "Your interesting-looking neighbor?" he said, as they sped off toward Pigeon.

"I only have the one neighbor," Billy said. "Very interesting-looking. But she doesn't seem to like my Irish good looks or my contemptible expression."

"Maybe"—LeFevre snorted—"she only needs a glimpse at your sensitive, spiritual side. Or you in a loincloth."

"Shut up, LeFevre." Billy was thinking of Miranda's bright orange jeans. She was wearing that old work coat with the sheepskin collar.

"Ooh, touchy aren't we?"

"Leave him alone," Scupper said sullenly, flipping the lights back off and reducing his speed. "Or we'll never get tomatoes again."

Everything was so quiet from the backseat of a squad car, and so beautiful, Billy thought. Maybe it was just the idea of staring out the window or being driven somewhere. It was peaceful. It was, he admitted, more peace than he'd had lately at home. His fish might be blissfully ignorant of any heightening in the emotional atmosphere—moving languidly in their tank just as they always did—but right next to them, a very powerful, very expensive telescope was leveled at the big picture window across the street.

Yes, he'd been spying on the only signs of real life in his neighborhood. Miss Straight as an Arrow, Miss Teacher's Pet. In point of fact, his interesting-looking neighbor not only interested him but drove him to distraction. And it had been a long time, a very long time indeed, since anyone had had that effect on him.

When Miranda had moved to town in the middle of a January snowstorm the year before, Billy had stared in eager surprise as the small, mufflered woman jumped out of a 1978 mint green Scout International with two dogs and posthaste started directing the movers on how to back their truck in. He'd half expected her to produce a pair of airstrip flashlights.

Then for three hours she carted boxes through the scourging snow into a house that could hardly have been called inviting. Abandoned would have been a more legitimate assessment. Dilapidated, cavernous, and crooked, and very much like his had been eight years earlier.

Billy, who had found out from the Piveys what his new neighbor's name was, wondered if she hadn't dabbled with it, dropped a letter here, added one there. Maybe her given name had been Miranda Blume or Blum. Blue as a last name seemed to him either highly suspect or very, very lucky. But then looking at her, he decided she wasn't the type to change her name for the sake of vanity.

On that welcome-to-the-ends-of-the-earth January day when a forbidding sun had finally disappeared altogether, the lights went on in a house that had been dark for a seriously long time. Billy, touched by the scene and inwardly festive at having what appeared to be an actual neighbor—not to mention an intriguing female one—put his boots on and his foul-weather jacket and headed out into the creeping night to make a social call. Under his coat he'd tucked a mason jar full of homemade, prespiked eggnog in the hopes that a little January cheer would not be rebuffed.

Knocking on the door, he waited as two dogs barked hesitantly, probably unsure of the exact procedure to use in their new house. A soft click, then the door opened all the way to reveal a woman wearing an entire closetful of sweaters. Noting that she had opened the door without caution whatsoever, he smiled. "I'm your closest neighbor, Billy Steadman. I thought I'd bring you some eggnog to take the chill off."

After giving him the once-over, Miranda peeked over his shoulder to confirm the direction whence he came. "My name is Miranda." She motioned him in, holding back two hound dogs by their collars. "Miranda Blue. Come on in. It's cold, but at least it hasn't started to snow in here yet."

Billy, one of those unfortunate enough to be charmed by

the sarcasm of others, stamped his feet and took a good look around the four-room house. Not as bad as he'd expected—wood floors, good solid walls, and windows capable of keeping at least a little of the wind out.

"I didn't think to bring kindling and wood in my overnight bag," she said, reading his mind. "The propane company was supposed to have come today, but it looks like they never made it." Glancing at him, she added, "The dogs actually think they're outdoors it's so frigid . . . Art started to lift his leg on that ficus over there. Of course, by morning it'll be frozen and his leg won't be feeling as friendly and limber toward it."

Billy laughed aloud for the first time in weeks and looked around. The house was laid out identically to his—kitchen, living room, bedroom, and bath. His old friend Sullivan Novo, from whom he'd won his house in a bet, had mentioned that the two properties had been built by feuding brothers. Pivey acquired Billy's house after the one brother died, sold to Sullivan, then bought the one across the street through a third party and held on to it.

"It's pretty sonofabitchin' cold," Billy agreed with Miranda, noting his own breath. Their houses were mirror images of each other, even down to window placement and size. "But that woodstove looks half decent. Let me go get you some wood from my place, I'll be right back." Before she could protest Billy shot out the door and returned in a flash with an armful of dry kindling and a couple of good logs.

"Thank you, kind sir," she said to Billy, who wondered what it would take to divest her voice of the caustic edge. He felt up to the challenge.

"You didn't need winter camping the first night in your new house." The fire started to crackle, and Billy, relieved that the stove still had a good flue, stood back. "Meanwhile, there's enough kindling for a fire tomorrow morning. You'll have to follow me home to carry some logs back though. But your dogs can come along to protect you." Turning to face her, he found her studying him.

"So should I be wary of strangers bearing gifts then?" Her tone melted a bit, hovering at softball on the candy thermometer.

"No, actually, you should be *aware* of strangers bearing gifts. It's a nicer word. Do you have any cups handy for some eggnog? That is, of course, if you drink eggnog . . ."

"Not on a daily basis," she countered, fetching the appropriate box. "Usually around the holidays, a glass or two, just to raise my cholesterol level to the December standard. But I didn't have any this Christmas, so I'm past due. Boy, that heat feels good!" Cheeks already brighter, she produced, like treasures, two plastic Roy Rogers cups, holding them up, then pointing with them to a couple of Victorian armchairs not far from the blazing stove. "Do you mind plastic?"

"A question I've never been asked." Billy was admiring the overembellished design on the mug-handled cups. He settled into a chair that was much more comfortable than it looked.

"Well, I collect plastic, especially the original stuff."

"And to what do you credit this predilection?" he queried, reexamining the lovely specimen in his hand. Full-color heads of Roy Rogers and Trigger framed by ovals of rodeo rope circumscribed the oversize vessel.

"My father never let us put plastic on the dinner table when I was growing up," she summarized. "The tackiness was too much for his sensibilities. No butter tubs. No yellow mustard containers like all my friends had. Nothing to squeeze. Absolutely no Tupperware. So in an effort to make up for time lost and plastic missed, I started collecting. At first I was indiscriminate—like all new collectors—and there was a lot of rebellion involved, which clouded my selections. Then I started picking and choosing and came to appreciate plastic as an art form. Now only the wineglasses and dog bowls are glass. The dogs seem to get chin pimples from the plastic."

"Besides, the plastic goes so well with the Victorian chairs." Billy was able to wedge in a little sarcasm of his own.

"Why yes," she replied, as if noticing for the first time. "It does, doesn't it?"

Having established a rapport between Trigger and Victorian petit-point, Billy then asked what brought her to Otnip and what she planned on doing here. "I'm just curious why anyone would move here," he added, downing the last of two fingers of extrastrength nog.

"What made *you* move here?" Miranda Blue looked him square in the eye, too much like a fellow escapee for comfort.

Defensiveness was his only defense. "This happens to be a good place for greenhouses. Which is what I do. I grow vegetables and herbs, designer stuff, like baby greens, sorrel, Japanese eggplant, lemongrass, heirloom radishes. And tomatoes. And, I feel at home on the range. Because of all the deer and antelope playing and stuff."

"Well, why this range? I mean you're quite a ways from anything—and there are plenty of other ranges just as homey . . ."

"I won the house in a bet, if you must know. And moved into it when the wanderlust subsided some years ago. I owned it, after all, and I discovered I really liked the lay of the land, which sort of breaks your heart in every direction." *The fact that my heart was already broken not being irrelevant,* he did not add.

"Why did the wanderlust subside? What was the bet?"

"I don't know you well enough to tell you those things." All she needed to judge him erroneously was to know he had won his house driving recklessly—suicidally—in a race and had moved to Otnip the mere carcass of a human being. "Maybe in twenty or thirty years when we've become good friends who wave at each other from our rockers. Maybe then I'll tell you, if you can remember to ask me. And you? What brings you to bean country? Not hydroponic farming, I hope: There's really only room for one of us."

With cheeks aglow from fire and eggnog, Miranda had become a picture of loveliness to Billy, he himself not immune to the confluence of warmth and bourbon. Here was an actual neighbor, the first one in all these years. Engaged in the removal of layer upon layer of sweaters, she could be stared at with impunity. An odd face, wide and open, but striking, and even splendidly so. Her hair was flecked with an abundance of premature white and cut unduly short and boyish. It gave one the feeling of self-abnegation on her part but also of vulnerability that contradicted the guard she seemed to have up at all times.

What took Billy's alcoholic breath away, however, were her eyes, set wide, framed by beautifully arched dark brows. Her eye color, or tint rather, was a pale gray and rayed with shards of white. Metallic. Martian. He wanted to think they were a shade of blue to go with her last name, but they weren't blue at all unless blue was the color of ice on an overcast day.

"No, I only grow houseplants and not very well at that. I'm an expert on propagating spider plants if that tells you anything."

"The mother of self-propagators?"

"You got it. No, me"—she was down to a plain ordinary white tee shirt and half her former size—"I came here to start a telephone business. Sort of a companionship service for older people who are lonely and need regular checking up on."

"Interesting, both literally and figuratively. You've come to the middle of nowhere to keep people company. It takes complete and utter seclusion—it takes Otnip—for that."

She smiled widely—extravagantly, he thought—and his heart thumped in response. "I bought this house because I like it out here."

"Ever since you were a little girl, roaming the range on your tricycle?"

"No, ever since I drove through on a driving binge trying to clear my head and was struck by it all—the sky and the fields, the different directions that spread out into different landscapes, the skinny cattle, the ravens, and the prairie-type wind. By that statement, you can see that I was at least old enough to drive."

"And where did you come from?"

She hesitated but only briefly. "From Aspen. You?"
"Telluride."
"Ah," she said knowingly, with a single nod upward.
"Ah," he answered, with one of his own.
That was the first time he'd met Miranda. Since then, they had become close—in distant and infuriating ways.

Now as he sat in the back of the patrol car, he relished further the idea of confusing the woman. She deserved it. She deserved to worry about the implications inherent in her house being the only one across from his. How the law and everyone else might view the involvement of his only visible neighbor.

She might even worry about him—the guy who had fixed things for her, given her gifts, shown her the secret handshake of the deerskin glove. She might very well worry.

It was then he wondered what life would have been like for Miranda Blue without him there. A bit more harshly real perhaps? Sure, Otnip was lonely, beautiful, and perhaps even seductive, but it was also the land of the reclusive crazy, the occasional lurid crime, and methamphetamine users outdoing pot smokers two to one. It was Navajo and White and Mexican and not necessarily a peaceable kingdom.

Maybe she needed to remember that. That neighbors, especially neighborly ones, served a purpose. Maybe it would all become clearer to her now.

Miranda's call waiting signaled her at 2:42 P.M. on the day they carted Billy Steadman away.

She was doing business on the phone with Rochelle Meyer, an eighty-three-year-old rabbi's wife dabbling in cabala, the mystical interpretation of certain Jewish texts. Actually, it was unclear exactly what Rochelle was doing in her husband's library: She admitted to having thrown herself into his books because the once forbidden territory was hers now for the scouring.

Recently, meaning to bridge gaps in her own knowledge of the arcane, Miranda had ordered *The Illustrated Book of Esoteric Knowledge* from the Cortez bookstore. Even though they were used to her special orders, this one made Janklow, the owner's, mouth stiff. "It costs $34.95," he had said, holding a magnifying glass to the page of *Books in Print.* "I'll need a deposit." He had never required a deposit before. Was it the subject matter, or the price?

Meditation for Beginners, which she had also recently ordered for Keeper Dix, a burn victim, had not been cause for alarm at all. In fact, Miranda noted they'd ordered several additional copies of the book. Perhaps Monet's water lilies on the cover had sanctioned it, or was it the MD's coauthorship? Maybe it had been the size: What harm could be done in ninety-six pages, a slim $6.95 worth of advice?

Mouth still taut, Janklow had put down the magnifying glass. "We have a lot of Carson Sung materials on hand. Most people are wanting to reread the works before he appears in person."

"He's appearing? When?" She'd just noted the promotional materials tacked up and all the books on display. Sung was a writer who had grown up not far from Cortez and, in addition to writing, still worked his ranch a bit. Miranda had always wondered where famous people lived. Sometimes, evidently they lived just down the road.

"Couple weeks." Janklow nodded. "The movie'll make a star out of him. I'm sure some big, huge publisher will pay off that university press and we'll start selling copies of *Wicked Sky* by the gross. Even the poetry's selling like hotcakes." It didn't look to Miranda as if the poetry was selling at all, judging by the tall stack of slender books before her. She picked one up, flipped to the first poem, noted the use of the words "blaspheme" and "barbed wire" in close proximity, and placed *Foibles* by Carson Thomass Sung in front of her at the register.

For the first time, he smiled. "Good choice." He rang it up with pudgy fingers. "Your other book should take about a week." He paused. "You a witch?" It was his attempt at both a joke and friendly conversation.

"No," she raised an eyebrow as high as it could go. "The book's a gift," she lied. "How do you know about the movie?"

"You're kidding, right?"

She frowned.

"It's been in every paper and on every radio show in the Four Corners. They're scouting a location." He reached below the register and pulled out a flyer for the reading, which he held up for her to see, then laid on top of her books. "In case you decide to come," he said, "wine and cheese will be served."

Miranda thought she might attend. After all, it was Carson Sung! She had started reading him in Aspen and had zipped through all the novels, *Wicked Sky* three times. Just thinking about it made her want to read it again. Would he read from that book—and which part? It had been months since her last social event, a mediocre movie she'd driven all the way to Telluride to see. How pathetic was that—calling the solitary viewing of a movie in a foreign town a social event?

Meanwhile, Rochelle had spent very little time recently debating matters spiritual or esoteric, no matter how many key words Miranda threw into the conversation. She seemed, not unlike Evalina, to want to focus on Miranda. In fact, Rochelle had just initiated a discussion concerning the effects of seclusion on a woman of thirty-two when Miranda asked if she would mind holding on a minute, that another call was coming in and she thought a friend might be in trouble.

"Oh?" Rochelle's eyebrows arched audibly. "What kind of trouble? No, go ahead dear, I'll wait. Time is only money . . ."

"Actually, you're right." Miranda thought for sure it would be Billy. "I'll call you back; we're not finished with this conversation."

"You're correct there, dear: I'm going to want to know about your friend . . ."

Miranda switched over, her mind swimming. What *if* Billy was making his one phone call from prison to her? What would he want? Help with his garden, help with his *crop?* Could she say no? Perhaps, and perhaps more significantly, there was the simple idea of Billy's placing a call to her—which seemed to have the startling effect, in spite of all avowals, of making her feel needed, wanted, and held in his confidence. Her heart was beating, and her hands had started to sweat.

"Hello?" Her voice held more eagerness than she might have wished.

But it was Lydia who returned the greeting, calling, as she regularly did, on her company's toll-free line. It had been a whole month since they had spoken.

"Are you in the middle of a conversation with a client?" Lydia's brash and familiar voice asked. "Because I'm wedging you in between a boring meeting and an insipid one to bring you tidings . . ."

Miranda, embarrassed by the disappointment she felt at not hearing Billy's voice, reddened deeply. Even sharper was the jab of self-recrimination. "Oh, hi!"

"Who have you got there with you? That man from across the street? Your voice sounds strained. I mean I can hang up right now if you need me to. Just tell me."

"There's no one here, Lydia. Yes, you did interrupt but that's okay, my clients are too nosey for their own good."

"Clients," she scoffed. "Who I *want* to interrupt is you and that man. I mean I've given you a whole month: Isn't anything new out there? No, I suppose that's an oxymoron." Though she had not yet come for a visit, Lydia had photos and knew many of the particulars of Miranda's life, an incomprehensible life from her point of view, one without power lunches or dinner parties, without movies or museums, without Saks and Lower East Side boutiques and discount drug stores, without theater tickets or concerts in the park. A life without conspicuous consumption, and a life without people!

"Actually," Miranda answered, "things are complicated right now."

There was a pause. "I usually don't like this word, but with regard to your life it has promise. What things?"

With some measure of reserve, Miranda filled her in on Billy's being dragged away in a squad car by the police. Finally, she took a quick swig from a purple Play-Doh cup of milky coffee. "I think he's going to call me. Ask me to do something for him. There are no relief workers in his life, and he's got plants to water, all sorts of plants. He may be about to put me in his vise grip, Lydia."

"Emphasis on the vise," came the snort. "Sorry, it's just—"

"I shouldn't have told you," Miranda interrupted. "If Billy knew you knew, he'd kill me."

"No he wouldn't. He's a man of principle, I've gleaned that much from what you've told me, possibly far more principle than you."

"How can you say that? He'll be the one using me; I'll get dragged into something."

"Well, on the legitimate side—he can't exactly let all of his herbs and vegetables die, can he? Emphasis on the herb—" She laughed again. "It would look funny if he *didn't* call you. Maybe he even trusts you; and maybe you don't know everything about him. Maybe he's been taken in for questioning on something completely unrelated."

Miranda could not wedge in a single word.

"Maybe," Lydia forged on, "you would discover all his redeeming qualities if you just decided to snoop when given the opportunity. This is the problem with all relationships, as I see it: we don't investigate our prospects. Your time has come—research the man!"

"I don't need to do that. Whichever way you look at it"—Miranda was weary—"he's guilty of something. And his appearance won't help him a bit."

"You said he was attractive."

"I never said that."

"Well, you described him one time and everything you said sounded attractive. *I* was attracted to him, just hearing about it."

"You're lying; you don't even like my type."

"That's just it, Miranda! He's not your typical type. You said he had sandy brown hair, a smattering of freckles, and a perpetually mischievous look. Remember, you've always gone for dark and egomaniacal over fair and upbeat?"

Miranda couldn't remember saying those things about Billy to Lydia, but then they were true, and how else could she have known them? Had she said *smattering*? "Well." She cleared her throat. "You certainly would *not* like his earring—his little hoop—and neither will the local authorities." What else had she told Lydia? Somewhere along the way, when you lived alone, the line between what you said or merely thought became blurred. "And his hair's too long for you," she added, to which Lydia laughed uproariously.

"You're protesting too much, you're jealous of my sec-ondhand attraction, *and* you're waiting for his call! I said it long ago, and I'm saying it now: You're attracted. Just admit that much."

"Uh-uh. This is a test, that's all, something to remind me that no matter how attractive he might be, it can all come toppling down the instant he gets carted away to jail. Be-sides, he does things I don't like."

"Like what?"

"Okay. He panders to the dogs, for one thing. He shame-lessly tries to get on their good side."

"You should hear yourself." Lydia lowered her voice. "So say he grows a little pot, Miranda, get *relative*, honey: This is a meth world, a speedball world we live in, and that makes him a traditionalist. Old-fashioned even. He's des-perate to get on the dogs' good side, bless his heart. But, here's the clincher and the thing that blows every objection to smithereens: He's right across the street. Plus he'll be home quick as a wink; people like him always make bail."

Lydia was sucking something from a straw, probably the sugary iced tea she swilled like an addict. "Now back to more important matters. When did Mr. Neighbor last make advances toward you?"

"That's an irrelevant question at this point." Miranda shifted in her chair, then stood up, pacing the three steps she could take without removing the headset.

"Tough. You've been hiding things, I can tell. Now talk. Otherwise, I'll think it's much more serious than I thought."

"Wrong. You know he's the one who regularly comes over armed with excuses. I never go over there."

"You've never used the word 'regularly' before. Go on. We're getting somewhere."

Feeling cornered, Miranda forced an offhand tone with the crowbar of will. "Actually, I can't right now. Otherwise, the client whose call I interrupted to speak to you will interrogate me—sort of like you're doing."

"I'd wager he's a goner."

"Did you miss the first part of this conversation? He's in jail. I'm not going to be Jesse James's girlfriend again. I can't do it! They always either get nabbed or get bored. They can't settle."

"This one is settled right across the street from you, Miranda: He's practically a homesteader, probably makes quilts in his spare time. He grows things and cooks; he concocts. Remember the basil lemonade you told me he brought to your lips? These are signs, signs of reliability, imagination, and . . . and gonership!"

Miranda should have never told her about the herbal infusion. Or that he had said, "I could fall into those eyes. And whatever world they're from."

"Guilty!" Lydia had yelled like a judge in need of a gavel. "Guilty not only of ending a sentence with a preposition but of being in love with you, Miranda. What did you say in return, you ingrate? What's the matter with you?"

"Whose side are you on?" Miranda now remembered feeling she had betrayed a secret even while owing Billy no such allegiance. "I said I did come from a different world, one with a different set of rules. Then I told him the lemonade was excellent and sent him home—"

"Gee-*whiz*, Miranda. Go read some romance novels, get a *grip*. This is God talking to you, in a language all women inherently understand. Who'd come back after that? Someone just like him. Right?"

Yes, he'd kept coming back, over and over again. She would not tell Lydia about the gloves.

"I have reasons not to trust—" she said now, hating how trite it sounded, how pat and overused. But it was true.

"Well, yes, honey, we all do. I mean what do we really know about people? I could be a klepto, a drug addict, a fetishist! There's no black and white, there's just wavy reams of tie-dyed gray floating around to confuse us. I'd also like to point out that white-collar criminals run this country and lead it to ruin on a daily basis. And in their rep and paisley ties, they're all considered marriageable and upstanding. Good catches. But they're crooks! I should know, I interface and network and do lunch with plenty of them. Doesn't that sound romantic?"

"I gotta go. Rochelle is going to pummel me."

"She the nosey Tree of Lifer?"

Miranda laughed. "Yes."

"Okay, okay, but just take that one piece of advice from me: *Research* him, Miranda, it's your opportunity. He's not only a goner, he's gone: go over and see what makes the man tick. Tell yourself it's the smart person's safeguard. The more you know, the better you can defend yourself. He's not a Johnny-*Costya*, I guarantee. Or a bore like Keith *Schmuckler*."

Miranda pulled off the headset and tossed it on the table. She increased the length and velocity of her pacing, then composed herself in the most effective manner she knew: by screaming with all her might into a soft pillow.

Art and Wayne came to sit beside her while her body

lay stretched out on the couch, her feet kicking like an infant's.

"Your voice, dear," were Rochelle's first words. "What, did you have a fight with this friend? Who is it anyway—a *man???*"

"I've been screaming into a pillow." Miranda was catching her breath, and felt a calm come into her straight from the realm of the exhausted lung. "I do it to regulate the tension in my body." This was true enough: She had discovered that migraines occurred with fluctuations in tension and that sometimes it helped to monitor herself, recognizing such variations and dealing with them as they occurred.

"Oh?" Rochelle's natural nosiness was taking on grander, more all-seeing and all-knowing proportions.

"No, my friend—my neighbor actually, and yes a man—wasn't the one who called. He was carted off to jail, and I sort of expected him to use his dime on me, because I'm the only one in his vicinity."

The physical gap between Denver and Otnip could be heard across the buzzing phone line. Rochelle, never at a loss for words, was probably refining her query. "Are you upset because he's in jail, because of what he's in jail for, because he's gone, or because of who actually called? Who was it who called then?"

"Oh, my friend from New York called just to chat. No," she answered Rochelle, whose insight was bone-chilling, "I'm upset because I'm thinking he'll ask me to water his plants." Musing, she contemplated how either way she was holding it against Billy. If he asked for her help or if he didn't.

"O-oh," crooned Rochelle, the wheels still spinning audibly. "So that must mean he's going to be in for a long, long time. And that you're feeling put upon. Are the plants really that important in the face of such a—crisis? Or maybe he needs to come back to living things rather than shriveled-up, dying ones. That I could see."

"No," answered Miranda, with a sigh. "It's not like that at all. I should think he'd be out soon. A matter of a few days. And he grows herbs, vegetables, and flowers. Sells them."

Rochelle perked up. "Really? What a delightful way to make a living." She thought for a moment. "You've never mentioned this man before, doll. I thought you said you didn't have any neighbors . . ."

"Besides him, I don't. I mean I do but he's right across the street, and the other neighbors are miles away." She wanted to drop the entire subject rather than have an interfering, hyperintelligent but bored Jewish woman rake her over the coals—which she would. "It's nothing Rochelle, just an annoyance."

Miranda could picture her client shaking her head, not swallowing it. Sure enough.

"It doesn't sound like just an annoyance, it sounds odd. A neighbor you've never mentioned who makes you scream into a pillow because he's going to jail and leaving you to water beautiful plants for a short period of time. This doesn't sound like an annoyance; to me it sounds like only part of a story. Not a bad story, either."

"—The rest of which is too ridiculous to go into right now. Besides I've got to get on with the day's clients."

Again, a wheel-spinning silence. "Miranda, doll"—she

called her My-randa—"I'm going to meditate on this one, and I'll bet you that when you call back in three days I'll have some answers for you. Maybe something randomly selected from Abe's library. Something is fishy here, and I would venture to say I sense heartache. The affairs of the heart, My-randa, they are the inner workings of the world. Good-bye, dear. And not too much screaming into the pillow, you of all people don't need laryngitis."

In truth, Miranda had only a few more calls to make and made them with all her heart—filling in cards with quotes and key words, and even the occasional necessary graphic.

At 7:18, after halfheartedly ingesting a dinner of fresh pasta with olive oil, sun-dried tomatoes, and Romano cheese, a meal served on early Chinese restaurant plastic, Miranda pushed her chair back and initiated a sigh that ended in a burp.

So why *hadn't* he called?

Was it because he didn't trust her, or because he had someone else to call? *You'd think he could call, just to let me know he was all right. Anyone in my position would worry, anyone at all.*

A nippy breeze wandered, like an old friend, through the house in its well-worn pattern, bringing with it a smell both of winter and of spring, slightly damp and chill but earthy, too. Momentarily stung by the change of seasons, she decided to step out.

Dogs orbiting elliptically, she trudged over the thawing ground with a cup of hot tea in one hand. She wore a Western hat, her soft gloves, a fleece-lined jean jacket and corduroy pants of deep tangerine plaid. Miranda dressed for the most part the way she'd always collected—eager to pit elegance against silliness, nature against artifice. It could also be said that in the past year she dressed to make an impression on her neighbor, the one who might be eating dinner at that very moment in the Cortez jail.

It was hard to picture Billy incarcerated.

Was he poking at pinto bean slop with his spork that very second? Would he be striking up a conversation with the person next to him? For the simple reason that she had never seen Billy Steadman relate to anyone but herself, it was impossible to imagine. She did not know how he acted in the presence of others. This occupied her thoughts for several minutes.

With the ultramarine sky deepening into an inky night, dark and cold once again conspired against the edges of things. Thus, under the blanket of dusk and with boundaries dimmed did Miranda begin perambulating the stretch between the two houses, tentatively pulling a thread from one domicile to the other like a spooling spider. Eventually, she found herself in the middle of the road, where she stopped—on her side of the yellow meridian—before looking both ways and stepping carefully over it like a puddle.

"Someone really should make sure Billy's door is locked," she said aloud to the dogs, who had joined her on the blacktop and stood scoping out the sweetly forbidden property on the other side.

She waved them on, and they bolted, beelining for the back of the house. Now, certainly it would be obvious to anyone asking that she had errant dogs to recover. Yes, she would briefly check to make sure the doors were locked, having come to capture her disobedient dogs. "Art," she barked out, playing her part. "Wayne!" No response.

Pitching herself headlong like a thief onto the driveway, she heard nothing but the sound of gravel crunching beneath her feet, and by the time she stopped in front of the doorknob, she had mentally willed it to give way in her gloved hand. Desperate now to go inside that house, yes, she would do what Lydia had advised and research the man.

 5

Billy was sitting on a banquet-type table in the lotus position, palms up, eyes half-closed, looking like a meditator.

What he was thinking about, however—when he should not have been thinking at all—was the expression on Miranda's face before she turned away and how vulnerable she looked in those orange pants. As if she were afraid that without something that bright on she might disappear into the landscape. Though she deserved to be misled a hundred times over, he felt guilty now.

Opening his eyes completely, he gazed upon the six people who stood before him in the dining room (the detainees, as Scupper referred to them), five of whom were dressed in green from neck to ankle. The sixth, Sharon Sawhill, a woman of about fifty with a perky face and frosted hair, had chosen white sweats and Keds with which to make her meditating debut.

Billy stood up and motioned for a big man with a palpable sadness just as big to come forward. Reggie Stoner was in for a DUI just like the other five. The man looked so miserable, Billy wondered what the rest of his life looked like.

"Stoner, is it?"

The man nodded and crossed his arms as if the cold had just started to set in deep.

"Stoner, what do you think the purpose of meditating is?"

"I don't know, man." He shrugged. "But I could sure use a drink."

Sharon was raising her hand like a little kid. Billy kindly acknowledged it but motioned for her to hold her questions.

"It's about relaxing inside, zoning out, getting really still, Stoner. Maybe you'd like to try it?"

The lumbering Reggie shifted from one foot to the other, eyes darting dully from one place to another. "Me? I-I don't know. I could use a drink. I could *really* use a drink."

Billy heard Sharon exhale loudly in frustration and smiled at her.

"Of course you could, Stoner. We're beginning to grasp that. It gives new meaning to the term 'oft-repeated phrase.'" Billy thought about what he just said and put one hand to his brow. "Listen, Stoner—do you like Reggie or Stoner?"

"Reggie."

"Reggie, then. The kind of meditating I do is pretty simple. One way to do it is to repeat a word or phrase over and over again until you're sort of hypnotized by the repetition of it. We could start you out by using the phrase 'I could really use a drink' since you already have that one memorized."

Billy hated to think what the purists would make of this one. "You'd just repeat that over and over while sitting comfortably. Let the sound of the voice in your head hypnotize you. After making a little progress, we'd move you on to a more productive phrase. It'd be sort of like an experiment—"

"I-I don't know—"

"Come on, man." It was Jim Begay, a Navajo. "If you don't want to, I do."

"Begay, is it?" Billy addressed him, receiving a tilt of the head in response. Sharon Sawhill looked crestfallen, as if she'd been passed over for the cheerleading squad.

"I wouldn't use that phrase though," Begay added. "Bad vibe."

"I-I didn't say I wouldn't try it." Stoner was coming around now that someone else had shown interest. "God, I could really use a drink."

"You got a good start on that mantra, Reg." Billy wondered what phrase Begay would use. "I can teach you both for our demonstration. As a matter of fact, let's use Mrs. Sawhill, here, as well. Three's a lucky number."

Sharon was beaming. "I have a phrase," she said, like the captain of a charades team.

"Yeah," said Stoner and smiled sheepishly as if he had finally gotten the joke. "I could really use a drink."

Billy had the three of them sit comfortably and took them through breathing, relaxation, and repetition, just as he had learned it years before in a hospital-sponsored program for cancer patients. Back then, he had confused meditation with desperate prayer. Nevertheless, he had managed to glean the mechanics of meditating, which he was able now to relate just as he had at the last behind-bars seminar.

Eventually, with all six students quietly sitting, Billy himself sat in the lotus position again, eager to return to his own thoughts.

Yes, Miranda was in his life—but not quite voluntarily.

Over a year had passed since she had moved in, and she had never set foot on his property, never called to chat— never even asked for his phone number in case of emergency (he had given it to her anyway). He began to wonder how someone could exist in such isolation until he remembered how, long ago, he had cut himself off from relationships of any kind. Only occasionally had he even succumbed to brief sexual liaisons; and though it might have been sex, and even satisfactory sex, it was never the right kind of passionate behavior, for it lacked the right kind of heart.

Then Miranda moved in, and, after a single encounter, his romance with isolation began to wither. Contact was what he wanted, more contact, in spite of their constant sparring. It had only been in the last couple of months that in desperation he had started pointing his telescope at her from his living room window. He needed to know—and thought perhaps this would tell him—whether or not she had any feelings for him whatsoever.

What he had seen were the normal, everyday things that stirred a lonely heart: her facial expressions when she talked to her old people, the fixing of tea, the brushing of dogs. A few odd things, too, like sweeping the walls with a broom and standing on her head. Several times he had seen her lower her face to a pillow and come up red-faced and breathing hard. It also appeared she liked to sing, and occasionally would stand still in the middle of the room, hands on her hips, to finish a song, after which, he noted not without a great amount of pleasure, she always took a bow.

Billy wanted to believe he deserved to watch because of her own bad behavior, that he had the prerogative because she had shut him out. It served her right if her world wasn't as private as she thought it was.

But even that wasn't a good enough excuse when he saw her change her shirt one day, in the living room. A lace undershirt came into view, which she inexplicably peeled off as well before slipping a sweatshirt over her head. Her breasts were not as small as he had imagined. The nipples were dark pink and erect, and Billy had closed his eyes, unable to take pleasure in the moment since this was a gift he had stolen rather than one he'd been given.

It was then he had to admit that he couldn't possibly gauge her feelings for him with a telescope—that he'd simply wanted to spy on her, and by doing so was throwing kerosene on the kindling of his own ambiguous desires. He had since repeatedly imagined his hands, his mouth, and his breath upon that body of hers. He wanted possession of her.

Well, it wasn't as if Billy hadn't tried making advances. Armed with one flimsy excuse or another, he would march over and parry with her, his guard up and hers up even more. Once he had taken her fresh lavender, rosemary, and thyme to hang in her kitchen, hoping she would ask him to stay for dinner. Her house smelled of soup, a kind of a carroty, steamy smell, but in spite of the brief blush of gratitude, she marched him back to the door with a polite but perfunctory "thank you."

"Miranda," he inquired, "don't you ever get lonely eating soup all by yourself?"

"I don't eat it all by myself," she answered. "The dogs get a little bowlful. Under different circumstances you would be slurping it up noisily as well."

"Oh?" Billy had to play up the sarcasm just to survive in her household atmosphere. "And what circumstances might those be?"

"They would be different. You know how. You would be without recrimination, and I would give you—a decent, upstanding neighbor—some soup."

He could not stop from raising his voice to say, "Oh, you mean the pot growing?" Truth be told, Billy didn't really know why he'd set himself up as an outlaw with Miranda—maybe because Elena had loved him as one and somewhere deep down he worried that any woman of substance would have to be able to love the outlaw in a man.

"The who-o-o-le lawbreaking scenario," Miranda amended.

"Well, Miranda Blue," he tossed the words her way like coins into a fountain, "I can't change my life for soup. For sex, maybe, but not for soup."

Her face went red and white, like a radish.

Before she could answer, he continued. "The relationship is young, however, and you may one day—"

"There is no relationship—"

"That," Billy summed up as he headed out the door, "is where you're mistaken. Think about it, sweetie pie." High off his old-movie-style delivery, he strutted off, happy with the upper hand, eager to play more reindeer games, to fan the fiery flames of repression, to bring the level of sarcasm to more heroic proportions.

Lately, however, he had begun to lose interest in his own sarcasm and to question his true motives. If he was so ready to get involved, then why had he not only set himself up for rejection but then held her harsh judgment of him against her?

Armed with an *Ondotoglossom*, he had knocked on her door at nine-thirty one evening very recently.

"Billy," Miranda said evenly, even as he noted the corners of her mouth tip up on their own.

She was an orchid, he thought, a pale, tantalizing flower. Perhaps, he should cultivate some of the subtlety he used on his flora with her. "This bloomed, just today. I thought you might be interested enough to bargain for it." So much for subtlety: Around her he seemed not to be able to control himself.

Miranda had stared at the voluptuous bloom with the long, bare stem. "It's beautiful," she said, unable to take her eyes off it, handily seduced by its snow-white body and pink private parts. But Billy put the bloom behind his back and cocked his head. "Ready to make a little bargain with William?"

"I don't require an orchid to survive, Billy." She sighed. "Well, come in, I just made a pie—"

There was that exasperation he'd counted on, that one-step-beyond-sarcasm place he wanted to work from. Perhaps she was warming up to him at last. Would he be able to handle her? "Don't think a piece of pie will buy you an orchid," he said as he stepped in, the flower still hidden. "I'll need to put this lovely bloom in the refrigerator for now."

"I don't expect your snooty orchid for the piece of pie. But just out of curiosity, what's it worth to you?"

"Oh, it's blueberry," said Billy with longing, head perched above the pie. "Only my favorite pie in the world. No, the orchid is a gift, actually. It's a gift for you. And although I realize it's wrong to expect anything in return, I can only say that if you had any heart at all behind that marble facade, you'd give me what I desire and deserve in return."

"Which is—"

"Which is a kiss." He said it with his guard nearly down. Maybe with sincerity he could fluster this woman to the point of complete collapse. She seemed enormously flusterable, and he felt enormously sincere.

"A-a kiss?" Horror-struck or disquieted, it was hard to tell which. "Why would I let myself kiss someone headed down the road of ruin, someone whose house I won't even step into?" She paused, then said miserably, almost to herself, "What if I liked it?"

"What if you liked my house?" Billy had to admit it, he adored her this way.

"No, not what if I liked your *house;* don't play dumb with me. What if my body, a rebellious faction of my rational being, were to go into full anarchy on me? My lips have betrayed me before. They might be betraying me right now. Besides all that, we're too different: It's that simple."

"I just don't see it that way. I think we're very much the

same, except for one minor detail. Here"—he opened his arms wide, indicating himself—"but for the grace of God go you."

"Not even close. You are a professional scofflaw. Even if I could live with it—"

"You're living with it now. You know I live across the street and you know I grow—a variety of things." Elena had smoked pot daily after she had gotten really sick. That was another reason he'd needed to defend marijuana, so as not to dishonor the memory of his wife.

"Yeah, but I'm not *involved* with you."

"You have the knowledge, whichever way you want to look at it."

"Yes, but I don't condone it; and by keeping you at arm's length I'm proving that I don't condone it."

"Oh, is that what you're doing?" He reached over and grabbed her by the arm, slowly, and just firmly enough to make a point. "And how hard is it, exactly, to keep me at arm's length?" If he was wrong about the chemistry, he wanted to know. Now. He wanted to feel her body mutiny against her mind.

She shook herself free, however, the force of which caught Billy off guard. "Not that hard. Don't flatter yourself that you're irresistible—I mean, where are the women in your life, Billy? Where are the people, for that matter?"

"Where are the people in your life?" he countered, thinking he might have squeezed her less hard, that instead he might have stroked her neck, which is what he'd wanted to do. Her teeth were stained blue from the pie. One delicate vein the same color as the berries pulsed at her temple.

"Which brings me to the point," he said quietly. "We *are* alike. Look at the way we live: out in the middle of nowhere, by ourselves. We both have resort-town pasts. You collect plastic, and I collect fish; we—"

"That's all beside the point. I don't know anything about you . . ."

"Well, that's your own fault. And where are your references? How do I know you aren't selling snake oil to old people?"

"As if I could ever do something like that. You can see I'm not that kind of person. Isn't it kind of obvious?"

"Ditto from my side: In the miniscule opening you've granted me, the crack I've tried to wedge myself into, can you honestly say you see a bad man? What's your problem with pot, anyway? What's the big deal?"

"Like other unlawful behavior, it makes people into fugitives; it drags their unwitting friends down with them. It makes you unfree."

"Well, shit, I guess I'm from the land of the unfree, then, and the home of the unbrave. I didn't know you were such an expert on how it affects people and their friends."

"Well, doesn't it?"

For a moment, it seemed to Billy she wanted nothing more than to be convinced otherwise. "If I answered yes to that, it still wouldn't make any difference to you. Do you see any people adversely affected by my lifestyle?"

"I don't see any people in your lifestyle, Billy. The addicts, wherever they might be, are adversely affected."

"Coca-Cola's addictive for God's sake, Miranda. So is eggnog and every other form of alcohol, including Aqua Velva. Maybe minds need to be altered a little, did you ever

76

think of that? What about sacramental drugs? What about peyote—"

"Oh, please, not the peyote lecture, rife with happy natives, roads to other dimensions, and Castaneda at the head of the earnestly searching masses like the Pied Piper of Hamblin."

"You're so categorical, just opening your mind would be altering it too much, right Miranda? It's Hamelin, by the way. The Pied Piper is from *Hamelin*. Have you ever even tried smoking pot?"

Yes, Billy's *meditation* was certainly going well this morning. An elevated heart rate, agitated brainwaves, and sweaty palms. He was so engrossed in recollection that he didn't hear Sharon Sawhill whisper his name from her spot, didn't hear her get up, come over to him, or put her warm and fleshy hand on his shoulder.

"Sorry, Sharon," he muttered, ashamed and yet greatly thrilled by the utter fakery of it all. "I was in deep. What can I do for you?"

"Well," she began. "I keep thinking about tonight's dinner. Like I can't stop." There was a long skinny notebook in one hand and a pencil in the other. She herself was posing as a writer; why couldn't Billy pose as a meditator? Seemed fair to him. Besides, he could teach these people how to breathe deeply without professing to be a swami.

"That's normal, Sharon," his voice was low. "Don't fight the thought. What's it going to be tonight, anyway?"

She couldn't tell whether or not to take him seriously. "Taco pie," she said miserably, as if some other dish might not have posed such a massive threat to peace of mind. Or

perhaps that some answer might have pleased Billy more.
All the perkiness was gone.

"M-m-m, a good taco pie." Billy squeezed her arm. "It's
okay. Just acknowledge the thoughts. It's all a part of
Sharon—what's your middle name?"

"Mystery."

"Mystery's your middle name?"

She nodded, and, sensing his surprise, beamed.

"Well, Sharon Mystery Sawhill, try to be aware of your
own unique thought processes, then let them go. Just let
things be. Okay?"

Gravely, she nodded and, having gotten the go-ahead for
contact between them, squeezed his arm back. "Thank
you," she whispered before heading off to her banquet
table to hoist herself back on top of it. Billy had liked the
feel of sitting on a table and had invited them all to do the
same, but seeing Sharon there he got the impression of
someone avoiding mice or waiting for the floor to be
mopped.

He watched her close her eyes, then he, Billy the Imposter, breathed deeply and closed his own eyes again.

Marijuana wasn't any more a part of Billy's life than boot-leg Grateful Dead tapes, bingeing on tequila, or talking to the man in the moon. But he had persisted with Miranda on the issue and—perhaps—gone too far.

"So you haven't ever even smoked a little weed." His tone had been smug. "What, are you afraid of losing control?" The question, he realized now might have been meant for himself.

At the time, of course, she had become indignant.

"I don't have to be afraid of anything to be opposed to getting involved with someone who grows drugs. Most people would find my point of view utterly and unequivocally comprehensible."

"Yeah, most people who live categorical middle-class lives next to other people with categorical middle-class lives. What if I didn't grow reefer? What if I just grew herbs and vegetables?"

Miranda paused long enough to set Billy's heart beating. "I don't know," she finally said, with what sounded very much like wistful overtones to Billy. "It's such a hypothetical situation; I already know what you do, it's part of my evaluation of you."

"No, it's all of your evaluation of me."

"So? What if you were a murderer—couldn't *that* be all of my evaluation of you?"

"Maybe, maybe not. But I'm not. And what if I based my entire view of you on your small-mindedness, your fear of losing control—"

"That's not it—you have no idea! Believe me."

"Really!" Billy looked her in the eye. "Then enlighten me, please." He had somehow managed to eat the blueberry pie while carrying on with this woman. In the complex part of his brain, the part that does things like silently tally the number of jets flying overhead in one day, he was able to appreciate the successful commingling of sweetness and acid in the pie, the fruit not prudishly firm as might be expected from someone so—prudishly firm. "Talk to me," he said to her soberly, doubtless influenced by the luscious coating on his tongue.

"No." She had put her fingers on her eyebrows and pushed them outward as if massaging them. "I don't have to prove anything to you. Now why don't you just take your stupid flower that's too beautiful for regular-room-temperature air and leave me alone. It's obvious you just want to torture me." Her voice got louder. "Isn't it just my luck I plop myself down across from the only bad choice for miles and miles and miles!"

Billy opened the fridge and slammed it without having taken anything out. "What are you talking about? There are plenty of neighbors you really wouldn't want to have,

Miranda. You should keep that in mind." He realized he had been standing in the middle of her kitchen arguing with her for well over ten minutes and shook his head, "Don't worry." He put down the empty plate he still had in one hand. "I'm going."

"Good, because all you ever do is insult me."

"And all you ever do is ignore me."

"For good reason!" She had regained the verge of a ferocious composure.

"Likewise!" Billy roared, and stormed away. He remembered feeling grateful, as he headed home, that he had his own bed, his own bathroom, and his own life. Because in that moment, he recognized how sticky it was between them. She drove him nuts.

As for marijuana, he hadn't grown any since he'd moved to Otnip. At first, his few loyal customers wouldn't stop pestering him. Maybe they thought they were doing him a favor by staying in touch, that after Elena's death he needed a reason for living, a purpose. That had been true enough.

"You gotta grow weed, man. Who's gonna supply us if you're out of the picture?"

He had only ever really grown miniscule amounts of marijuana, but his people had always clamored for it. "Humanity needs you, man. *We* need you." And, "You owe it to us, man."

That had been the last straw. "How do I owe it to you?" he wanted to know. "Really, I'm interested. How do I owe it to *you?*"

"Us meaning humankind. Us meaning the black-market

economy. Us meaning those with irreparable proclivities to the product. You have a greenbud thumb, man. It's your calling. You know how we feel about Billy-bud: it's right-eous product because you care, man. It's totally the essential *kind.*"

They had always sworn it was better, stronger, purer than anything around. He had no idea what they were talking about until he had started growing tomatoes in Otnip, using the same techniques, and had watched people start to react in the same catnip-addicted way. His secret weapon, once a silly experiment, was now a reality. It was worth noting that he had never offered Miranda a tomato; that he had perhaps saved that offering as a last resort.

"Well, I don't care anymore," Billy had finally told them all, loathing the language of the smoker. "Things are different, in case you hadn't noticed. And I'm into Bonsai now. Bonsai's my calling." This pronouncement had pretty much shut them all up. Clearly, he was out of his mind, a man destroyed by the death of his wife and living in a Japanese dream world in the middle of a flat Southwestern plain.

Only later did he think to try out this confabulated excuse pulled wholly from the inside of a hat. Bonsai. He bought books on it. Bought his first specimen, a small juniper in a crackle-glazed vessel. Then a holly. And a miniscule fig. Some years later, after giving away the trees, he found himself experimenting with Bonsai techniques on his last remaining pot plant, which he had named Dolores. *Pain.*

Eight years later, only Dolores remained as a testimonial to his Bonsai years; and there, still under the grow lights (technically, she should have been outside), surrounded by his tomatoes, she bore the look of some distant cousin of a dwarf maple. It was quite remarkable if a little perverse.

Now, while sitting cross-legged in the county jail, Billy could not help comparing himself to the small plant he had named pain, snipped and wired and forced not to grow. His defects were as obvious as the plant's, easy to peg, and certainly reason enough for any woman to stay away from him. Not all women responded to the walking wounded; he could think of one in particular who seemed not to have that proclivity.

Billy made a resolution then: that upon returning home he would move Dolores to the window ledge in the kitchen next to all his clippings and rootings. There, on a cheerful tile shelf, Dolores would receive the natural warmth and light of the sun's rays. He would stop pruning her, pruning his own past. Dolores would simply exist.

Upon completing the two-hour introduction to meditation, Sharon Sawhill came up to him flashing a copy of *Meditation for Beginners*. "You were much better than the book!"

Billy grinned, pointing at the cover. "Nice water lilies. You take care now, Sharon." She seemed ready to pop, and he knew why and raised his hand quickly to stop her. "Don't tell me your phrase, they're secret!" He gave her a hug. "I'm sure it's perfect."

Meanwhile, he followed Begay out the door.

It was apparent this man had had no trouble shutting everything down and going in deep, and Billy found himself wanting to know more. "Hey, Begay. What did you feel when you got there?"

"Nothing," answered Begay matter-of-factly. Then, "Emptiness but not emptiness."

Billy, conversant on the subject, considered this as good an answer as any. "Yep." He forced out a cheerful response. "That's what it's supposed to be. Nothing wrong with a little beginner's luck."

"Seems pretty simple to me," Begay said in a monotone. He turned the hyphen-smile of his mouth into more of a dash.

"Well, then you're just an advanced human being, Begay, what can I say?"

"Well, I'm not White. That might be an advantage."

Billy, unlike Begay, was prone to bristling at an insult, and had to struggle not to show his feelings. "In terms of your spirituality, it probably does, Begay. White people exploit resources and other human beings. We break treaties and steal native artifacts. We have blue eyes, and Jesus had brown." He launched his most dazzling smile at Begay who seemed to digest words at his own slow rate.

"Bill," he finally said, "I'm just a Navajo trying to survive in America."

The ashes of glibness were giving birth to the phoenix of honesty. "So what do you do in real life?" Billy asked. "If you don't mind my asking."

"Counsel people. What is it that you do?"

Begay seemed to be asking just to make it obvious how inadequate a question it was. "I grow vegetables in a greenhouse. Sell them to restaurants."

"You grow things," the big man summarized. "And what is it you seek?"

Unsure of his footing on the blunt terrain, Billy bought

time by pulling a pack of warm Juicy Fruit from his back pocket. "Actually," he said slowly, "right now I'm seeking a woman." His tone became flat with candor and Begay looked up. Sheepishly, he continued. "I haven't been meditating, I haven't been able to do it right in years—maybe never. I'm a fake. What are you in search of?"

Begay thought for a moment. "A place. Among my people. Outside my people." He shrugged then, almost imperceptibly but Billy saw it. "A woman," he looked off into the distance, "is a far more complicated project."

"Jesus, that's for sure."

Begay really smiled this time, revealing small, white kernels of teeth, then lifted a hand, which he laid on Billy's right shoulder heavily, like a paw. "Sometimes I think a good woman is the only way a man can learn to reconnect. To everything. To make him forget about the world's heaviness. To make it light again, and beautiful. What's her name?"

"Miranda." Billy peeled a piece of gum. "Miranda Blue."

Begay smiled again, then turned and walked away, not looking back when he said, "Good mantra."

Meanwhile, Billy's own heart throbbed so loudly in his chest, he wondered how just the sound of Miranda's name could affect him so. He had not told anyone about her before, maybe that was it. Maybe Begay had that effect on people.

He tried to imagine his return home.

Would he fetch her? Stand before her and confess? To what? To the fact that his one remaining pot plant was a budless, Bonsai'd shadow-of-her-former-self named Dolores? That he had just liberated her with a move into sunlight and a promise that she would warp no more? That his wife and best friend had died at the age of twenty-six after just two years of marriage, and it had taken him eight years to recover? That he had never been interested in another woman until she had moved in? That in spite of the fact that he desired her, with a longing so sharp and miserable he had resorted to peeping, he had set himself up to be rejected because he was afraid of the consequences of involvement?

With a tight feeling in his chest and his breath shallow, Billy took himself through his own formula. Breathe in for four, hold for seven, exhale for eight. In for four, hold seven, exhale eight. Relax shoulders. Feel the ground. Breathe in: Miranda. Breathe out: Miranda. Miranda. Miranda. Good mantra.

By the time Scupper and LeFevre approached, he had composed himself and stood there idly chewing his gum.

"How about we drive you home?" LeFevre said, studying Billy. "We need an excuse to stop at MinuteBurger, and nothing else requires our presence in Pigeon."

Billy happened to be boycotting MinuteBurger. Despite the fact that he offered to give them a good deal, they wouldn't buy his tomatoes. *No tomatoes on burgers* had been Travis Ardner's decree. It wasn't traditional. Billy, once MinuteBurger's most ardent spokesman (fries were made on the premises and beef-buffalo burgers cooked a perfect medium every time), was keeping his distance.

Nor did he want to be pestered for tomatoes by Scupper and LeFevre or tormented and teased about the attentions of Sharon Mystery Sawhill (who, bless her heart, had made him smile).

Finally, he did not feel inclined to go home just yet.

"Other plans, guys," he said, reaching in his pocket to jingle some change. "I'm sure there are some dogs fighting in Pigeon—you could break that up. In any case, you're on your own."

He headed toward the pay phone to call Sullivan. Chances were slim that Sullivan, who lived not far from Cortez, would be at home, but he carried at least one cell phone at all times. All of a sudden Billy wanted to see him, needed the company of someone who knew him, had known him.

"You're just now getting around to your mom?" LeFevre asked, sidling up to the pay phone.

Billy froze: He had forgotten his mother, completely forgotten. "I called her already." He turned his back. "She's fine. Sends her best. Now let me get on with my life, LeFevre."

"Not that there's much to get on with," he mumbled, causing Billy to wince as he dialed not Sullivan's number but his mother's.

"Hey, Mom," he whispered as he watched LeFevre swagger down the hall, probably to the soda machine.

"Billy." His mother sounded relieved as well as irritated. He immediately pictured her small frame, her bony, lotioned hands gripping the phone as if he himself were in it. "Did it take them this long to come and get you? Next time, I won't tip them at all. And they seemed so nice and dependable."

"You *tip* them?" They had never said a word about it.

"Well, of course, I do, sweetheart. You don't get something for nothing, you know. It's worth it to know you're safe."

"How much?" Billy felt like the heel he was. His mother was sending money to the police so that she could make sure her boy was okay.

"Oh, not much at all. Your father sends them wine, and I write the thank-you note."

Jesus. "Well, it's my fault the call is late. Just for the record. But I sort of pay them for this little service, too. Is everything okay?" What was next for the boys in blue, a Parma ham?

"What wouldn't be? Of course, *we're* okay. Your father just hired two more salesmen, and Bobby [Robert Frost Steadman] is planning his next wine tour. He loves the south of France. You're the one we worry about, dear. Are *you* okay?"

"I'm fine, Mom," he said, then added, "better than fine, I guess."

There was a pause. A pause filled with silent desire and prayer. "You met someone." No inflection at all. "Didn't you?" Dead serious hope.

Billy thought maybe it was the afterglow of the Begay effect that was making him confess. Or maybe it was all due to his mother's having called the police and their exacting of the meditation workshop—which had shown him just where his mind went, given the opportunity. Where his obsessions smoldered.

"Maybe," he said to his mother, who bit down on her joy by solicitously dropping the subject and hurriedly updating Billy on his sister-in-law and nieces, his grandmother Lewisia, and the state of gardening in New Hampshire in the month of March.

"Please don't get mad at those nice policemen, Billy," she

concluded. "They should work the angle from both ends. I bet I probably would." Another pause. "Does she have a name?"

"Yes, Mom, she does," Billy said simply.

"That's all I need to know. You take care of yourself. And call, if you feel the need."

Standing there with the receiver in hand, he dropped in another quarter and dialed Sullivan's number. It rang only twice.

"Willie Word!" Sullivan roared, then stopped short. "You okay, man?"

"I'm fine," Billy said, looking down the hall to see if anyone might be listening in. "I need a favor, though."

"You name it."

"If possible, I need a ride home from the Cortez jail."

Sullivan was momentarily silenced. "Jail? What are you doing now, teaching them how to cook with fresh herbs?"

Billy laughed. "Close," he said. "Meditation seminar. I don't want those deputies driving me home again, pestering and profiling me the whole way."

"Well, lucky I'm at home. Actually, I'm on location right now, but arranged to take a couple hours off to go to Cortez for reasons I will explain later. Then I had to come home because I was in the middle of a story and somehow left tape three at home, as Providence would have it. So . . . I can come get you, but you'll have to swing by the set for a couple of hours. You might want to spend the night after you see the place. I've added a little something to my line of work."

Sullivan was a locations scout for TV commercials, a job that impeccably matched his natural affinity for dazzling, dramatic, hard-to-reach settings with a superior sort of organizational genius. He was the local guy, the one who matched up native people and businesses to the production companies. He loved his job, made the most of it, and was never without a stack of "bots," as he called them—books on tape. He *read* more, he told everyone, than most college professors even if his library consisted not of spines lined up but of boxes of tapes piled high. He had just recently begun collecting rare taped readings, much in the manner of an opera buff collecting old 78s of Caruso.

"You could probably use a little diversion," Sullivan continued. "As a matter of fact, you could use a little of anything. And I need an ear to bend."

"I know exactly what I need a little of," Billy said. "But I'll come anyway. Where's the location?"

"On the northeast border of Navajoland, down this one road nobody's ever even numbered. Beautiful. Private canyon, water, trees, the whole works. You will *dig* the spot, Billy, even if it bears the scars of three other truck commercials. No hotels for miles: I have them all set up—well, you'll see. The whole thing will blow your mind."

Ten minutes later, Sullivan pulled up in the Rugmobile, a vintage silver Cadillac convertible, custom-painted and upholstered entirely with Navajo rugs. It was Sullivan's pride and joy and his vehicle of choice for exploration, for the ticking off of every prospective unnamed, unnumbered road in the Four Corners area.

The top was down. He got out of the car wearing a fringe jacket and beaded boots up to his knees.

"What do you think?" he asked, doing a pirouette as an

actor's voice continued to narrate from inside the vehicle. Sullivan—an unlikely cross between a cigar store Indian and an Italian mobster—gave Billy a bear hug, then looked him up and down.

Billy knocked a black baseball cap that said CHEVY ROCKS off Sullivan's head, grinning ear to ear, and put it on his own. "Now you look a hundred percent," Billy said. "And I needed a new hat. It's really good to see you. What's with the costume?"

"Long story. Having to do with the filming of *Wicked Sky, The Red Badge of Courage* by Stephen Crane—and other things." Sullivan pointed to the door of the Cadillac. "We are at a critical point." He punched the stop button on the tape player to give them time to settle in. "I have to say, it's not as good as the live storyteller I hired for evenings around the campfire. The guy is superb. I think he's actually *from* the nineteenth century."

"What are you talking about?"

Sullivan leaned close to Billy. "And you are not going to believe some of the girls working craft services on this shoot."

"I always forget what that is," Billy said. Sullivan had never stopped pushing women Billy's way even though he knew it was pointless. "The food?" Billy had only been on a couple locations. Once, Sullivan had hired him to provide flowers for all the talent, which consisted of ten cheerleaders hired to pile into an SUV.

"Yeah, the food, Billy. Craft services is the food, the Evian, the snacks, the candy, the *food,* the nonunion people. Anyway, these girls are from yonder." He waved toward the mountains, the direction of Telluride. "I guess the skiing is getting thin—and they need that extra cash for off-season. They're babes, Bill. Verging on *hot*."

Billy smiled and pushed in the tape. He propped a fully upholstered set of pillows behind him and let his head tip back to meet the sun. Within minutes, Sullivan had taken his first shortcut turnoff, and while the dust blew up behind them Billy listened to stones pinging up from the dirt road onto the low fenders of the Caddy like BBs fired randomly at tin cans.

He wondered what Miranda was having for dinner.

A sudden flood of brightness flicked on right as Miranda's hand reached for Billy's doorknob. Startled, she froze like a deer in headlights before quickly reminding herself that this kind of sensor light was either meant to bid welcome or scare the skunks away. No one was there, no one but her.

Up close, Billy's house was more innocuous and friendly than she could have anticipated. It was so remarkably like hers in every way—prairie shack posing as California bungalow—she felt as if she were approaching her own threshold. How had she managed never to come over, not even once, in all the months she had lived in Otnip? It struck her now nearly as ridiculous as it was heroic.

In a sense, however, she had never given herself a choice in the matter, since a mere two weeks after she had moved to Otnip Billy had plopped his problematic sideline proudly into her lap. She had been cutting a pecan coffee cake with her best knife, enjoying the feel of blade through velvety flour. The attractive and amusing man before her was about to have a piece. The whole thing had seemed just shy of miraculous.

"Why would you think it appropriate to tell me this?" She pulled the knife out like a sword from a pierced heart.

"I don't really know." Billy crossed his arms, stepping back. "Somehow, I thought we should be straight with each other. I mean I'm not what you'd call a big-time criminal. Why, do you have a problem with it?"

"Well"—she set a stingy sliver down in front of him—"you never know what will happen with criminals, big-time or small-time. I like to know what will happen." Furthermore, she told him, the disappointment beginning to make her irrational, she believed rebellion was more often dumb than original, and it bored her. And she did not have time in her life anymore, she said, for such types. *What a bunch of crap! She had loved the fringes and its rebels and had gorged herself on that particular smorgasbord for years.*

But he had stood there, nodding, slowly nodding as if he were able to make sense of what she'd said.

"You're reforming your life," he summarized. "I can appreciate that."

Enraged, Miranda felt she had been cunningly betrayed. Because, not only had she sworn off bad boys and been dealt another one right away—even one who appreciated self-righteous women!—it had taken much less than two weeks for her to discover that she was attracted to Billy. That had taken about two minutes. Shouldn't she have guessed though? A single guy in the middle of nowhere with a greenhouse? It seemed so obvious once he said it.

Billy looked at her sadly then but with a certain unmistakable admiration. "I figured you might be that kind of girl." Almost relief, even.

"I'm not any kind of a *girl*, for one thing." Even though her ears were burning, indignation rose to meet his admiration. Eventually she had to admit she liked the fact that he seemed to admire just the kind of woman she thought she should be, one pitching herself toward self-improvement. On the other hand, it induced a panic in her so great that when she thought about it she had to struggle for control, for she had not yet become that worthy person and might never become her.

Thus had Miranda set herself up as the spurner from that second week in their relationship. As such, how could she have possibly ever visited Billy, flagrantly disavowing everything she'd said she stood for?

He, on the other hand, had come over many times (many more than she had confessed to Lydia). Excuses seemed to come naturally to him. In fifteen months, he had befriended her dogs, thinned her irises, fixed the tool-shed door, even added LPs to her collection—a Dinah Shore and a Peggy Lee. Plus he'd populated her house with plants, presumably surpluses for which he had no use. Handing her a rococo-looking ivy with six-foot-long vines one day, he told her that one little *Hedera helix* freed the average house of virtually all benzene in the air.

"Should I worry about benzene?"

"No, Miranda." He fingered the vine like a long necklace. "You should let me worry about it."

Usually it took about twenty minutes for her to start heading him toward the door. (She'd calculated approximately fifty hours of actual relationship time between them.) In addition to sticking to her guns regarding the kind of men in her life, she supposed she feared that were he to linger, she would be discovered somehow. Shooing him off seemed a far easier, if in many ways more frustrating, alternative.

The pattern had come to a head one recent evening when Billy had come over with the most beautiful flower Miranda had ever seen, an orchid, half-dangling half-propped on a delicate stem. Everything about the flower was erotic, from tongue to cavity to color, and here was this man wanting a kiss in exchange. A kiss. But—did he truly want a kiss or did he want to see her react in the way they both knew she would?

Duly provoked, she had barked at him. He, in turn, had grabbed her arm, saying something about trying to keep him at arm's length. Voltage had shot through her so unmistakably she had blushed scarlet and had to yank herself almost brutally away from him to keep her edge. Meanwhile, she wondered darkly if she shouldn't have had some kind of response to his having seized her like that. Was he violent?

What did Billy want, that was the question. Because even though he persisted in visiting a couple times a week, he really seemed to like the fact that she had made herself inaccessible. Yes, he seemed to thrive on that.

The door was unlocked.

Ever so fleetingly, Miranda entertained the idea of turning around and returning home at a high clip. She might have, too, had it not been for an incandescent glow she noted coming from the next room. Curious, she moved cautiously in its direction. Perhaps something had been left on that needed to be turned off. Perhaps she could actually be of use.

She crept the four steps into the living room where she was met not by a random watt-wasting lamp but by an enormous tank teeming with fish, which rose up to meet her like a living wall. The aquarium easily measured ten feet in length and five in height, and, dwarfed by it, Miranda could only stare mutely at the multicolored swarms moving about, some languidly, some with seeming purpose. Because of its location at the back of the room, Miranda had never seen even an insinuation of its glow from her house, staring across from her picture window toward his. Back and forth they paced. Back and forth, about-facing at intervals both random yet highly synchronized. The same contained sort of chaos that brains are made of.

Unfamiliar with the ways of fish, she wondered if they were hungry or if pacing was simply their way of life. Feeding them, she reasoned, might be another handy service for her to perform. Yes. She would first check on the rest of the house, then come back and feed the fish on her way out. *I fed your fish,* she could offhandedly say upon his return. *They were practically on the verge of starvation.*

Back in the kitchen, she turned on the small light over the stove and glanced around. An open vintage paperback, *The Maltese Falcon,* lay facedown on the counter. The leaky faucet spattered in slow drips onto a pile of dishes (old-fashioned roses on porcelain) left over from breakfast. Miranda picked up a chunky coffee cup and saw crumbs in the bottom: He was a dipper.

The walls, papered in pale blue gingham, gave the room

a touch of the frontier woman. She thought of Lydia's comment about quilt making and frowned, shifting her gaze to a refrigerator covered with magnets and bits of paper, postcards, and snapshots. Photos of family and friends, presumably, and of Billy in various shades of the same wide grin. In one taken at the beach—possibly Mexico—she noted a scar on his right shoulder, then noted his shoulders themselves, broad and muscled. She counted two moles before pulling her head back and telling herself to stop.

Peeking out from behind a postcard of a rabbit with antlers was a photo of Billy and a dark-haired woman, very beautiful. She had a round face, coffee-colored skin, and big silver hoop earrings. Her smile, spread across her face and up into her eyes, sparkled and radiated outward, out of the picture even. Billy's arm was around her, and he was looking at her while she gazed directly into the camera.

Miranda, heart beating, stared at Billy staring at the woman. She could feel the love in his heart, she could feel it. Her own face was hot. "This is the kind of woman any man would truly love," she thought. "Someone free, easygoing, big-hearted and full of life. Someone who's not afraid to love outlaws—or to get over them—who doesn't beat herself up or let others beat her up, and who most certainly does not lie about who she is."

In that moment, Miranda forgot why she had alienated herself from Billy, forgot why she had alienated herself from the world. All she felt, in fact, was a sense of having alienated herself and for no comprehensible reason at all. What was she doing? Other people were living lives out there, engaging themselves, eating dinner out, going antiquing, taking voice lessons every week. They were feeling, even if that meant feeling pain. Quietly, she replaced the postcard. She should go. Why had she come?

She was nearly out the door when Billy's phone list, next to a buff-colored rotary on the wall, caught her eye. There, at the bottom of the list—right there at the bottom— was her name. Miranda. 248-8828. Nothing more. His handwriting was small and neat, and straight up and down, just as it had been on that receipt. He used periods.

Above hers were the names of restaurants, in Telluride and Cortez and elsewhere. Someone named Sullivan with many crossed-out entries beside it. Someone named Audrey, and Phil, and Parker Pivey, too. A FedEx number. The post office. She looked at the answering machine. No messages.

Without thinking, she punched the outgoing message button.

"Looks like I'm out with a hose in my hand—no strike that—I'm out in the greenhouse tending tendrils. Leave me a message, unless it's Miranda—in which case come over and find me and message me in person. Thanks a lot."

Miranda blushed but could not move. She hit the button again and listened. She thought she detected emphasis on the words *find me* and thought she heard him smiling as he spoke. Did he actually want her to come over, or was he teasing her?

When she finally moved, it was not toward the door but the bedroom, her heart pounding terribly as she pushed open a door that had been painted a thick, glossy, enamel white.

The small, messy, west-facing room was so full of plants that the air met her in a heavy mass. Miranda inhaled deeply, and, under some sort of oxygen spell, found herself making the bed with nurse's corners and sheets pulled to straightjacket tautness. She picked up the few pieces of clothing that had unsuspectingly been left on the floor and sneaked a sniff at his shirt before hanging it up in the closet, even briefly running the underarms by her nose.

Danger, Miranda, her inner neon flashed. *You're sniffing the shirts of a man in jail. The shirts of someone who believes you to be better than you are.*

She just could not imagine him in jail, though, with other criminals. It was then Miranda admitted that he did not seem to belong to the genre to which he had assigned himself.

"Perhaps," Miranda thought as she headed back out, "I should take a tour of the greenhouse. Perhaps there I'll see evidence of the person I've renounced, and I'll be brought back to my senses."

After negotiating the path from the kitchen door toward the back of the property, she flipped on the only light switch she could find, right outside the heavy glass door of the greenhouse. She hardly expected the whole building to light up, but it did.

That was when her perspective shifted as well as her balance: For there in the greenhouse it was hard to see Billy as anything but a cultivator, a person whose thumbs and eight fingers were all as green as grass stain. Miranda stepped inside, where the luxuriant atmosphere enveloped her, wrapped itself around her in ribbons of color and leafy fragrance.

As she gazed around, stupefied, it occurred to her that this was the kind of place where people might be too happy to remember that they were sad. Then it occurred to her that if she was having this thought, she might be sad inside— and so might Billy be since he was the one who had created it.

Very slowly and as quietly as she could (so as not to seem like anything more than a visitor), she walked the flagstone paths, which guided her between the rows of herbs, and vegetables in all phases of development, and finally flowers, mainly roses, and some of them tiny as fairy buds.

In the far corner stood a sort of half terrarium half cage filled with mossy stuff and orchid plants. The few visible flowers seemed to be leaning toward her, looking at her. "So that's where these things grow," she said to her dogs who had arrived, freshly drooling, from the outdoors. In her stupor, she had forgotten to close the door. "Go play," she said sternly, noting a humidifier spewing mist at the plants. The dogs sat instead.

"Go," she repeated, sticking her face in the mist. It was obvious dogs belonged to a clumsier world, one filled with trees and sticks and flat fields of durable objects for them to knock over. Was she from dog-world as well? Did she have clodlike, simplistic pain instead of the exquisite torture represented here? Maybe in her cruder world, someone had had to knock her to her dull senses.

Tropical fish complemented this world. Here, blossoms donned the colors of the spheres, and orchid plants strained languorously to break free of their beautiful cages. Miranda sighed as she sat on a central stone bench, staring at the tidy ranks of vegetables silently growing, growing.

What would be the effect of eating a salad consisting entirely of greens plucked in the glory of preadolescence? Sitting there, she was overcome by the feeling these tender vegetables represented everything most desirable on earth, everything sweet and nourishing and good. That if she ate them, she, too, might become all those things. And who would ever know if she picked a few young carrots or baby peas to gobble down?

She stood up and looked around, having forgotten again why she had come. There were no marijuana plants in view, nothing betraying criminal behavior of any kind. Seeing a hose nearby, she picked it up and held it in her hand. She thought of Billy's outgoing message and made her way to the spigot, which she turned all the way on. She started spraying things indiscriminately then, just spraying. She tilted the hose up, and, with it raised high in the air, imitated a child imitating rain.

Five minutes later she returned to the fish room, picked up the food, and carefully scooped out a full measurement. She began to scatter the flakes on the surface, her idea being that the fish would come up one at a time and quietly nibble, acquainting themselves with the floating food before ingesting it.

Consequently, nothing prepared Miranda for the feeding frenzy of the larger fish who rose to the surface of the tank like sharks at the smell of blood, causing the water to churn and roil and even splash out of the uncovered sections of the top. She backed away.

"Nice fishies—" She resealed the can of food and tossed it onto the floor near the tank. "Nice denizens of the un-deep."

While backing toward the kitchen, Miranda saw the blue-green glow of the fish tank being reflected in the metal parts of some large object near the picture window. It was a telescope, an expensive-looking instrument. Miranda wondered what celestial bodies Billy gazed at, then noticed that it was not aimed upward at all, it was aimed in the general vicinity of her house. No, directly at her house.

Not possible, she thought as she approached it. But as she bent toward the scope, it was her own desk—close enough to her eyeballs to count the colored paper clips in their little plastic tray—that rose to meet her.

"Oh my God—" She yanked up her head and then just as quickly reconnected with the eyepiece for another look, this time moving the lens ever so slightly each way. Her index cards, her opened mail, a coffee cup, and a framed picture of Vivianne taken two years earlier in a Batgirl costume.

"He can see everything!" She continued to stare at her living room, doing an inventory of what he'd seen. He was just like his fish—ravenous, even if he appeared just to be pacing. She had a vision of herself in the living room then, in her slippers and patched-up clothes. Had she picked her nose? Left her pants unzipped after using the bathroom?

Bleakly, she began to rationalize. Lydia would have said he had been driven to it, that he'd become desperate to get to know her in any way he could, poor man. Vivianne would have laughed, citing again the ridiculous premise of utter seclusion. She would have defended Billy's spying, praising the telescope as the perfect tool for lonely, alienated, desperate people trying to connect in any way they could. Miranda shuddered to think of what Rochelle's commentary might be, something having to do with stymieing the natural course of the heart and the consequences thereof.

Planting herself on the stool next to the telescope, she looked through his window toward her own house. She pictured herself there and pictured him poring over her at close range. She pulled the eyepiece down to her eye again to see how much of the other rooms were visible. A little bit of the kitchen and virtually none of the bedroom or bathroom. That was a relief. Her shoulders dropped, and a breath was expelled after being unconsciously held in.

It was then she felt an unmistakable twinge in her right eye, followed by a dull ache at the base of her neck. She dropped her head forward and rolled her neck. Another twinge. She rubbed her eyebrows. *I don't need this now, I'm trying to think. No headache. No headache.* She breathed in and out quietly, trying to relax her shoulders. She would have to go home.

In attempting to shift the sight of the telescope too quickly back to where she had found it, Miranda knocked it upward toward the night sky—where it should have been in the first place. Curious, she looked in. It was black, everything became black. With a little shifting, she saw the blurry bright specks of stars cross her view. Then, somehow, she found the moon and her mouth involuntarily fell open; and when she finally left Billy Steadman's, it was with the telescope firmly planted in her arms.

At home, she prepared herself an espresso, for she had read and confirmed that caffeine could sometimes deflect a migraine. She lay flat on the floor trying to think of nothing, trying to follow some of the meditation techniques she had gone over with Keeper Dix. She tried to empty her mind, which was difficult given the chemistry of coffee and the fact that she had waited too long, wasted those critical moments looking at the moon.

Resigning herself to the onset of pain, she moved into her bedroom, where she lay in the dark for two hours, a dull throb vying with sharp stabs for control over the right side of her head. Fully clothed, she eventually fell into an exhausted sleep.

At eight o'clock the following day, Miranda put on some white overalls and went outdoors, Art and Wayne clambering behind her. It had been three days since her last trip to the Otnip post office, and though mail was usually minimal, it was her habit to go every day during the week. Today, driving down the road, she would also be able to see if there was any activity in the greenhouse across the street. If he was home, she wanted to know.

In addition to the overalls, which hung loose and bagged at her feet, Miranda sported large, extradark tortoiseshell sunglasses to conceal her right eye, still badly bloodshot from the headache of the night before.

Keith had landed his blow slightly to the right of her nose, about two inches below the ocular socket. Though her nose seemed to have healed completely, especially given that she had never done the wise thing and gotten medical attention, the headaches had begun occurring within weeks after the incident. From what she could gather they were neither classic migraines nor cluster headaches even though elements of each were present. They affected one side, deepened into the eye, and were generally triggered by a quick release of stress after its equally quick onset.

Though drained from the ordeal, Miranda was happy to be outdoors. Trampling the ground in thick-soled boots, she kicked the clods of dirt that stood in her way and crushed them, enjoying the sensation of clumped earth giving way and turning to dust beneath her feet.

A few brave bulbs had decided to make their spring debut. Miranda, still new to seasonal joys such as this one, squatted, seduced, beside the midget spears. Then she stood and gazed past her grove—four giant cottonwoods in desperate need of pruning, a weeping willow, and a row of lilac bushes massive enough when in bloom to intoxicate even peripheral neighbors—to the pasture. No longer dormant, a shy green infused the field, a flush of life that seemed to deepen even as Miranda stood there feasting upon it.

Things were growing not only in the greenhouse but outside; and as she stood there, she felt sure she could feel the bulbs burgeoning under her, pressing up, tiny, tender, and yet volcanic in strength. How did such a delicate force of nature break through the earth's crust? How did a carrot send its threadlike root downward as its feathers shot up?

She flashed on a teenage Vivianne (in glasses that looked more like goggled microscopes) telling her for the first time (of many) that technically bumblebees should not be able to fly if one were to pit wing size against volume—that every time they flew, the laws of physics were defied. Miranda wondered, calling the dogs to her car, if the odds were not equally stacked against tulips.

Billy did not seem to be at home. Driving by, she saw no signs of movement in the greenhouse or outside, but in craning her neck backward to get a good look nearly ran off the road and into the drainage ditch. Overcorrecting, she swerved manically across the meridian and into on-coming traffic, of which there was none. Now, she prayed he was not at home, because any car passing by in Otnip was as visible and noteworthy as a jetliner roaring its white contrail across the empty blue. He would have seen her biff.

Well, if Billy had been home, wouldn't he have been at her door at the crack of dawn for a certain item blatantly missing from his living room? He had done so once before, knocked on her door at the ungodly hour of 6:58 in the morning. He needed coffee, he said, staring at her flannel Bullwinkle pajamas with a crooked grin on his face. He had actually marched over dressed in his robe.

"We open at seven," Miranda said back, wondering why the dogs hadn't gotten up and why she had answered the door at all. Well, who else could it have been? "That's when the coffeemaker goes on."

"All by itself?" He was incredulous, as if she had been the one to invent the wonder of the timed appliance.

"Yeah. It goes on, all by itself, at 7 A.M. every morning. I hear the noise of the water dripping and feel all cozy inside. Like I have company. Then I smell the coffee and swoon."

"You actually swoon? How can you swoon if you're al-ready lying down?"

"It's an interior swoon. A sort of emotional swoon."

"Ah. But you don't have anyone to make you toast. Wouldn't that be nicer?" The dogs arrived, going to Billy first, as if he were hiding treats under the velour of his robe. She watched as he played absently with the velvet folds of Art's jowls, the softest body part of them all.

"Maybe I should invent the timed toaster." Wayne must have sensed she felt betrayed, for he'd come over to stand beside her.

"That would be a lot harder. Butter has to be administered immediately for toast to be perfect." Halting, he cupped a hand to his ear. "Listen—I hear it!" He made his way toward the kitchen. "Now why don't you go back to your room, and I'll bring you your coffee? You can have it bedside. Cream and sugar?"

"Cream," Miranda called back. "But I'm going to get dressed. I'll have it in the kitchen."

When she emerged, however, Billy had already gone. Her sharp feeling of disappointment was interrupted by the sound of the phone.

"Hello?"

"You had your chance to be served, but you turned it down. So I went home." He hung up immediately.

Somewhere deep inside her, Miranda admitted Billy had figured her out. If anyone was keeping score, he had just won that hand and lots of others before it, and despite her caustic analyses and visceral notations, she could not have told you what the game was called, what the strategy was, or how to win. Naturally, that tormented her.

In truth, Miranda did not need to go to her mailbox more than once a week. In that amount of time a few bills might collect, a few payments from clients, random catalogs, maybe a flyer from the grocery store since she had signed up to be on their list. But the same Miranda who grasped at papers flying in the wind clung to the notion that important news might at any time be delivered to her via the US mail. One never knew when. Maybe people would track her down and write. Friends from New York, from Aspen. People finally answering her change-of-address notice.

What met her, however, as she pulled at the twisted key in number 23, was a box overstuffed with correspondence of all kinds. Unwedging it took some doing, and in trying to maneuver her hand within the compartment, she managed to knock a few envelopes back onto the floor of the inner sanctum. That was when she heard a voice ask her—for there was no one else in the matchbox-sized building—if she wouldn't mind picking up a package. For Billy.

Miranda did not answer right away.

"Unlike *some* folks, he doesn't come to pick up his mail often enough," the voice continued, through Miranda's mailbox slot. "This one says 'perishable' and it's been sitting here for two days. You live right across from him, don'tcha?"

"As a matter of fact"—Miranda pulled herself together—"yes. But how do you know that?" A PO box didn't tell where someone lived: Miranda guessed this woman had simply pieced together—i.e., researched—where every boxholder in Otnip actually resided. They were interrupted by the sound of a fan coming on, a hangar-sized monster used to circulate the air in the suffocating space. Miranda peered into her box and saw lips moving.

"Come to the front desk, we can talk there," the mouth said. Miranda noted a single dark mustache hair over the upper lip before noiselessly closing her mailbox, wishing that she could just as easily close herself off from the Otnip grapevine. Obviously, they knew she and Billy were neighbors. What did this imply—that they were friends? More than friends? More than just neighbors?

Somewhat timidly she presented herself to the postal clerk, who had already lined up a signature spot and laid down a pen marked US GOVERNMENT before her. There was a small box on the counter indisputably marked "perishable" and with Billy's name indisputably indicating that it was his.

"This way, his plants won't die." The woman was as matter-of-fact as they came. "FedEx usually makes these deliveries. I'm not sure why it came here this time . . ."

Miranda stared at the signature line. "Isn't there some law against me picking up his package? I mean, is this legal?" You never knew until you asked.

The woman looked up over the tops of her small, rectangular, frameless reading glasses and through clumped strands of Big Hair, hair sometimes referred to as *fried, dyed, and then shoved to the side.* "No, hon, it ain't. But by the power vested in me—and for the sake of Billy's tomatoes and whatever else he grows—I'm authorizing you to drop this off. *If* you don't mind." She pulled off the quickest, tidiest smile Miranda had ever seen, then made it disappear like a penny from a palm.

"Of course not," Miranda parried with an award-winning smile of her own. "I mean why would I mind?" She signed her name while feeling the woman's stare, the

111

words *and whatever else he grows* circling her head like a germ-carrying mosquito.

"What is it made you go gray?"

"Hm-m?" Miranda looked up.

"The white in your hair. Did it all happen at once?"

"Well." Miranda reached up and ran a hand through her hair and suddenly, feeling her glasses on the top of her head, realized the woman was looking into the one red eye. She had forgotten to put the glasses back on after reaching in the mail slot. "Yes. As a matter of fact. It did." That was an outright lie, but Miranda wanted to divert the woman's attention away from her eyes.

Meanwhile, she was instantly taken with the idea of being someone who could change overnight—who might change today, for all they knew, these whispering people who had already figured out what her relationship was with Billy, even before she had. They didn't know her, she could change. Overnight! She wished she had never taken that telescope from Billy's. She wanted him to aim it at her and watch as she became a different woman before his very eyes, one he could never figure out.

"You're lucky it suits you so well." The woman, whose name was Vicki (*Vicki Schuster, Your Postmistress* was stenciled on the back wall home-sweet-home style right above her softball ribbons), smiled and handed Miranda the package. "Goes with the eyes. Dave D. over at MinuteBurger told me about them and he wasn't exaggerating one bit. Although the one"—she leaned forward—"could use some Visine." She extended her hand. "I'm Vicki. I don't think I've ever introduced myself. You sort of slip in and out of here."

Miranda took the hand, feeling the pressure and warmth of what she could only assume was a prize-winning softball player's grip. But her nails were beautiful—trimmed, shaped, and shiny.

"Anyhoo. You can tell Billy we can't always do his bidding for him. That he needs to pick up his mail more often or sign a release to have you pick it up in his stead. But tell him I was nice about it. I suppose you get tomatoes from him even in winter, huh?"

After muttering something about "No, not really," then "Well, yes, sort of," Miranda exited, struggling to balance not only an armload of mail but her newly invented relationship with her neighbor. Back in her car, she endeavored to jam the mailbox key in the ignition several times before fumbling with the correct one.

"Hey, Miranda!" Vicki had come outside waving her arms. "Drop off that heap of mail in your arms at his house too while you're there! I forgot to tell you it's all his! Catalogs mostly, nothing for you! Bye!" She actually spit in the dirt before disappearing back into her realm—where the power was, without question, great indeed.

Next time, Miranda told herself, slamming in a Doris Day tape, *I'll ask more questions about Billy. I'll be as nosey as everyone else is around here. How good can tomatoes be, for pity's sake?* She took a moment to fan the slippery stack of mail on her lap. Catalogs for seeds and greenhouse supplies. For fish and aquariums. A bill from the electric company, and one from Eldridge Rubber and Plastic Hosing. Something from the Four Corners Nurse Veterans of the Vietnam War. She stared long and hard at that particular envelope, wondering what Billy's affiliation was, what had drawn him into their cause.

Throwing the mail onto the passenger's seat, she finally turned onto the highway. With the wheel in her hands at ten and two, she drove a demure thirty miles an hour all the way home, thinking tenderly of nurse veterans, then of Vicki Schuster.

In order to counteract a vague feeling of loss and hurt, she envisioned herself for the first time as someone, part of a very select group, whose winters were tomato-rich. They had already decided that, the grapevine people. And were you not, to some extent, what people made of you, said of you, thought of you? It had seemed Otnip might be the perfect place for the reinvention of herself. And yet, oddly, it now seemed that the people populating her life—even sparsely—had been the ones inventing her.

She drove down Billy's driveway and, with the engine running, jogged in and placed the mail and the box on the kitchen table. At the last moment, she reached for the Nurse Veterans letter and tucked it under her arm. She was eager to get home.

The dogs, however, had seized their opportunity to leap from the open door of the Scout and bound off, disappearing in the blink of an eye. They would not come when called or even threatened. Reluctant, however, to loiter at Billy's house when he could return any moment, she made haste to leave, gravel grinding and flying as she backed out.

Once home, she remained in her parked car for a few moments without opening the door. She remembered fish and plants and everything she had seen in Billy's house.

She wanted not only to return the telescope but also to rip apart the bed she had made under the influence of too much leafy greenery and oxygen. And where were the tomatoes she had lied about receiving?

Back at her desk she took out Gregory Vogt's card. With new people, she checked in almost every day; and at the moment she relished the idea of Gregory's deep, soothing voice. There would be no personal questions like what made her go gray and was it all of a sudden that it happened.

In the middle of dialing the number, she stopped to stare at that one piece of Billy's mail she'd taken. Quite deliberately then, as if it had been her intention all along, she sliced it open with her letter opener. An honest mistake—she could say she had not realized prior to opening it that the name and address were not hers. Did he really give money to Vietnam nurse veterans? Was there a sweeter cause for a man to champion? She could not think of one.

She finished dialing and withdrew the envelope's contents, scanning for the upshot. "Thank you for your donation . . . $400 . . . tax deductible. Supporters like you . . . possible . . . continue with desperately needed assistance for these forgotten heroines still trying to cope with life after trauma." Miranda felt a lump forming in her throat just as Gregory answered the phone. Why should this touch her so?

"I want to read something to you, Miranda," Gregory plunged in. "Turns out I did have a book of poetry here, just an anthology. With a single Whitman excerpt." He did not wait for any answer, but took a breath and began.

"This is the female form,
A divine nimbus exhales from it from head to foot,
It attracts with fierce undeniable attraction."

Gregory both spoke and sang the poem, the rhythmic delivery slow and sermony like a preacher's.

"I am drawn by its breath as if I were no more than a
helpless vapor, all falls aside but myself and it,
Books, art, religion, time, the visible and solid earth,
and what was expected of heaven
or fear'd of hell, are now consumed,
Mad filaments, ungovernable shoots play out of it,
the response likewise ungovernable,
Hair, bosom, hips, bend of legs, negligent falling hands
all diffused, mine too diffused."

Miranda had stopped fiddling with index cards, pencils, everything. What kind of selection for an anthology was this? He read on.

"Ebb stung by the flow and flow stung by the ebb,
love-flesh swelling and deliciously aching,
Limitless limpid jets of love hot and enormous, quivering
jelly of love, white-blow and delirious juice,
Bridegroom night of love working surely and softly
into the prostrate dawn,
Undulating into the willing and yielding day,
Lost in the cleave of the clasping and sweet-flesh'd day."

Not a tremor, no pause of doubt interrupted the flow of the cadenced sentence that the old man had infused with life and longing. Miranda felt the rush of a pilot light igniting all her burners. The phone line buzzed as blood rushed to her face.

It had been over a year and a half since she had loved a man, been held tightly, been desired and desired someone in return. Such was life after her own trauma. Three months after Miranda had moved in, Lydia had FedExed her a vibrator (next-day delivery for a life-size-lingam model which she kept in the toolshed), along with some personal lubricant and a book on Kegel exercises. Vivianne had, after her own fashion, sent twelve novels recommended to her by some professor friend at Stanford as paragons of smoldering literature. Both gifts had come in handy, even if one required furtive trips to the shed.

A vision rose in Miranda's mind then—a wash of familiar faces all looking at her with disbelief. Vivianne, Lydia, her friends from Aspen, Vicki from the post office, the clerks at the grocery store in Cortez, Cherise Pivey, even Majesta Fein—they were all shaking their heads at her. "At least take care of your physical needs," was the unanimous consensus from the sea of females picketing her frontal lobe.

"It's something, isn't it?" Gregory's normal voice brought Miranda back to her desk, her hands, her headset. Everything was tingling. "It's from *I Sing The Body Electric,* a nine-page poem. I can't wait to get the rest . . ." He coughed. "I hope you're not thinking me unseemly for sharing that. It's a bit bold, I know . . ."

"Body electric is right," stammered Miranda. "No, no, you were fantastic. The *voice* . . ."

"It's like another voice came through me there—" He stopped, self-conscious of his own enthusiasm.

Miranda, however, did not by any means want it quelled.

"All poets"—she slipped a bit of Agatha Colgate into her tone—"would tell you that poems were meant to be read aloud."

He paused. "It made me feel heathen—a pagan—for reading it!"

"Well, now, *that* might have been the particular poem," she ventured, smiling, and heard him concede. "Gregory," she continued quickly, "why don't we just use our time to give you an audience?" She waited a moment. "You need to practice your reading, and I need to practice my listening."

"You mean I'd—I'd just recite poetry? Like the entire 'Body Electric,' from beginning to end?" He waited a long time before saying, "Let's give it a go, by golly!"

"Good," she said, flipping through the *Webster's Collegiate* on her desk. "And by the way, 'heathen' comes from 'from the heaths' just as 'pagan' means 'from the village.' There's nothing ungodly mentioned."

"My children might disagree with you there. Don't get me wrong, I love 'em; but they seem to be missing something of the joy of the spirit. If I'd realized this when I was far younger, I might have lived a different kind of life. I might have been an outlaw, in the good sense of the word. Well. I should let you go. Whatever happened 'bout that police car next door?"

"The police car?" Her voice escalated by three-quarters

of an octave. "Oh, they carted my neighbor off, it looked like. Not sure what happened there."

"Carted him off, you mean took him in?"

"Yeah. Probably a misunderstanding of some sort."

"Took in the hydro-farmer?"

"That's right."

"Well, I could hazard a guess or two. With a *hydro-farmer*. Any chance he's a grower?"

This is not happening, Miranda thought, *just simply cannot be.* She thought she'd been safe with Gregory—that his curiosity would stop just short of her neighborhood. "Evidently, he grows hydroponic tomatoes. Is known to have caused wars over them."

Gregory laughed. "Now *that* I could see. Warm. Pendulous. Begging to be clipped, salted, and eaten rapaciously as if its juices could not stand further containment." Gregory, suffering what appeared to be a lusty contagion of Whitman, cleared his throat, then shifted his voice out of overdrive. "A good enough excuse to befriend the—"

"Oh *shit.*" Miranda blurted, interrupting him. "Excuse me."

"What . . . what is it?"

Miranda squinted. A vintage Cadillac with the top down had just pulled into Billy's driveway. Billy was getting out, as was the driver who looked like a New York model fresh off a Civil-War-era photo shoot. With him was a young woman in suede jeans and a cowboy hat looking around as if she'd landed on the moon.

"He's back," she said, distracted by the van-art landscape painted on the side of the car: Canyonlands in sepia tones. "From jail."

"Cops bring him back?"

"No, no cops." Miranda's monotone was distant.

"Well, maybe you should mosey on over and make sure everything's okay. You're not in a wheelchair, too, are you? He a nice fellow?"

"Yeah." She turned the word into a shrug. "I don't really know him that well. Anyway," she cut Gregory off, "I'll keep you posted. Your poetry books should arrive in two days. How about I call you then?"

Headset off, Miranda stared across the street wondering what to do. She was tempted to set up the telescope and have a good look; instead, she eventually dialed the next number.

Lael Vanderpin, who was trying to set a world record on the number of paperback mysteries read in one lifetime, was sounding frisky today. "Why isn't there an *old* person confined to a *wheelchair* as a detective?" With Lael, all important words came highlighted. "Don't you suppose lots of people like *me* would identify with that? *I'll* say they could. Right now I'm reading one where the *detectives* are *cats* of all things, and these are *successful* books, very popular. You'd think an old person confined to a wheelchair could get more of a *response* than that."

"*Ironsides*," Miranda said distractedly, wishing she had her binoculars handy for a quick study of the Cadillac.

"What?" Lael irritably queried.

"*Ironsides* was that Raymond Burr show where he was confined to a wheelchair. You need to add another element to it, you know, to make it your own. Something truly— original."

"Oh," Lael said, surprised. As if she never expected to

be taken seriously. "Well, yes, I guess you're right, there was such a show. But you see, *my* detective is a *woman*, Miranda, an o-o-old woman. And she has a secret *weapon* . . ."

"Now you're talking," Miranda said, wondering how long the three of them would be inside and how long it would take Billy to discover he had been robbed. She did not have to wonder long, for moments later they emerged, Billy eating an apple and fringe-jacket-man smoking a cigar, his free arm around the girl. They did not go to the car, however, or head back to the greenhouse; they began walking toward the road. Then once they got to the road, they began crossing it. The yellow line was nothing to them!

"I want you to keep working on your main character," Miranda told Lael with great urgency. "I want to hear more about her in three days. Make her special—make her come right at you—Good-bye, Lael." It was the shortest check-in call she had ever placed.

They were walking down her driveway!

She ripped off the headset, bit her lip, tucked in her shirt, and felt her teeth for scum. Shit. Shit. *Shit.* She hated herself for reacting. Who were these people anyway? She ran to get the telescope and opened her door, the object in her arms like a missile-sized hot potato.

"Here," she said, thrusting it forward before anyone had a chance to say anything. "Here, you voyeuristic, fish-loving, orchid-flaunting problem person. I don't care if I'm admirable or not. What you see is what you get, okay?"

"She's prettier in person," the fringed man said, stepping

forward to take the telescope and putting it right back down on the boot bench. "The picture in your brochure doesn't do you justice. Sullivan Novo," he said, moving past his woman friend, past Miranda, and into her house. "I'm inviting myself in."

Billy confessed lovesickness to Sullivan while on location in Navajoland with Chevy Trucks.

It was the drive over that had primed him, cracked him open like the great gaping land all around. Pure seduction was Sullivan's cavalcade of canyons, arroyos, and long stretches of sage; bridges, mesas, and notable pullouts; caves, ridges, water holes, and secret archeological sites. In addition he could tell you, at any given time, which direction they faced and what lay ahead both immediately and far beyond.

"We'll be coming up on this little *arroyo seco*," he would report. "Then in ten minutes we hit the desert. If you were to keep on going west-northwest, you would eventually be in Provo, Utah. But that would take three-quarters of a good novel." Things were never measured in miles but in *bots*.

In the Cadillac, with the top down in spite of the early-spring chill, Billy felt connected to the wind, the dust, and the disappearing sun, and he let himself be driven, amenable to the idea of being elsewhere for a night. He had forgotten how natural it was to be with this friend, with whom he had spent so much time in what seemed like another life. They had first met in a bookstore in Santa Fe, where Billy had indulged a desperate need for Raymond Chandler. "Ever heard Elliott Gould *read* Chandler?" With half a dozen audio books in his arms, Sullivan had looked at Billy's paperback edition of *Farewell, My Lovely* with skepticism, as if books should only be entrusted to great voices.

"So," Sullivan was saying now, as he fumbled through his box of tapes and pulled out some Bill Monroe. "The famous Carson Sung was at the Cortez bookstore for a reading just hours ago."

Sung, a literary but popular local writer, was Sullivan's hero whom he quoted relentlessly, memorizing long sections of both prose and poetry. Billy had known about the reading, which had been heavily advertised in the area, had even briefly considered going. "Oh yeah: So how was he?"

"Frankly"—Sullivan shook his head—"I was hoping he would read some of his poetry. Or a little of *Long, Dry Cry of the Desert.* Or *Blessed Beat.*" There was disdain in Sullivan's tone. "He's shamelessly pandering to the future making of *Sky.*"

A movie was about to be made of his most affecting and successful book, *Wicked Sky,* one of the few novels Billy had read twice. "He's entitled to pander a little, isn't he?"

"Listen, Billy, I'm his biggest fan, you know that. I've listened to everything he's ever written three times. I couldn't believe he was coming. I'd been thinking about it for weeks, dreaming of the meaningful conversation I could have with him, the one where he tells me he's always hoped to be understood *that* well."

Billy could hear an unfortunate end, like the crack of distant thunder. "You put him on a pedestal. How surprising can it be that he wants a movie to be made out of his book? I mean, Sully, who wouldn't?"

Sullivan was hardly listening. "I am surprised he wants to ruin his neighborhood. They'll be scouting a location out here. The *movie people*. They're going to make some beautiful, empty, unsullied section of range famous. They'll ruin it."

So that was it. Sullivan's personal playground dirtied. "You scout out locations for commercials, Sully. Take them places you shouldn't. What's the dif?"

"The difference is big. No one associates a commercial for a truck with anything of meaning. *Wicked Sky* is everybody's favorite book and for good reason. They'll want to know where it was filmed and then they'll want to *come.*" Sullivan paused long enough to let Bill Monroe finish a tune.

"How was Sung, though?" Billy was curious. "I mean what was he like?"

"The undisputed master of Western pathos? Better even than his tapes." Sullivan sounded dejected. "Great reader, deep resonant voice, intelligent—and though pedantic, polite. He didn't ridicule the Colorado cabernet. Or the cheddar cheese served with chicken-flavored crackers."

Billy laughed.

The sun, rushing to set, struck red cliffs in a fleeting moment of warmth before dark. Sullivan, all tour guide, pointed to it, as if drawing attention to a little something he had created. "He does, however, seem to have a weakness for the young women. The coeds from Durango were drooling all over him—as if he were a rock star or something. Maybe women want their fathers. Is that it? I mean, what do you think women really want, Billy?"

Sullivan did not make a habit of analyzing women, in spite of his vast number of conquests. Billy was surprised at the question. "Beats me, Sullivan. I should have asked Begay for more insight."

"Who's Begay?"

"This Navajo who learned to meditate as fast as most people learn to lick a spoon."

"Maybe he was just pretending."

Billy smiled. It was just like Sullivan to think so.

Shaking his head, Sullivan pulled the car back onto the road, hitting fifty so fast Billy's cheeks pulled backward. "Maybe we're all just pretenders. I mean what if I get older and the women keep staying the same age? And for some reason, unfathomable to me, they keep liking me in spite of my pretensions, and my pandering, and my faults."

"And that bothers you? That they'll keep liking you?"

"Yeah. It bothers me. What if I need a woman who can call me on my bullshit. Not fall for it every time. Challenge me."

"You smoking pot again, Novo?"

His look was one of disgust. "I'm a cigar man, Bill."

Even though Sullivan had hauled marijuana from place to place earlier in life, like Billy he had become indifferent, except in allowing that the experience had acquainted him with the far reaches of the Four Corners. By the time Billy met him, he was working for FedEx, further researching little known roads, sometimes with his camera and always with a map.

"Well, maybe in looking at a lonely author pandering to Hollywood and to women young enough to be his grand-daughters, I'm realizing I may be lonely for real companionship one day," Sullivan said. "Which is something you of all people should understand."

Billy sighed. "Why don't you just find someone closer to your age, Sullivan? Here you are, the first thing you say to me is how hot the girls serving the food at your shoot are."

For a split second, Sullivan did not speak. Then he got defensive. "Well, it's not like we control who we're attracted to."

"No," Billy agreed quickly. "That's for sure."

Evidently, that was all either of them wanted to say, for when Sullivan reinserted *The Red Badge* Billy didn't argue.

One and one-quarter chapters later, they arrived at what Billy could only describe as history meets a kinder, gentler Hollywood. The tidy encampment on the edge of a stream consisted of six Civil-War-era tents, surrounding a central campfire and chuck wagon. While a uniformed beanpole of a man played the fiddle, a handful of horses were being brushed by people dressed in period costume. Occasionally, busy-looking, clipboard-holding individuals wearing base-ball caps would emerge from their tents.

"Wow," Billy said, as they pulled in beside a row of rental Jeeps. "When did you start doing things this way?" Sullivan seemed to have superimposed an additional theme on his brand-name production.

"This is my first time!" Sullivan gazed lovingly at his handiwork. "See, ever since I heard about *Wicked Sky*, I've been thinking about how this empty landscape lends itself so naturally to pockets of time travel. You don't have to ruin things permanently with a full-on movie to get a sense of . . . stage." He smiled widely. "And I'm good at it! People eat this shit up! Truck-selling assholes are nicer to each other surrounded by the Civil War!" He waved at one of the girls standing beside the food wagon. "My tepee's off behind that clump of cottonwoods. It's already set up with two cots."

"Expecting company?"

"You never know." Sullivan grinned, as if their previous conversation had been nothing more than a fleeting moment, a cramp, easily rubbed out by a return to the company of women.

Billy looked around. "It seems so peaceful here. Like you've *drugged* these people."

Sullivan laughed, nodding. "You utterly captivate them with natural beauty—then bring in the heavy artillery of artifice. I had no idea. Think of the possibilities! Are you hungry? Tonight it's beef-barley casserole and corn bread, dandelion greens, apple pie, hard cider, and cowboy coffee. Designer water goes without saying."

Sullivan spent all of dinner flirting with Beth and Savannah, the two young women who had been hired to facilitate food preparation. They were in their twenties, athletic, and very pretty, and seemed mesmerized by Sullivan's endless supply of tall tales, which they took for the gospel truth. Billy, who had seen the act many times, feared Sullivan would end up actually dandling the two of them on his lap.

Billy remained quiet throughout the meal in spite of his

friend's efforts to make him sound like the most charismatic baby greens grower on earth, someone who *grew* dandelions. A lie!

Later on, in the tepee and settled in their cots, Sullivan, sounding not so angry as perplexed, confronted him. "What's the matter with you? Don't you like women at all anymore? I mean, just to enjoy? Aren't you ever going to snap out of it?"

"I could ask you that same question, Sullivan. The same one you asked yourself an hour and a half ago. Two just isn't enough of that kind of woman anymore. Not for me, attraction or not."

It was a nasty comment and quite unlike Billy, who appreciated the whole spectrum of women. He moved from his cot to the fire and in choppy movements pushed a stick at the smoldering coals. Outside, the cottonwoods rustled.

Sullivan sat up in his own cot angrily. "You are never, ever going to find another Elena," he said, each word wading through the silence as if it were thick and deep. "She was unique, Billy, I'd be the first to say so. But you've shut everyone out for so long, I don't think you know how to open up anymore. Yeah, okay, I have my own tired proclivities with women. But I think I still let people touch me. My mother calls me whenever she wants. My friends know where to reach me and can count on me answering my messages. I play softball in the spring and hang out at the coffee shop talkin' dukey with the locals."

"Have you tried to leave me a message lately?" Billy interrupted. "Huh? Have you heard the message on my machine?"

He opened the flap of the tepee and stared out into the

night. Then he turned around and confessed to Sullivan what had been consuming him for weeks, months, he had lost track—that he was in love.

"In *love*." Sullivan was silent for several moments, the word hanging in the air like a long-forgotten but familiar tune. "Oh," he said finally, eureka belying the flatness of his tone. "It's the woman across the street. I mean who else could it possibly be, man, you don't ever go anywhere except to make deliveries. It's like she dropped out of the sky—and looks like she dropped out of the sky, too. Those eyes. She split up with her boyfriend?"

Billy had pocketed a *Respect for Your Elders* brochure on one of his many missions to Miranda's. Sullivan, who occasionally came to visit, had seen it on the kitchen table once and studied it carefully. "Do you think I could call up and ask her to read stories to me? I think I need her, Billy. I need her bad. You ever spend time with her?"

Jealousy had come up like metallic spit in his mouth. "Not much. She has a boyfriend somewhere. Merchant marine or something. She calls me if her toilet's plugged or needs a shingle renailed to the roof. Besides, she's too old for you."

"Well, I don't think so. In an icy cold way, that woman verges on *hot*."

"There was never any boyfriend," Billy said now. "I made that up. But from the very beginning, I sabotaged myself. I told her I was a grower."

"A grower—"

"Yeah. She thinks I grow pot in the basement."

"Why'd you tell her that?"

"I don't know exactly. Lots of reasons. But bottom line? Because she wouldn't accept it. And then I wouldn't have to worry about getting involved. She'd keep me at bay."

"And so?"

"Almost ferociously, the woman has kept me at bay. It drives me wild with desire."

"Why didn't you just tell her you had lied? That you were famous for tomatoes? That you didn't understand your own reasons for bending the truth?"

"I don't know. I'd gotten this fire going, and to come clean would have doused it with water. She would have hated me."

"She hates you anyway."

"No. No, I wouldn't say that. There was something from the first moment. Maybe it scared me so much I trumped up the lie real quick."

"Uh-huh. So now?"

"Now? Well, she saw LeFevre and Scupper come and pick me up. I'm sure she thought I was being hauled off on a charge of growing with intent to sell. I kind of liked that, I have to admit—like, I wasn't playing around after all. She would feel bad for me and stuff."

"But how do you know you're in love with her if you've never spent any time with her? I do that shit, man, not you."

"I never said I didn't see her. I go over all the time, trying to work my way in. Bring her stuff, fix stuff, putter around her house." He wanted to mention the telescope but lacked the courage. "The thing is, she's so different from Elena, about 180 degrees. But they seem to be able to coexist peacefully in my head and in my heart. Like ballasts or something, black and white, and balanced."

Sullivan whistled. "That's nice. That's a nice thing to say, Bill, so nice it almost breaks my heart to hear you say it." The whole tone of his voice had changed, dropped like a medicine ball down the staircase of honesty breaking treads along the way. "I take it she doesn't know you were married and that your beautiful, incredible wife died of cancer? That the evil weed was what saved her when she was so sick . . ."

"No. She doesn't know." As obtuse as Sullivan could be about his own life, he didn't miss a trick with regard to Billy's.

"Well, dude, maybe you should tell her. Maybe there's something you don't know about her, did you ever think of that? Like maybe she's removed herself from civilization for a reason. Are you ready for whatever her life throws at you?"

He thought of Miranda marching around her property with her dogs and her orange pants, talking to herself. Miranda pinning up laundry, picking up garbage, and singing songs to an invisible audience. Miranda looking out over the plain like a sailor waiting to sight land. "Yes," he said simply. "I am."

"Jesus, Billy,"—Sullivan had gotten up out of the cot and took his turn poking the fire—"it's about time, man, that's all I can say. It's about fuckin' time. After the way you acted tonight, I thought something might be wrong with your *dick*. I mean I've always been terrified you would die brokenhearted but not celibate." He produced the stub of a cigar and lit it. "The effect women have on us. It's frightening, isn't it?"

"Good use of the word 'frightening.' " Billy laughed.

"That one, Savannah, she slipped me her phone number while handing me coffee after dinner."

"Tonight?" Billy liked the smell of the cigar here in the canvas tent.

"Yeah, just a few minutes ago. So I immediately start thinking about taking her to this deserted spot I know, this cave dwelling where you can look out over the entire world. Now why would I want to do that? I like that spot alone. It's my spot. It's where I feel most connected to myself and everything else. Why take a twentysomething there?"

"Who should you be taking there? Someone who can point out your faults?"

"Well. *Yeah.* Or no one at all." He took a couple of puffs. "I need to go on a woman fast, Bill, that's what I need. Give them up, cold turkey. I pick the wrong ones, and I think it's getting worse. I mean why would I want to take someone named Savannah, fifteen years younger than me, to my favorite place? That scares me. The name Carson Sung, ex-hero, comes to mind."

Billy burst out laughing.

"I do *not* want to share that spot!"

"Maybe you should be thanking Carson Sung for stirring things up inside you."

"I don't want to be like him, Billy."

"You're already not, Sullivan. Not only are you not a great writer, you're not that polite. You're not portly or professorial. I don't think you should worry about it."

"Thanks. I think. And true, Savannah is a person, a unique individual, just like I said earlier. Maybe I shouldn't be so quick to toss her aside."

"That's not exactly what I meant." Though heavy on sarcasm, the humor wafted right over the top of Sully's head with the cigar smoke.

Sullivan, satisfied with his own conclusions, however, put out his cigar and lay down on his cot. "Tomorrow's another day," he intoned in his best Vivien Leigh. "And we're having grits in the mo'nin'. After breakfast, I can duck out again and drive you home. I want to meet that woman across the street. What's her name again?"

"Miranda," Billy said. "Miranda Blue."

"Blue as in blue?"

"Yes."

"Does she tell you what your faults are?"

"As much as she possibly can."

"She doesn't know the half of it. Good night, Bill."

When Billy fell asleep, it was not the thudding, black sleep of the depressed but the light-footed, buoyant slumber that took you places. He dreamed of the open road and wind. The only image he could cull upon arising was a split-second cameo appearance by Sharon Mystery Sawhill dressed in her white meditator's sweats and holding up a pit-stop variety sign that said, DON'T WORRY BE HAPPY. It was her phrase.

He was still smiling when he showed up for breakfast.

"Where's Sullivan?" he asked Beth, who looked at him as if for the first time. In honor of the theme, she sported a lace-up, low-cut blouse (wardrobe, anyone?), full skirt, and boots.

"He and Savannah went horseback riding," she said in a pout. "He said to tell you he'd be back at eight and to help yourself to breakfast if you wanted." She began seeing to his needs: a plate, some silver, a tin mug. "Have you known him long?"

"Sullivan?" Billy said. "Yep. A long time."

"What's he really like?"

"Well." Billy scratched the day's growth of hair on his chin. "His writing pretty much consumes him."

"Really? He writes? I knew he was deep. What does he write?"

Billy affected a tone of resigned confession. "Erotica mostly, very well written. Don't tell anyone, though. People would be all over him, especially women."

"They already are," Beth said, pouring Billy more coffee.

"What do you like about Sullivan?" Billy thought he might relay any complimentary articulations to his friend later on.

"Well," the woman purred, "he's got this incredible imagination . . ." She brandished her own coffee cup toward the encampment. "It's unreal. And he swears he's under budget. Even with the storyteller, fiddler, horses, staff, everything. It just makes you want to be near him. Share his world."

Billy smiled at her, studying the smooth oval face and the perfection of dark eyebrows against creamy skin.

"So you grow vegetables," she said out of politeness, looking off, scanning for horses and riders returning from their morning romp.

"Yes, I do," Billy said. And that was that.

When Sullivan strode up on his pinto (Billy never knew he rode) there was a twinkle in his eye. Savannah, he said, would be accompanying them to Otnip: She needed a break and the first director's assistant had released them until later that night. Beth, he said, could handle the midday snacks.

Probably as peevish as Beth, Billy got into the backseat of the sedan and stared at the tape caddy. "Got any Carson Sung?" he asked innocently, as they settled themselves, Beth staring at them sullenly from a distance.

"Carson Sung? I love his work!" Savannah crooned. "You know they're making a movie of *Wicked Sky*—"

Sullivan shot a piercing look at Billy. "This A.M. it's a little more Bill Monroe. Stay in character, that's my motto."

"I look forward to reading your work, Sullivan!" Beth called eagerly from camp as they pulled away. This elicited a look from Sullivan that Billy wished he could have captured on film, or in a can. For once, the man of mystery, surprises, and fabrications, was caught off guard. He waved at Beth, then told Savannah to scoot on over closer to him, which she did without hesitation.

"What work?" she inquired sweetly.

"Didn't Sullivan tell you he was a writer?" Billy leaned forward with the query before reclining in the back as if it were a chaise lounge. And while Sullivan finessed himself around Billy's lie like a slippery eel in a net, Billy wondered what Miranda would think as all three of them pulled into his driveway.

 10

"This is the man I won my house from," Billy said, following Sullivan and Savannah into the house as Miranda stepped back. "As well as one of my oldest friends," he continued. "And this is Savannah. Thank you for making my bed, by the way."

Once they were all inside, Miranda eyeballed her guests, wondering what drove a man to dress in period costume. The woman was too young for him, which caused Miranda to reassess the kind of friends Billy had, therefore the kind of person Billy was, ergo the kind of women they both probably liked. Perhaps she was too old for these men. She stuck out her hand anyway.

"Nice to meet you, I guess." The face, not handsome in the regular sense, was nevertheless oddly compelling with its combination of full lips, Roman nose, high cheekbones, and slightly sunken bright hazel eyes. His grip was not only firmer than average but longer lasting.

"Ditto," he said, the corners of his mouth curling up. "I *guess.*" His eyes roamed the room. "You a collector? Fifties stuff?"

"Not really." She shrugged, then impulsively dipped her head toward the Cadillac in the distance. "I noticed you yourself have proclivities of some kind."

Sullivan took off his coat, and gave her a good long stare. "We all have proclivities. Jeepers, girl, where *did* you get those eyes?"

"You ask a lot of questions," she mumbled, as Sullivan continued to pick up objects and put them down. "Which could be viewed as intrusive. Are you the one who bailed out Billy?"

Sullivan put down her wing-shaped Lucite ashtray and picked up the Gumby pencil holder. "Billy," he called out, "you were right about what she would think."

Billy had disappeared into the kitchen, wishing he had been the one to ask for the genealogy of her eyes. Long ago, in fact. Now, however, he had already become Sullivan's straight man. "Well," he called out, "she assumed, and you know what happens when people assume . . ." Though sounding flippant, he was nervous as hell. "How about we have a little brunch together?" He attempted a new tack. "An omelet!"

"I would love an omelet," Sullivan said.

"Personally, I'm starving." Savannah spoke more to herself than anyone else.

"What do you mean, right about what I would think?" Miranda marched into the kitchen just as Billy opened the vegetable bin. The others instinctively followed. "Didn't you get hauled off to jail?"

The carrots he pulled out of an otherwise empty bin were bulky and crude when pitted against his fragile Lilliputian varieties.

"Geez, Miranda"—he held up the bag—"it looks like you just got back from big-rabbit camp or something. Where's the food?"

"I was about to go—" she protested.

"Because this is grim," he cut in. "I'm going home just for a second to pick some sorrel, which is nice in omelets. Sullivan, talk to her—but not too much. Savannah, could I convince you to help me?" *I'm in the driver's seat,* he thought, *once again.*

Savannah, plainly not interested in removing herself from Sullivan's flirtatious interest in Miranda, nevertheless conceded. "Sure," she said, running her fingers through her long red hair. "Whatever."

For a moment, Miranda saw in Savannah a younger version of herself, enamored of people like Sullivan and scared to lose them. She was about to pity her until she remembered Savannah had at least found someone to sleep with at night.

"So you *didn't* bail him out then?" There was cross-examination in her manner. She had begun retrieving coffee beans, a grinder, an espresso maker, and some frozen English muffins.

"On what charges?" Sullivan tittered, removing the suede coat and rolling up the sleeves of his white grandfather-shirt. "Billy's mom regularly calls the police station and begs them to get Billy to call her. It's lunacy."

"Billy's mom?" The words did not register. Miranda had made Billy an orphan, someone unattached to anyone anywhere. Like her and like everyone else in Otnip.

"Yeah, he doesn't list his number, and he won't give it to his parents, who—worry about him. It's absurd, but it's Billy."

She watched Sullivan sit in her favorite chrome-and-linoleum chair. "So then why did the cops come out in person to pick him up? With the lights flashing and everything?"

"I don't know about the lights. But this time, it turned out they wanted him to lead another meditation seminar. The chief of police's wife is in search of peace of mind, and there aren't that many meditation teachers in Montezuma County. They threatened to release his number to good old mom if he didn't show."

"Meditation—" Miranda remembered seeing such books on his shelf. It was an act of great will, however, to hop the mental lily pads from jailbird . . . to cosseted son . . . to practitioner of things elevated. At this rate, he would end up a delegate for the UN.

Sullivan nodded, arose, and made his way to the cupboard. "He got the idea"—he began fingering things just as he had in the living room—"the first time *we* were in jail together. Before your time."

Back one lily pad. "For what?"

"We'd gotten into a fistfight over something pathetic. He broke my nose, it turned out. I had a weapon on me. We were too tired, drunk, and beat-up to do anything but sleep it off. The morning after, sort of as a joke, Billy sits cross-legged and closes his eyes, and the next thing you know, he's teaching a few inmates to breathe deeply. He does know the fundamentals, I'll give him that."

"I don't believe it." Miranda shook her head. "I thought—"

"You thought he was being hauled in for growing reefer—"

"Well, I—"

"He doesn't grow reefer. Hasn't for years. Even when he did, it was always just a little sideline for someone with a supernatural aptitude for growing anything at all. He had a remarkably devoted customer base for miniscule quantities of *sinsemilla;* now, he has people starting wars over his tomatoes."

"I've just recently learned as much," Miranda said primly, just as Billy and Savannah reappeared with four fistfuls of what looked like perfect, young spinach.

Miranda's exotic-flavor stare stopped Billy in his tracks. "What did you tell her? What did he tell you?"

"I told her you were abducted to call your mother and teach peace of mind." Sullivan put his arm around Savannah's waist and reached his fingers to her belt buckle, which he fiddled with. Unflinching, Savannah removed his hand, but not without couching her delight with a first-rate look of dismay.

"Which is the most ridiculous thing I ever heard," Miranda said, raising her voice above the loud whine of the coffee grinder. "I never saw any tomatoes in your greenhouse. You've never brought me tomatoes."

"You're right about teaching peace of mind," Billy said sweetly, charmed by her reaction. "An utterly ridiculous idea. I merely instruct in calming the mind. As for tomatoes, Miranda, that's another story. They are in high demand and cannot be wasted on ingrates. They grow under special lights and secret conditions in the basement. I'm touched you went into the greenhouse, by the way. I feel sort of—violated by it."

He regretted it the instant he said it, for it somehow

brought invasion of privacy and the whole telescope issue to mind. "I don't suppose you have any salsa?" He reassigned his irritation to her lack of condiments.

Without saying a word, she pulled a bin out of the bowels of the refrigerator, an extensive assortment of hot sauces of all kinds. Jalapeño, tabasco, picante, ranchera, habañero. Mexican, New Mexican, Louisianan, Coloradan, Arizonan. "You led me to believe—" she began.

"She's a salsa-holic—" Sullivan quipped gaily. He had begun carefully lining up plastic cups. "And a plasta-holic! These are really nice." He chose a Barbie mug for Savannah who, Miranda thought, verged more toward Skipper in coloring and proportion of long hair to total body height.

"Sass-aholic—" corrected Billy. "Her engine runs on sass. And she led herself to believe just what she wanted to believe."

"You lied to me, Billy—"

"You wanted to be lied to! You wanted to believe what you considered the worst about me."

"What about you? Laying things out in the open from the very beginning—that you were growing pot? Truly an honest beginning, I must say. Bravo."

Billy glanced at Sullivan, who raised both eyebrows high up as if to say: *Just tell the truth.* "I was defending it theoretically, Miranda—at least in part. You set me up to do just that, because everybody needs a foil. Prim exists because of prurient. Rule because of defiance. Wasn't it just like you to assume the worst?"

"Well, maybe you wanted me to, did you ever think of that? You think you know so much," she said dully. "Well, you don't know *me!*" She startled herself and him by pushing him, hard, in the shoulder, like a third grader picking a fight. It was an act of frustration, of having misunderstood completely and of being completely misunderstood.

Billy grabbed one wrist, just as he had months before in a similar impasse. "I know you, Miranda." His voice was low and intimate. "I know you better than you think."

"You've studied me through a convex lens." She slowly wrenched her arm away. "There is no psychology in that."

After pulling free, though, she remained acutely aware of the warm place on her wrist, the specter of his hand. There had been so little human contact in Otnip, so pitifully little, that as she stood there her tingling wrist seemed to be relaying the message to other neglected body parts, the same ones Whitman had recently enumerated.

Miranda felt tired, weak, and confession-prone: She wanted to tell Billy that she was an orphan, that she loved tomatoes, that she had smoked pot—lots of it—in high school, that she had crippling headaches and was worried about brain tumors but couldn't tell anyone, and that she deeply feared the part of herself that could not judge a good-anything from a bad-anything, from houseplants to lovers. But she could not say a word. Not in front of a drop-in audience. And certainly not given Billy's cavalier manner.

"There's plenty you *can't* see through a telescope," she said instead, rubbing the folly from her wrist with her other hand.

From an early age, Vivianne had always had microscopes lined up in her room. She believed to see things preternaturally close was to truly understand them. By her senior year, however, she had made a baffling jump from insects to faeries. Now Miranda finally understood: microscopes and telescopes were ultimately sad, ineffectual tools that filled you with longing, distanced you, removed you. They did not help you get close but made you feel far away, small, and weak-eyed. "It provides you with an incomplete assessment of things."

"I never did that much assessing, Miranda," Billy said. "I watched. I guiltily admit to that. The night sky is boring in comparison."

"Kinky," Savannah chirped merrily, as if someone had finally had the good manners to get her attention with something worthy. "But cool. Do you two like each other or not?"

"Yes, Savannah dear, they do," Sullivan patronized. "Very unkinkily. But Billy, by his own doing persona non grata in Miranda's life, has had to resort to the desperate measures of a peeping Tom. Now that we've established he's a good citizen, however, things are different. Unless, of course, Miranda here can ante up some kinky but cool behavior of her own—"

Billy had begun sautéing the sorrel. Sullivan found the silverware and was removing plates from the cupboard: two Velveeta plates in orange (Miranda's favorites), one that said Shell Oil, and a black-and-white-checkered commemorative plate from Michelin tires. "I like this stuff," he said, holding each piece at arm's length. "Very much. Have I made myself clear on that point?"

Miranda, meanwhile, had begun a mental inventory of her underwear and of herself in various phases of undress in the living room. "Stop trying to flatter me," she snapped. "It's not working. You are not what you collect." Most of her panties were tattered. Bras and camisoles? Decent but uninspiring.

"I didn't have to try at all," Sullivan said, grinning at her. "Is she always so snarly? I like that in a woman—"

Billy, his back toward the others, both resented and appreciated Sullivan's trying to muscle things. "You can't handle snarly, Sullivan, and you know it. Yes, she's snarly, sometimes even unkind. But then, she is a woman of principle." In a glass bowl he began to crack eggs one at a time.

Largely without being aware of it, Miranda had become tense in these proceedings. Hadn't he liked that principled part of her? Dropping her shoulders, she began breathing in slowly. "If your purpose today was to come and insult me," she said, briefly closing her eyes, "you've succeeded."

"I can assure you that wasn't his purpose." Sullivan had taken Savannah by the shoulders and was pushing her gently into the closest chair, briefly touching her long expanse of hair. She flipped her head as if to shoo a fly.

"I wasn't talking to you, spokesperson-man," Miranda said, trying to release further shoulder tension.

"No, that *wasn't* my purpose." Billy, remarking the hurt in her voice, wanted to assure her he had not planned on coming to her this way. Why had he confessed to Sullivan? He'd wanted Sullivan to meet her, not lasso her, tie up her feet, and present her to Billy—showing off for both of them—in record time.

Miranda opened the kitchen door to let the dogs in, who immediately scurried to Billy's side, shoving wet noses toward the pan.

"And you have hounds, too," Sullivan crowed with approval. "Can I move in? I'm comfortable here. I can see why Billy persists and persists in the face of—what did you call it—principle?"

"Billy," Billy clarified icily, "can speak for himself. I will say I love the dogs. They also happen to like me. Very much."

"They're animals and respond indiscriminately to kindness and/or food in any form. Human beings, the emotional cripples and contortionists of the vertebrate kingdom, are harder to mollify."

Platter in hand, Billy arrived. "Miranda," he said, looking at her with all the accumulated longing and weakness he had ever felt, "I love it when you talk that way. It makes me feel—at home somehow."

Miranda was focused on the food in front of her, still hopeful that she might ward off a headache for a few more minutes, just long enough to get them out of the house. The sorrel, bursting with tartness, seemed to have almost enough of whatever it might take to realign her body chemistry, and she chewed quickly and thirstily, crushing greenness into the juice of an antidote.

But between the third and fourth bites, her eye twinged. She did not look up but swallowed the mouthful carefully, fearing it might stick in her throat. As ravenous as she had been moments ago, she was now just as desperate to stop eating, and with a trembling hand, reached up to cover her right eye as piercing pain shot through it again. She stood up.

"Miranda?" she heard Billy say, the words crossing a chasm to get to her. "What is it?"

She stared at him through her good eye and took a deep

breath. "Nothing." Another sharp stab. "Everything!" She let her hand drop, even though the tearing of the eye had begun. Her vision blurred with water. "We're both screwed-up people, people who lie and can't be normal."

Billy was up and had his hand near her eye in an instant. "Did you get something in it—"

She jerked back sharply as if he were about to assail her. "Please," she said, closing her eye, "can't you just . . . go?" In all these months, this was where she had gotten: flinching when he approached her, ordering him to leave but half-wishing he would stay. Pain shot through her skull. She wanted to be alone, without witnesses. "I don't need you in my life right now!" Head down, she fled, wishing only for her clumsy feet to get her out of the kitchen without stumbling.

From her bedroom, however, more desperate and honest perhaps from the impending incapacitation, Miranda questioned if alone was really how she wanted it; because to a person alone, everything—emotions, melodrama, even beauty—reflected loneliness back. Before she was able to answer herself truthfully, a stream of gunfire exploded through her eyeball. With the pillow over her head to screen out both light and sound, she succumbed, trying to breathe carefully, in and out, as if taking baby steps with broken feet.

Two hours later when she awakened to the sound of the phone ringing, she was miraculously pain-free.

"Respect for Your Elders," she slid into her chair and answered, hoping to avert any accusations of truancy by keeping it businesslike.

It was the retired doctor, Frank Fujima, healthy neither

in body nor spirit, who generally used his time to examine life's unfairness, above all to the noble profession sworn in the name of Hippocrates to do good.

"I was concerned," he pinched the words out, "that something had happened to you. I suppose that's the doctor in me—"

"Sorry, Dr. Fujima," Miranda fumbled for his card, then glanced out the window. The Cadillac was gone and so was Billy's truck. She tried to remember what she had said in the throes of pain. "I was dealing with some neighbors."

"You've never forgotten me before."

"I'm so sorry," she repeated, "to have caused you concern. I didn't forget. It was just a little matter of—electricity. A short." That is, after all, what her headaches seemed to approximate.

He grunted. "Have you never wondered," he began, as if the conversation were already halfway done, "why doctors get paid so much? Because of the crap they have to put up with. We're not sensitive enough, we charge too much, we don't know what we're doing, we're too specialized." He coughed dryly. "I never cared what people thought then, and I care even less now."

Although he never mentioned his ailments, Miranda imagined some ugly degenerative disease turning his insides black. Her greatest challenge had always been to remain even with him. Now, however, freedom from pain incited an honest response, just as its onset had a few hours earlier. "I wish I were more like that," she said. "I think I care too much what people think."

Dr. Fujima was thrown off by the personal comment and paused a moment. "That can get you into trouble." His words were careful. "Though it seems only human to care about how you are perceived."

Miranda looked at his index card. While other clients were on their third already, Dr. Fujima barely had five lines to his name. Maybe it was her fault there were no makings of a character sketch here. Maybe she hadn't tried hard enough.

"I had a patient once," he remarkably continued, "a young woman. Kept coming back with the same complaint, plantar warts. I kept burning them off, she kept coming back. One day I asked her why she thought she was getting them. 'High heels,' she said, 'but don't tell me to change my shoes.' "

Miranda smiled, then asked Dr. Fujima if the lesson was that people didn't really want to change. "No," he said, "I think the lesson was never to act taller than you are."

Miranda laughed and wrote down *high heels* before signing off, words that looked funny next to his name. Then she brainstormed and scribbled in as many descriptive words as she could come up with for the man. Eight lines, ending with *surprising*. That was better.

Late for Rhea Phynos, Miranda nevertheless chose instead to punch in Evalina's number. Evalina would worry, and Rhea, who kept the television on all day, could only be bothered with accurate scheduling of her shows.

"Oh, Miranda," Evalina said, "I was going to call *you.*"

"You were?" Evalina had never called Miranda before.

"Because today I threw the I Ching for you, Miranda, dear."

"Really." She had only herself to blame for having given this woman a diagnostic tool. "Wherefore?"

"Oh, no reason," she announced. "Boredom. Interest. The combination of the two, I don't know. Anyway it was Fixing, the eighteenth hexagram. Kiu or the wind below, the mountains above." She paused and whistled, something Miranda had never heard her do. A wren sound, very high and clear, the antithesis of her speaking voice. The voice of the soul.

"What?" Miranda asked, wondering meanwhile where Billy could have gone, especially with all that remedial gardening to do.

"You may be in for a little change, my dear. Since you got a moving line in the first position, you need to be extra careful of the kind of change you make. A close friend may help you see clearly. Be patient."

A weary sigh escaped Miranda's lips. Today, oracles might just be on a par with headaches. "You're not supposed to throw them for someone else, are you?"

Evalina ignored the query. "Did you know that green tea is better for you than black? I'm drinking Gunpowder Green right now. From China. Anyhow, dear, I don't blame you for thinking guidance complicates matters."

"I never said that!"

"No, but that's what you think." Evalina had never been so outspoken before.

"I don't know what I think half the time."

"Well, good point. Interpretation is 90 percent of an oracle. Sometimes, as you say, you *do* need help correctly interpreting, knowing what to think."

Miranda felt that words were being put in her mouth. "Are you trying to tell me something, Evalina? I feel advice coming on."

"Me?" Shock and dismay. "Heavens no, dear, I'm just a stubborn old thing trying to keep my brain engaged. Now my friend Kitty—have I ever mentioned Dr. Kitty Dragoo?"

Evalina never mentioned things without a reason. Miranda started taking deep breaths with her hand over the receiver. "Nope." She tipped her head back, loosening her neck vertebrae.

"A psychologist, brilliant woman. Of course, she's retired now—lives with her granddaughter. But every once in a while she sinks her teeth in for a spell. Still sharp as a tack. We were at Smith together about a million years ago."

Miranda said nothing, still gauging Evalina's motives in moving from oracle to therapist.

"Because," Evalina slurped her tea, "being so comfortable with old people and the phone, it occurred to me you might benefit from her and she from you. In addition, you would meet one of my oldest and dearest friends. Most of 'em are dead by now but not Kitty." Miranda heard the clink of porcelain cup against saucer. "That eighteenth hexagram validates a possible connection between you two."

There are moments in life when too much is going on. Maybe too much is always going on, but in the middle of the open range the illusion is one of manageability, one thing happening at a time. Miranda stared across the street and willed her brain to become a fish tank, clear inside with tranquilly colored thoughts. Chaos, but contained. What Evalina was saying to Miranda, clear as a bell, was *Get psychological help*.

"You think about it, dear," she squawked as if the hearing aid had just failed. "Kitty knows you're the one who

151

matched me up to the I Ching. She'd like to meet you. I'll let you go now." She clucked a good-bye and hung up the phone.

Miranda removed the headset and went to the kitchen. The table was clear and wiped, the dishes stacked neatly in the sink. Someone had put Saran over her plate, which she removed carefully. She poured reheated coffee into the cup left out for her and took everything to her desk, ready to call Rhea. Only after sitting down did she realize that Sullivan had chosen the rare and valuable Wizard of Oz cup for her and frowned while staring at it. She had never liked that cup.

Yes, Savannah had gotten the Barbie cup, and Billy the Lone Ranger. For himself, Sullivan had chosen the only automotive cup in Miranda's collection, a classic Mustang mug in powder blue from the Ford Company.

What did he know about Miranda? What did anyone know? Only after switching out Snow White for Dorothy was she able to continue on with the day's calls. Now more than ever she liked the idea of dwarf men who came already labeled.

 **11**

Billy didn't come back that night; nor did he return the next day or the day after that.

Miranda, who had never even considered the possibility of his going away at all, was in shock. Wasn't he a gardener? An attendant? Someone needed on the premises? Feeling vaguely responsible for his absence, she nevertheless held what she maintained was reckless and unreliable behavior against him.

Seventy-two hours later, she concluded that her neighbor had not gone away, he'd moved away. Abandoned carrots would be withering into threads soon. Orchids would droop, desiccate, and evaporate into thin air. And the fish? They would slow down, become still, then permanently float to the surface. Eventually, the water in the tank would evaporate and leave nothing behind but sand, a miniature shipwreck, and assorted fish bones. Paint would peel from the front of the house. One morning, she would awaken to find the windows boarded over and garbage stuck to every surface like lint.

Miranda found herself brooding. For though she might have described her previous state as one of solitude, she realized now that she had not really been alone at all. She had had a neighbor, an audience, someone to pester her, pursue her even. This had made a difference, and one, it was obvious, of immense proportions. She saw now that what she had wished upon herself had finally occurred: She was alone, with nothing but a phone line connecting her to the world. Though she continued to make calls to her clients on her lifeline, she deflected personal questions like sunbeams off a mirror.

Solitude was hardest at the end of the day, that critical time regular working people punched out and returned to their families. For the first time, she wondered if she might not be better off having satellite TV like everybody else around. In the middle of a storm one evening, as trash careened by her window helter-skelter, she thought at length of all the people she had neglected since her move away. Was it too late to touch base and finally say where she had gone? She retrieved her collection of blank postcards and picked out a dozen.

How are you? she wrote. *What have you been up to? I'm finally settled in Otnip*—as if she'd been so busy and so much had happened between then and now she was lucky to get off even a quick scribble.

Only Majesta Fein received a copy of the brochure and an actual letter in which Miranda apologized for having remained uncommunicative, then tried to approximate her life in Otnip, mentioning her clients, her routines, the lay of the land. At the bottom of the page, realizing she'd omitted mention of Billy once again, she put the letter aside, unsigned, unfolded. At that point, if he wasn't in the letter, the letter wasn't completely honest; and Miranda didn't feel like fabricating fresh lies anymore.

Then she put on the Dinah Shore LP Billy had given her, ran a hot bath, lowered herself into it, and drank two cans of Schlitz Malt Liquor through a mud mask caked and hardened on her face. Billy had given her Dinah's *16 Most Requested Songs* on a rainy day in February. A rainy February 14, as a matter of fact. Though he hadn't made mention of the V-word, he had brought over a Thermos of hot chocolate and put on the album without showing it to her. They'd listened to "Willow Weep for Me" and "Mad About the Boy" and had said very little to each other, sitting there in the living room as the rain pelted the roof and made lakes of the plains outside. Miranda had liked the company, the surprisingly silent presence of him.

But after about the sixth song he'd gotten up. "I'd better go," he said, checking his watch. He'd never checked his watch before.

"Okay—" How could she have asked him to stay and listen with her though? How could she have asked him, after a year of pushing him away, to hang out a little longer—just to keep her company? "You have plants to tend."

"No."

"Deliveries to deliver."

"Nope."

"Calls to make."

"Uh-uh. None of the above." He'd stood there biding his time and tucking in his shirt, a yellow button-down that was frayed on all fronts.

"So what are you looking at your watch for then?"

"Well, my time's up here, Miranda. You've trained me so rigorously, I can sense just when to go so that I won't have to suffer being kicked out; and it will take some effort on your part, now, to get me to stay longer than the twenty minutes you've always allotted me."

"I'm surprised you keep coming back."

"No, you're not: You might be surprised if I didn't though. That dire scenario can remain hypothetical, however, if you somehow manage to ease me into staying at your house for longer and longer periods of time."

Dinah Shore, she thought as she submerged her face to soften the mask, *can buckle one's knees with longing.* "Well," she'd said to him then, "I do sort of owe you. For the sublime vinyl disc. Which I love." And the next time he'd come over, with his Scrabble board, she'd told him if they were going to play they would have to play to the end. That had elicited a smile big and fetching enough to warm Miranda's frosty manners: she had offered him a tuna sandwich and had let him win the game, which was difficult for someone who had once memorized hundreds of obscure two- and three-letter words.

Limpsy now as well as inebriated, she merged with the cool bedsheets, wondering what a particular man—one who would further sabotage himself in Scrabble with words like "want" and "you"—would actually feel like next to her. A calf touching hers, a heavy arm strewn across her rib cage.

The next morning, as she dropped her postcards into the slot, she asked Vicki Schuster if there was anything she could do for her.

"Like what?" Vicki was struggling with a roll of tape, picking at the end with her long nails. She handed it to Miranda to try. "Yeah, you could find me a real man in this godforsaken territory, someone who could love me tender at night and clear the yard of storm debris in the morning—"

Miranda blushed and waited. There was a pile of donuts on the counter. Why had she never thought to bring donuts to Vicki? "Billy seems to be out of town," she ventured. "I was thinking I could take his mail if you needed me to."

Vicki picked up an old-fashioned glazed, broke it in half, and handed Miranda the bigger portion with a smile. "Audrey's going to come in every so often for Billy's stuff," she said. "But it's nice of you to offer."

Miranda shrugged. "Oh," she said, trying to figure out who Audrey might be. "You don't happen to know when he's due back." She stuffed the donut into her mouth. "Or anything, do you? Because his friend Sullivan was asking, and I really didn't know."

"Sullivan Novo?"

Oh-oh. "Yeah." She feigned delight in the smallness of the world. "You know him?"

Vicki nodded, crossing her arms at the mere mention of the man. "Of course. He used to be on my softball team. Helluva hitter . . . Hit on all the young women, too, as a matter of fact." She grinned, clearly fond of him. "Anyhoo, I could ask Audrey when she comes in. Or tell her to call Sully, she knows him, too. Why don't *you* just call her? Real nice girl."

"I suppose I could."

"I mean out there it would seem stupid not to talk to whomever for whatever reason, right?" Vicki shook her head. "I'd go nuts in Otnip, to tell you the truth. I mean, even this post office . . ." The words drifted like a loose dinghy from the shore. "No coffee shop, even. No running out to grab something."

"I like living alone," Miranda said, feeling a sudden need to defend the recluses of the world.

"*Really,*" Vicki said, looking at her squarely, as if for the first time. "Well, I tend to find that suspect. You don't strike me as by nature withdrawn. Or hostile. Or even weird."

Miranda didn't want to know how she struck Vicki Schuster. She glanced at her watch and scooped up her one clothing catalog and grocery store mailer. Frozen catfish was on sale again: Why the never-ending surplus of catfish in the Rocky Mountain states? "Oops, I've got to run. I'll see you—"

"You bet," Vicki answered, resigned. "Take another donut, I'll just eat 'em—Take one for Audrey!"

Sure enough, the morning of the third day of Billy's absence someone Miranda assumed to be Audrey pulled her small yellow Datsun pickup truck into his driveway.

Dressed in old work pants and wearing a purple scarf in her curly red hair, she let herself in and did not reemerge until four in the afternoon when she drove away. She showed up the next day, and the next, always arriving around nine in the morning, usually leaving by late afternoon. On the sixth day, she carried half a dozen small crates to the pickup, loaded them, and drove off.

How, Miranda wondered, did someone know just what to do to run Billy's life? Was she eating lunch in his kitchen and napping on his bed? Had she taken up *The*

Maltese Falcon just where he'd left off? Added a few fish to the tank? Goldilocks had moved in and taken over the porridge-making operation—and in one seamless maneuver it was as if Billy had never existed at all. It made Miranda sick. She considered phoning: How are the orchids? And the tomatoes, how are they faring in the bowels of the basement? But somehow she could not make herself do it, and the longer she waited, the more contrived it became.

After nine days, Miranda opted for outside counsel and called Vivianne in Philadelphia, where her message machine indicated she would be. A conference, most likely.

"These cartoonist-people are weirder than my average audience," she said, answering Miranda's initial queries. "But I have to say, it's all very refreshing! And they seem to be responding to my topic—Cape Versus Wing in Heroic Action. Cape as a symbol of concealment, power, and magic—followed by brief parallels to the magic carpet. By the way, Aunt Raye was asking about you the other day. So prepare yourself for a call."

"How about I just let the machine get it—"

Vivianne paused, finally acknowledging a deviation in the normal proceedings. "You don't usually call me. Is the nothingscape finally getting to you?"

"I'm fine," Miranda said too quickly. "Spring in Otnip is a mixed bag, though. You wait and wait for the first truly warm wind, one without pockets of cold. Then you wait some more. If I knew what the term meant, I would call it existential."

"I would call it depressing, which might be the same

thing, who knows. You need to get out of there. Take a trip. See some sights, meet a man, or a woman, even— Hang on a minute, there's room service. Hang on." Miranda heard the phone hit wood. "I ordered breakfast for dinner," she resumed as silverware clinked on porcelain. "It cheers me up."

"So, *you* need cheering up."

There was a pause. "Well, if you must know, I'm smack in the eye of stormy conflict with Ivo. Which I thought I could explain to Aunt Raye, but she'll never understand me, not like Mom did: Why do I call her?"

"Blood is thicker than fairy plasma . . ." Miranda chirped falsely; she still did not like being reminded of Vivianne's ten extra years with their mother. "Go back to that conflict part, though, that sounded interesting."

Vivianne laughed her particular laugh, a *ha-haaaaa: ha!* straight from the jungles of Brazil. "I'm sure it did: actual human conflict. With actual humans. Of course, over where you are that would be impossible."

"Not entirely impossible. Because there are other humans."

"Really. Like who?"

"Like my neighbor who isn't here right now and the woman who has taken over his life as if she had been waiting in the wings to do it."

"Rocky?"

Vivianne had taken a liking to Rocky Torez (who had not only responded to her dead-on eye for plumb but, being a beekeeper, to her knowledge of insects). "No, not Rocky. Although he's named a honey after you now. Nope. Billy Steadman from across the street."

The shock of saying the name out loud filled her with a sort of delicious panic, as if she were about to become weightless, then head, heavy as lead, down the steepest part of the roller coaster.

There was a pause. "The old one-legged guy with the greenhouse and all those cats?"

Vivianne had never seen Billy, and Miranda had seen fit to alter the truth a little. Now, this deeply frustrated her. "No," she articulated with care, "the young guy who's been knocking at my door ever since I moved in, the guy I lied about so that you wouldn't get involved or give me advice. The guy I've been keeping at arm's length: the handsome-but-not-in-a-dark-oily-way witty guy with the green thumb who sells herbs, vegetables, and flowers to area businesses. Who's gone right now. Which seems to be driving me crazy even though I fear I may have driven him away." If she had said as much to Lydia, she would have had to suffer through all the anguished I-told-you-so's and feel like a failure. At least with Viv it was all so new she wouldn't have the wherewithal to make quick judgments.

Vivianne had stopped her amplified chewing. "I need to come for a visit." She cleared her throat. "I should have remembered that men always find you, Miranda, no matter what. They look into those eyes and . . . I want to check him out."

"I thought *I* was the one always running after a certain type."

"The two things can coexist but usually not very well." She sighed. Miranda waited. "I'm not going to lecture you. He's certainly handy, I'll say that much. Just be prepared," she added, "for the wars that inevitably follow."

161

"You're talking about Ivo now."

Vivianne grunted. "The man is a tyrant," she unleashed. "Fastidious to a fault, borderline obsessive-compulsive. A brute."

Ivo, a tidy and rational man sporting London-made tweed jackets and round glasses, seemed anything but brutish. "Did he yell or—or get aggressive?"

"See?" Her tone was triumphant. "You suspected, right? It's so *obvious.*"

"He didn't hit you, or anything—" Miranda's voice was almost a whisper. It barely concealed her need for solidarity in the realm of the beaten woman.

"Of course not!" Vivianne laughed. "What do you think I am anyway? No, I'm talking about mental tyranny and violence. He's such an empiricist!" *Scum* was implied.

Miranda, face red from the quick relegation to some sadder category of women who got hit, clenched her jaw. "You were once quite the empiricist yourself, Viv. All those microscopes, the notebooks, and slides, and specimens. It's as if you've forgotten who you once were . . ."

"I had a *conversion,*" Vivianne continued, as if Miranda's job were simply to facilitate her address. "I took high school physics solely to learn insect aerodynamics. In the humble bumblebee wing I learned science was not so much defied as taken to task. I could have clutched tighter to my microscopes and formulae, but instead, I loosened the empiricist knot. Or corset, as it were." Miranda heard a bite of crisp toast, the squeaking of sausage gristle between teeth.

"So, what does this have to do with Ivo?"

"Everything. We were having a lovely candlelit dinner in our matching pajamas. Scallops. Champagne. His reminiscences of a lonely Prague childhood culminated with an epiphany: One summer night, having caught a moth for company, a careful study of its wing structure changed the course of his life. It seemed fitting to share my own insect-based metamorphosis. Long story short? Full disparagement."

"So you kicked him out? In his pajamas?"

"I told him I thought we should date other people." Sip of coffee. "Which is why I'm meeting someone later in the bar." Another sip. She sounded nervous, like she hated the game she had to play.

"A car*toon*ist?" Miranda knew her heart wasn't in it.

"An animator." She emphasized the difference.

"But—but what about Ivo? I mean, why choose a guy like him in the first place? You knew he studied bugs, and he knew you studied faer—mythical winged creatures."

"I'll give you a hint, little sister. It's not Debate 101. It's not physics and it's not biology. It's called chemistry. Can't be helped. Which is why I'm about to torture Ivo by seeing other people. He needs to worry about me never coming back. He needs to buy me a large gift having to do with bees or moths—and apologize. In fact, I may just pop in on you without telling him where I've gone. Lord knows, people can't locate you if you're in Otnip, Colorado."

Vivianne threatened often to come out but never had, not since that first time. Yes, it was hard to get to—a nothingscape. And without Billy it was getting lonelier and lonelier all the time.

The next day, Miranda devoted herself to her clients. Fannie Bartnik, Benjamin Boy, Keeper Dix, Rowena Marx, SueEllen Tonnager, Pipsi Cooling, and lots of others. Diligently she demanded the very best of herself and of them and, not surprisingly, they delivered.

Gregory had started *Song of Myself,* and for the first time Miranda asked him for a bit of commentary on the text. Pipsi Cooling, having finally memorized all of Psalm 19, quaveringly obliged a request to recite. Miranda even managed to get Rhea Phynos to summarize some of her soaps, which had the unfortunate derivative effect of once again raising the Television Question in Miranda's mind.

Only Keeper Dix, a firefighter burn victim to whom she read *Les Misérables* almost every day, pointedly asked why she was being so "gung ho" about everything. What was she hiding, he wanted to know. *Nothing,* Miranda answered, hearing the apprehension in her own voice, *Can't a person be effusive without getting the third degree?* Instantly, she regretted the use of the term "third degree." Keeper, however, had gasped raggedly in delight at the gaffe.

During her lunch break, Miranda took the down comforter from her bed and began beating it to a pulp outside. She heard the phone ringing but only just as the machine kicked in, and though she arrived with plenty of time to pick up, upon hearing Lydia's voice decided not to. A conversation with Lydia would either entail lying, which she was not feeling up to, or telling the truth, which seemed even harder.

It occurred to her, standing outside again with a dust mask on and a broom in her hands, that there was no one she could just tell the truth to—without editing or embellishing. She couldn't tell Lydia that there was no longer anything to hold against Billy. She couldn't tell

Vivianne that a blow to the face and a broken nose had sent her running. She couldn't tell Billy that she'd put a wall up not because of his offenses but because she was afraid of loss.

What would she tell a psychologist of ninety-two, if the opportunity were to present itself? How much she had kept from people? How much that had compromised not only her character but the course of her life? How much she had learned? In spite of these brave but dispiriting insights, she wanted to run away again. Even farther this time, to a lighthouse or a stone cottage on some craggy outpost of rock.

She realized, however, as she played therapist on herself, that her reasons for wanting to run away might have changed: Didn't she just want to see if someone would come after her? What an infantile mind—so transparent! She would embarrass herself on a couch; then, given a professional's insights, she would fall apart.

She returned to her afternoon clients eager to prove herself again. She was caring. Capable. And professional.

"I'm a new woman, Miranda," Lael Vanderpin, the mystery writer and first on the list, gushed. "What a difference oxygen has made! I'm giving my protagonist O_2, and nixing the wheelchair. Both would be too much to burden the reader with, don't you think?"

"Absolutely," Miranda had never heard Lael so buoyant. It was infectious. "Very original. Tell me more—"

"Well," Lael lowered her voice, as if patent were pending on the character, "midseventies, a widow with an oxygen tank. Alone in an assisted care facility—except for her lovebirds and a head full of memories. Collects cacti. Of course, being a chronic asthmatic, she's always been a voracious reader, and her natural turn of mind is to question irregularities, to piece together the slimmest of clues . . ."

She paused. For a drag on her oxygen? Miranda had to cover her mouth with her hand to smother the erupting grin. No one gave these people credit! Forcing the corners of her mouth down, she queried as to Lael's writing methods.

"I write longhand," Lael replied primly. "On yellow legal pads just as many writers before me have done."

Frank Fujima, Evalina Peguy, and Cassidy Knewth all responded to Miranda's ministrations. Her triumph, however, came in getting Gustave Robbins, a retired calligrapher, to talk about Waterman's first fountain pen and the miraculous juxtaposition of capillary attraction and atmospheric pressure. *Interest*, she thought, recalling Evalina's comment. *It's all about pitting interest against boredom.*

At the end of a full day, she took the dogs on a walk, and noticed that tulips had come up at Billy's. Hundreds of them, close to the house. She had never seen orange tulips before and stared long and admiringly at this novel showing of her favorite color. *Could he have known*, she wondered, *or am I living in a dream world?*

Later that night she retrieved Billy's telescope and set it up, pointing it randomly at the cosmos before peering into the eyepiece. What she saw was blackness, an endless sea of black sprinkled with lonely white flecks. The dark cold of the sky permeated her chest: There was no beyond: It was all beyond: Where am I?

Compared to the cosmos, the bosom of Earth was warm,

and drawn back to it, Miranda slowly let the lens fall like a leaf until it touched Billy's roof, and then inched it downward toward his window, before stopping herself. *What are you doing, Miranda?* She lifted her head and stared across the street. *What are you doing?*

 12

It had been Evalina's brilliant idea, about a month earlier, to attempt contact with Miranda's other clients. She had begun to worry about Miranda and did not really know to whom else she might turn.

Yes, of course, there were women who struck out on their own, pioneering types, chopping wood, bushwhacking their way through life, butchering hogs, doing it all, and hardly sleeping at that. Tough, thick-skinned women. That was not Miranda, however. Miranda had isolated herself, but then reached out again, thereby sending as mixed a message to the world as Evalina had ever received.

But Miranda was also stubborn as a mule. It wouldn't do Evalina any good to talk further with Kitty about her; and certainly Miranda couldn't be forced to talk to Kitty. Really, the only thing to do was to seek out other people with whom Miranda had had contact. All together, they might be able to solve a bit more of the puzzle of Miranda Blue.

So she ran an ad in the same magazine Miranda used for

her advertisements, an ad in which she cryptically alluded to pale irises in spring. All she could do was hope for the best.

The first call Evalina received—approximately three weeks earlier—had been from Rochelle Meyer, a woman Miranda had mentioned several times, as if she eventually wanted them to meet.

"The code word is Blue," were Rochelle's first words. "As in, how Miranda has been sounding lately."

Evalina, relieved, had concurred. Rochelle had then initiated a brief discussion on Miranda's virtues, ending with a mention of the brochure photo. "With eyes like that it's obvious that girl is connected to the world of spirits," she said, to which Evalina replied that if the eyes were the window to the soul, why Miranda's shutters were nailed open. Rochelle then further noted that the picture looked as if it had been taken at one of those curtained booths requiring no photographer, causing them both to think quietly for a moment.

"I feel sad for Miranda that there is no picture-taker in her life," Rochelle had summarized, thus tersely initiating their twice-weekly conversations.

Satisfied with her single new coconspirator, Evalina had canceled the ad, and was therefore surprised to receive another call, just ten days later, from a Gregory Vogt, who confessed to having been behind in his reading of *Advanced Age*.

To their profile, he added his views not only on her spirit but her voice, one a vocalist might call a chest voice, emanating, he said, from the diaphragm rather than the head. A radio voice. Except that in her case every emotion seemed to register, even the ones she tried so valiantly to hide. What her pale irises might attempt to belie, he believed, her voice never could.

By the time Gregory joined the group, the police had already come for Billy, and they all knew that there was a someone in Miranda's life, someone glaringly unmentioned even though he lived right across the street. The mysterious neighbor instantly became the focal point of their conversations.

Rochelle, Evalina, and Gregory were set to teleconference the Wednesday after Easter. It was approximately six-thirty in the evening. All across Colorado, clouds pitched by in big broken-up masses, and the sun was streaking down onto the Earth in fanlike rays, radiant and soft.

Rochelle had just finished a dinner of bow-tie noodles and broiled filet of halibut and had brewed a tiny pot of decaf for the phone conversation. She particularly relished the thought of filing a report with her friends, for she had done some homework and come up lucky.

Evalina had had a rough morning trying to coddle bones that seemed at once brittle and dense with pain. By midmorning, however, she had managed to read a few pages of the *Wall Street Journal* and feed the cats, Tick-tock and Talulah, a special can of lamb stew. Happy cats gladdened her, and she threw the I Ching with a light heart. By six-thirty, she had finished her cold supper and chosen ordinary Lipton tea to which she was about to add honey and some heavy cream left over from yesterday's strawberry shortcake.

Gregory had spent the entire day working on an article about rediscovering poetry late in life, something Miranda, in fact, had suggested he do. He thought he just might send it off to the local paper but worried about portraying himself as some kind of zealot. Perhaps he was. Pen still in hand, he wondered if a person could be overtaken by a poet's soul and felt for a moment that Whitman had chosen to speak through him, a lowly whittler, a man who had gotten many things wrong in life.

At 6:12, just minutes before conversing with his two new friends, he finished his first real meal of the day, a ham sandwich, while staring at the half-whittled sparrow he would someday complete. Miranda came to mind.

Rochelle was eager to get down to brass tacks: "Well, I had an idea to call the county sheriff's office out there. I don't know why I didn't think of it sooner. I found out why William Wordsworth Steadman, Miranda's neighbor—and the man she seems to be taken with if you ask me—was hauled into the police station."

She paused, anxious not to sound too pleased with herself, which was simply impossible.

"Good gravy, why?" Evalina inquired, slurping her tea.

"Is he growing marijuana?" Gregory asked bluntly, having come back again and again to the same conclusion, and this having mainly to do with the magazine *High Times* being his most frequent source on hydroponic growing.

"Heavens, no! Whatever would make you ask such a question?" She paused. "He was hauled off to call his *mother.*"

"His mother?" Evalina's blue baseball cap shielded her eyes from the bright glare of the 150-watt reading lamp perched above her favorite chair, where she sat taking notes.

"That doesn't make much sense—". Gregory was disappointed his theory was incorrect. He liked the idea of the rebel farmer. Recent reading had acquainted him with both the hemp plant and medicinal uses of marijuana. "How does it play out?"

"Plays out strange," Rochelle went on. "Seems his wife died of leukemia some years ago." She paused just long enough to silently utter *May she rest in peace*. "And ever since, he's kept to himself, the poor dear, to the point of never listing his telephone number. His mother calls the police station to relay messages to her son, and he pays them for the service with tomatoes. This time as compensation he was asked to teach prisoners to meditate, something he's evidently done before."

Neither of them said anything. Finally, Gregory spoke up, unsure of which part to comment on first. "Put all that grief and energy into tomatoes, did he? But why would the police tell you this, Ro?"

"I wondered that myself," she said. "But evidently, it's no secret. *Everybody* knows about the deceased wife, and about the unlisted number. Old news."

Evalina was deep in thought. "Does Miranda know, though?"

"Well, I don't think she does," Rochelle continued. "I spoke to a deputy LeFevre about it. Rodney. What was my 'stake,' in it, he wanted to know. So I told him we were Miranda's old clients and were trying to look out for her. We didn't know what the situation had been and didn't want her living across from a felon or otherwise unsavory character. I mentioned Miranda was just as sweet, charming, beautiful, and smart as she was lonely. I said I thought something had sent her out, solitary, into the world, and that by accident—I don't know why on earth I told Rodney LeFevre this—by accident she'd landed across the street from the one person who could drive her crazy."

Gregory laughed out loud and noted that that's pretty much how relationships worked, wasn't it?

Evalina, draining the last of her tea, made a mental note to extol the virtues of heavy cream to Miranda. "So what did he have to say to that? I agree with you, by the way, Greg, that Cupid's arrow usually has a little curse on it. Anyway, go on Ro, what did Rodney LeFevre say?"

"Well, he said he liked my nerve. Then he remarked that Billy had asked them—jokingly—to turn on their flashing lights in order to confuse Miranda, that she deserved to be confused."

"So they're teasing each other," Gregory offered brightly, "which would indicate disinterest on neither end."

"A good sign," Evalina agreed. "Anything else?"

"Nothing except that I got his number." Rochelle threw the bomb with glee.

"They gave out his unlisted number?" Evalina was as surprised as she sounded. "That seems wrong." She lowered her voice. "Did you dial it?"

"Not yet. And to be fair to LeFevre, he didn't really give me the number. He merely mentioned the name of Billy's company, Try a Little Tenderness—which the parents are unaware of as well, evidently. I called up directory assistance and voilà. . . ."

"Boy howdy, woman!" Gregory barked. "I'm glad you're on our side! Meanwhile, I'd like to hear the man's voice, see what kind of person he is. He's not at home, we know that, and the girl leaves around four; we could listen to the message machine."

They got the answering machine after the third ring and listened: "You've reached Try a Little Tenderness. I'll be away until the third week in April. Audrey Fromm, who is filling orders, will be answering messages or can be reached at 865-8121. Happy spring to you . . . And if by some miracle this is you, Miranda, I want you to know I'm going to leave you alone from now on. For the record, I would *like* to understand you and to accept you, but you've got to meet me a fraction of the way. P.S., your dogs come to visit me all the time when you're not looking." Bee-ee-eep.

"He's most definitely smitten." Evalina sounded both thrilled and truly put out. Still," she mused quietly, "we don't know everything about her. She's hiding something. We know why he moved to the hinterlands. We don't really know why she did."

"No," Gregory agreed.

"I liked his voice," Evalina continued, deeming it sweet and down-to-earth. "Did you, Greg?"

"Nothing not to like. It was the voice of someone you could talk to. Honest, I thought. Rochelle?"

"I liked him." She made the leap from three recorded sentences to character appraisal.

"I wonder if Miranda has heard that recording," Gregory pondered. "I'd wager she hasn't. I bet she doesn't know when her farmer is coming back, or even if he's coming back. She has been so—guarded—lately."

"Locked up," agreed Rochelle. "Won't answer a single question tossed her way."

"I've even gone so far as to try to set her up with an old

psychologist friend of mine," Evalina said. "I'm waiting for her to say she wants to call the woman, who I'm sure could open Miranda up, pry open the oyster shell. But," she concluded, "I don't think Miranda's interested."

"Well, my feeling," Rochelle said, "is that we should call this Audrey. Ask her for the date of Billy's return. See what's what. What's the worst that could happen? We have no one else to call, unless either of you can think of anyone on Miranda's side we could interrogate."

There was no answer. Rochelle said she would call Audrey, then call everyone back.

"Audrey," she told them twenty minutes later, "a farmer herself, made friends with Billy years ago at a local open-air market. She called him a great, if lonely, guy—her words—and said he did miracles with anything green. She was nervous, she said, about his crops not doing as well under her care, especially the tomatoes, but had been lucky so far. She said she hadn't met Miranda but had seen her walking her dogs and had waved on several occasions. I asked if she had any idea where Billy had gone, and she answered he'd gone to visit his parents back East. She didn't have a number.

"What about in case of emergency?" Evalina asked.

"Yes, exactly," Rochelle said. "I asked Audrey that very question. In case of emergency, she said, he told her to call his friend, someone named Sullivan Novo, who lived in Cortez and who always knew how to reach him."

"Did you call him?"

"Not yet," Rochelle said. "I needed to ask you both. Do you think we should?"

 13

Another week went by, and Billy's orange tulips came into flamboyant bloom. Though the wind blew them from side to side like bells, the tulips did not topple or break, nor were they devoured by deer thanks to Audrey's aggressive squirting of the periphery with something from a green bottle.

Miranda had gotten up the nerve to wave to Audrey several more times, always receiving a friendly wave and smile in return. She thought perhaps one day soon Audrey might pop over, but it never happened. Of course, she never summoned the courage to fabricate an excuse and march over there either.

One afternoon, while hanging up laundry on the line, wet sheets and towels flapping around her cold fingers, Miranda did have a visitor. Well, a default visitor. Amidst the racket of the fluttering linen, she did not hear a car drive by, turn down Billy's driveway, back out again, or park alongside her own fence.

"Yoohoo," she was surprised to hear a call as she stood

grappling with the curves and puckers of the fitted sheets, which never did seem to hang nicely enough on the line.

A woman in pastel pink sweatpants and sweatshirt had gotten out of a white Ford LTD, and stood at the picket fence waving. Miranda put down her basket of clothespins and walked over while the woman mouthed a big but silent "Hi" and reduced the intensity of the wave to a flutter of fingers held close to her chest.

Miranda's first thought was that finally Pigeon had gotten another Realtor, for Cherise had the same perky familiarity as this woman. A den mother or welcoming-committee chairperson out to become a professional—someone who had not been informed that a cowboy hat and boots most winningly accessorized hocking whatever was left of the Wild West.

"Hi," Miranda said, rubbing her hands together, then shoving them in her pockets. "Can I help you with something?" Was Billy about to list his property?

"Well," the woman's tone was even more death-defyingly chipper than her wave, "you might be able to. I was looking for Billy Steadman. I thought I'd pop in on him—you know, unannounced, but no one seems to be home. That is the house, isn't it?" She pointed across the street.

Pop in, unannounced? In Otnip? "Yes, that's his house. But he's not home. Hasn't been home for a couple weeks. Are you a Realtor?"

Her face fell to the floor. "Oh," she said. "That's too bad. I had something perishable to give him. A gift." She paused, just realizing Miranda had asked her a question. "A Realtor? I wish I was! No, just an acquaintance."

How could she ever think he would sell his house? "Well, I could put whatever it is in my fridge."

She beamed. "Could you? In your freezer? I'm Sharon, by the way. Sharon Sawhill. Billy taught me to meditate a couple weeks ago."

Miranda smiled. "Miranda Blue," she stuck out her hand. "So, he was a good teacher?"

"Oh, my, yes. What a *sweetheart.*" She blushed and began fiddling with the hair around her ears. "Of course, I had no idea what to expect. Now I meditate every day—you can tell him that. I'm up to twelve minutes! Same phrase, too."

Placing the foil-wrapped square in her freezer, Miranda wondered what a woman like that was doing in the county jail to begin with. While hanging up the towels, she came up with a list of possible crimes. Shoplifting came in first, followed closely by credit card fraud, poisoning food, and finally *popping in unannounced,* which Miranda could see as a *modus operandi* of sorts, one eventually leading to some kind of misdemeanor.

Then she thought of Billy meditating and wondered why he'd begun doing it in the first place. She knew he didn't grow marijuana and that he had lied, which made him not the person he'd wanted her to think he was. That much she knew. But she still didn't know what the real story was.

On the phone circuit with the elderly, Miranda continued to deflect any and all personal queries. Billy was gone, she said to those who asked. That was all. In fact, the only person to whom she still occasionally leaked personal details was Keeper Dix, the firefighter. At forty-two, he was her youngest client and the only one who lay bedridden in a hospital. He never spoke of the future, nor did he speak of the past.

To Keeper, she read forty-five minutes of *Les Misérables* three or four times a week, a service miraculously covered by his insurance company. The story sidetracked them—as only the truly magnificent nineteenth century could—from the ghastly realities of his own condition.

"Happy Easter, Miranda—" Keeper said one Sunday (for him, Miranda occasionally made exceptions to the no-weekend-calling imperative). "What did the Easter Bunny bring you?"

Last Easter, it was Billy who had left her a little present.

Keeper heard the smile materialize on her face and asked what was so funny. If it had been Rochelle or Evalina or Gregory (who had stepped up the inquisition lately), or even Frank Fujima, she would have brushed off the comment, winging the ball back in their courts. But Keeper was different. You couldn't do anything but the truth with Keeper Dix.

"I was thinking about how my neighbor sprinkled my lawn with hundreds of jelly beans last year. It looked as if it had rained them."

"Miranda," he said after a moment, in the tight-skinned way people with facial burns and bandages and things too heartbreaking to conjure up talked. "Smiling agrees with you. What did he do this year?"

"Thank you," she murmured, feeling aforesaid smile fade in spite of the effort to leave it at half-mast. "Well, this year the Easter Bunny is not around," she cleared her throat. "He went away without saying where, or when he would be back. I suppose Easter is the worse for it. Don't tell anyone though. Most people my age don't believe in Easter Bunnies."

She heard the sound of oxygen being sucked in. "Did you and the Easter Bunny have a falling-out?"

She swallowed hard. "We've never really had anything but. He thinks I won't have anything to do with him. Which might have been true before—but for twisted reasons too complicated to explain. I think he might be damaged goods—" The instant she said it, she winced, ashamed at the sound her thoughts made as they burst into audible speech.

"Miranda—" Keeper interrupted with more strength than he had, "we're all damaged goods!" It would have been a volatile outburst from a set of healthy lungs and an untaped mouth; for Keeper such an eruption was the source of much distress. Surprised by the force of his reaction, Miranda held her breath, waiting for his irregular gasps to subside.

"Read to me," he finally said with far less volume and air. "But listen to me, woman: if the Easter Bunny makes you smile, *believe in him*. I'm in love with Cosette, Miranda. Without her—and you—I would become more of a ghost than I already am. Live more shapelessly in my head, in my gauze wrappings." More sucking sounds. "Trust the people . . . who . . . give you . . . *form*."

Miranda, her heart aching for the man on the other end of the line, told him she thought it was excellent advice and would follow it if it weren't too late. Then she found her bookmark at page 773, a chapter entitled "The Battle Begins," and let herself fall into the pages of the book, happy and relieved by the sensation of Keeper falling in right behind. Cosette had become a woman; she was about to fall in love with Marius. Now that Miranda knew Keeper was in love with her, she prayed Victor Hugo would not let him down.

Another week passed, and the summer winds finally arrived, a massive swell of warmth rolling in as if from a distant land.

At dusk on a Thursday in April, the thermometer still hovering at seventy blessed degrees, Miranda put on her running pants and shoes and headed east at a full gallop. She ran for an hour and a half, arriving home not only parched and panting but utterly exhausted. Even the bewildered dogs drooped visibly as the home stretch came into view. After feeding them, she got into her Scout and, famished herself, drove to MinuteBurger about twenty minutes away.

It was a mob scene at the small, locally owned diner, a zoo. From families with kids, to teenagers and laborers, to the kind of motley stragglers this part of the West was famous for. No one she actually knew, but how surprising was that?

Waiting in line, she surveyed the counter for an empty spot, then watched, salivating, as large quantities of freshly cut potatoes were dropped into roiling baskets of fat. By the time she reached the front of the line, she had almost decided to order two Junior Beefalo Burgers but then came to her senses at the last minute.

"I'll have . . . a regular cheese Beefalo, extra onions and pickles. Lettuce. No tomatoes. A small order of fries and a medium chocolate shake."

"Dark or milk on the shake?"

This was new. Miranda raised her eyebrows.

"There was a demand," the bald-headed man said as if to answer her question. She thought she detected a smile but could not tell under the shamelessly coifed handlebar mustache concealing his mouth. Though he wore the same white-and-brown uniform as everyone else, his name tag read *Travis*, and under that *I Own This Joint*. "We try to please," he kept staring at Miranda. "Dark is richer."

"Dark," Miranda dutifully answered.

"We don't serve tomatoes on burgers. But, just out of curiosity, why no tomatoes?" He glanced up as he loaded her orange tray. MinuteBurger's color scheme delighted Miranda every time she saw it: orange plastic, pink-and-white paint, occasional brown accents here and there. Personally, she would have been happy if the fifties had lasted fifty years instead of ten.

She shrugged. "I love *good* tomatoes, so I only like *good* tomatoes on a burger. Otherwise, what's the point?"

He grunted and gave her change from her five, adding too many napkins to the tray as an afterthought.

She sat down at the far end of the counter, in between an older woman gorging on a kid's meal and a bulky man finishing up what looked like three Junior Beefalos and a large shake, the color of which she did not recognize.

"Now, what kind of shake is that?" she heard herself ask, intrigued by how fast things were changing at the venerated establishment. She had been away too long.

"Maple!" he answered with great enthusiasm. "I don't think I'll ever go back to chocolate." He gave it a few swirls with his straw. "Here," he picked up the cup. "See for yourself."

Miranda, not wanting to seem rude, moved the straw to the left in order to take a sip, then raised the cup to her lips. Instead of oozing down slowly as it should have, the remaining inch of milky ice cream plopped thickly down in a mass, hitting her squarely in the face. Eventually, after having extricated herself, she forced a smile, groping for the pile of napkins eerily provided by Travis. "Smells *and* tastes good," she said. "Inhales remarkably well, even." She blew her nose, then dared to look at the man. His eyes registered hilarity.

"Sorry," she told him. "People rarely take me out for this very reason. I eventually have to take myself out, in spite of the obvious risks."

"You're that girl from down 47X Road, across from Steadman."

Had Vicki Schuster been at it again? "Do I know you?"

"I'm Rocky Torez's brother, Buddy."

"Buddy Torez," she said, sniffing some residual milk into her nose. "I'm Miranda Blue." She smiled at him, then turned to her food. "Please forgive me, but I'm faint with hunger." She took the first bite and nearly collapsed with pleasure. The onions were minced to perfection and spread evenly on the bun. Rarely did you get onion with the first bite of any ordinary fast-food hamburger. "What do you do around here?" She said it with her mouth full. It was a line she'd heard Vicki use at the post office. *What do you do around here?* As if doing anything, anything at all, were commendable *around here.*

"I'm a teacher at the high school in Cortez. Shop and industrial arts. Rocky tells me you call old people up, check in on 'em. I like that."

"Well, yes." Miranda picked up a bundle of five or six fries, lined them up, and bit off the ends all at once. "But really, they check up on me. Or try to." It had been too long since she'd gone out . . . This was civilization. This was life! She looked around again in disbelieving joy and gratitude for the simple things so close at hand.

"You like living alone?" He had started crumpling up foil on his tray, making neat balls of trash, the kind of trash that would never be airborne enough to land in her yard. Then, instead of leaving them on the tray, he put them in the pocket of his coat, which made Miranda think of Rocky, who never threw anything away either. She pictured a shed full of foil balls.

"No," she said, satiety momentarily sparking her honesty. "As a matter of fact, I don't. But I needed to do it."

"Uh-huh. You friends with Steadman? I guess you'd have to be, the way those houses are lined up. Kinda nice, I'd think, to have someone there to watch out for you, huh?"

"He hasn't been around lately." She avoided the question.

"Oh right—gone for a spell. Audrey's taking care of the greenhouse. You met her?"

She shook her head. "Not really. I mean of course we wave." *I am his closest neighbor,* she fumed from within, *and the last person to know anything.*

"Real nice, friendly girl, especially once you know her. Does farmers' markets. Peppers, squash, eggplant, some tomatoes—nothing like Bill's, of course. I guess he pays her pretty well to step in for him." He stood up and stuck out his hand. "Anyways, nice to meet you. See you again."

"Drop by if you're ever out Rocky's way," Miranda offered, trying to prove she was from the same friendly planet as Audrey. It was suddenly imperative that she attempt an increase in the actual number of human beings in her life.

"Love to!" he called back, and, for a moment, Miranda felt normal, like a regular person in a regular place. She could befriend Buddy who would have patience with her wood-burning and metalworking skills. She might even audit his class, go back to high school again—maybe get it right the second time around.

Because on the first go-round she had done plenty of things wrong, even with Viv censuring her for each and every one of them as they occurred. She'd taken too few science and math classes. Not applied herself enough. She'd smoked pot and cigarettes and drunk fortified wine and slept with Charlie Caparzo when she was fifteen. Worst of all, she'd categorically refused to travel during the summer with her father and mother and stayed with friends instead. Why had she done that? Why had she denied herself both the experience and the consequent memory of it?

It might have been fatigue or hunger, or the contrast of too little human contact and then the bustle of Minute-Burger, or the fact that Miranda had never allowed herself full rein when recalling the past—whatever it was, thinking of her parents on this day, on this stool, in this place caused a lump to form in her throat and she stopped chewing in order to take a deep breath.

Travis appeared just in time to force her to swallow and to regain her composure. "So," he said, picking up the saltshaker from its corral to wipe it clean, "you're Steadman's neighbor?"

She nodded. "Rocky's, too."

"Well, you give him a message for me, since he probably put you up to the tomato comment in the first place . . . Tell him I did a survey, and the public was pretty much unanimous: tomatoes on burgers, if used at all, need to be tasty and ripe. Well, nearly ripe. Tell him I'll be calling him. I may be stubborn, but I listen to my customers, that's one thing you can say about me. Lord knows I'll be doing a pinto bean burger next. You like the dark chocolate?"

"Um, yes," Miranda replied, by then convinced that tomatoes had replaced the gold standard in these parts. "Very much. Thank you." She needed to be nice to this man if she planned on becoming his most frequent customer. "I'll pass along your message as soon as he gets back. Which should be soon."

"Dave D. said you had the eyes. I had no idea eyes came in that color. Well. Enjoy the burger."

Once home, Miranda sat in her armchair, belly full, and listened to the clock tick louder and louder on the wall, that special trick it did just for her. Briefly, she imagined she could smell her mother's jasmine perfume and see her father rearranging the ropes of beads and stones she habitually wore around her neck—and doing it decisively, as if there were a correct way for ornamentation to be administered. Miranda had not been able to speak at their funeral. While Vivianne had stood there dressed in white, speaking of the wings of Death, Miranda's ears had buzzed, drowning everything out. She had missed her chance to say she loved them, so much, and then to list the reasons why.

Would she continue to let opportunities, big, small, and in-between slip by?

At the moment, for instance, it seemed glaringly obvious that there were messages (from Travis to Billy) and meals (from Sharon to Billy) to deliver. After all the times Billy had come over, rubbing his life against hers like a flint stone, perhaps it was her turn to make an effort, find out where he was and when he would be back. Passivity, her old friend and ally, seemed now to have all the sharp advantage of a rusty blade.

Despite the fact that she had misled him and he had misled her and that they both knew very little about each other, she admitted that, yes, in very unstraightforward ways, it could be argued that around Billy she felt slightly more in focus. Not focused, but in focus. Was this form, or was it just the beauty of someone's interested and watchful gaze?

Without being conscious of her actions, she had retrieved the phone book and flipped to the Ns. Before losing her nerve, she found the number she was looking for and dialed it.

"Novo!" a voice screamed, above the noise of a large crowd from the sound of it.

"Hello. Sullivan?"

"Who's this?" he said, amidst the clanking of plates and loud chatter.

"Miranda Blue," she yelled. "Billy's neighbor. I hope I'm not interrupting!"

"Miranda! Sure enough, I recognize that sultry, sassy voice of yours. No, it's just dinnertime here, and everybody's desperate for food." He covered the mouthpiece, but

Miranda heard him saying something about the director wanting a massage before dinner. And to get the wine out of the cases. He was on location.

"I dialed your home number," she said to him.

"Oh: forwarded. It's how I live my life. You're not inter-rupting." Another covering of the mouthpiece, the sound of women's voices, directions being given and taken. "In fact, Providence had a hand in your calling me. More about that later. You wondering about Billy?"

"Well . . ." she began, noting that the inference was that she should be wondering. "Yes, I needed to—"

"Well, I need to talk to you about Billy, too," he cut in, the mild Doppler effect of voices receding as he moved away from the crowd. "But not on the phone. You need to be here: See, it was *your* house that inspired the current brainstorm. We're not that far from Pigeon. A couple hours max."

Miranda, having freshly renounced passivity, toyed nervously with the idea of driving two hours to do what Lydia would call "researching the man." It was more bla-tant a move than she was prepared for. On the other hand, that little trip to MinuteBurger had whet her appetite for getting away, for seeing new faces and learning new things. "I have clients, people I have to call every day; I can't just leave—"

"You've already proven by moving to Otnip you can do your job from anywhere on earth. Call them from here! I have thousands of free minutes on my cell phone—"

She hesitated. She had never been on location before. How had her house inspired him? Were they doing a fifties theme?

"In addition," he added casually, "I've just recently had a call from a certain Rochelle Meyer, rabbi's widow and dabbler in the arcane."

Shocked by the sound of a stranger uttering the name of one of her clients, Miranda only half heard him say, "And if you don't come out, this Rochelle will know more about William Wordsworth Steadman than his own neighbor does . . ."

 14

Hopping out of the truck, Billy realized how desperately happy he was to be home. Hardly having cast a sidelong glance at Miranda's empty driveway, he was greeted by her frothing dogs, the unbridled joy of liberty nowhere more evident than in the spinning, whapping tails. He stroked them eagerly before wondering, not without some apprehension, why they had brazenly crossed the meridian when they had always been so sneaky about visiting him before.

Audrey was in the greenhouse pinching pansies and nasturtiums for the salad mix when Billy arrived with the dogs. She greeted him with open arms, then addressed the animals. "Go on back out," she said, pointing to the open door with a velvety flower of deep violet. "Or no bones later on."

"You know these dogs?" Billy inquired, leading her back toward the house.

"I'm taking *care* of these dogs, Billy," she answered emphatically just to clinch his cluelessness. "Until this very moment," she continued, "I've been doing it all for the dueling homesteads on 47X. Her dogs. Your plants and fish. Not that I don't like the dogs—they've been sneaking over for weeks. Your fish, on the other hand, are just as charmless as I remember."

"Oscars have too much personality for most people. They're piggish, and they like to play."

"Whatever. They're too big. Their rabbit-sized poop makes me uncomfortable. They'd go for my hand if I got it close enough to the water. *And*—they stare."

Billy laughed. It was all true. "They know a beauty when they see one."

"They stare at my hand," she corrected. "Do not try to flatter me just because I was here for you in a time of need."

Billy had slept with Audrey once years before, after Rocky Torez's annual hard cider party. With no prior knowledge of the giddiness contained in bubbly apple juice, he drank three pints, after which his organs had begun tingling and his heart turned inexplicably light for the first time in many months. How was he to know—as she mysteriously indulged him—that she generally preferred the company of women?

Sullivan naturally had been the one to edify Billy and congratulate him. "It's a first step," he'd said. But at their next encounter, Billy was so mortified all he could do was ask Audrey's forgiveness with his eyes. Meanwhile, he wondered secretly if he hadn't somehow sensed Audrey's inclinations and slept with her in spite of them, or for those very reasons; because he knew she would never want involvement, that he would never really interest her, that there would be no threat of regularity or permanence or passion. This made him feel even worse. A frank word about it was never exchanged with Audrey (the frankest person on earth). Nevertheless, they had become friends.

Now he wondered if Audrey hadn't fallen for Miranda: Why wouldn't she? Why wouldn't anyone? Maybe Audrey had come on too strong and sent Miranda virtually running for safety. Miranda was a known runner, after all. But then why would she have left the dogs with Audrey?

"I won't take your aversion to my fish personally," he said. "But I would love to know exactly why you're on dog duty." Noting the dank smell of the empty refrigerator as he pulled open the door, he slammed it quickly after grabbing two beers. He should have stopped at the grocery store on the way home, but that would have dashed his plan to knock on Miranda's door in need of something. Now she wasn't even home.

Audrey shrugged. "Sullivan called to ask me if I wouldn't mind feeding them for a few days, and putting them in for the night on my way home."

Billy tensed. "Sullivan? What does he have to do with anything?" It wasn't Audrey on the make but his best friend.

Audrey pulled a pink bandana from around her head, wet it in the sink, and washed her face thoroughly before taking a swig of beer. Then she sat down at the kitchen table and told Billy Miranda had been invited to go on location. That she had called after Sullivan to thank Audrey and tell her where the dog food was. Looking at Billy hard with her pebbly eyes, she asked, "What's Sullivan up to, anyway?"

"Hopefully, not the first thing that comes to mind. Miranda never called here otherwise?"

Audrey shook her head. "Uh-uh."

"Didn't you ever speak to her, have a conversation with her when I was gone?"

Another shake of the loopy red curls framing her face.

"It just doesn't sound like her to up and leave: I mean who's calling her clients?"

For all these months, Billy had been able to rely on Miranda's being there. The wanton abandonment of her dogs, her plants, her clients disturbed him, shocked him even. It was irresponsible.

Now, in addition to not knowing where Miranda had gone and for what reason, he realized he also felt gypped: He had dreamed of being the one to liberate her from her endless weeks of routine, from winter winds and spring and summer winds to less windy frontiers westward and eastward. When she finally did venture forth, he had seen himself as the escort of choice. He had pictured them driving together to Mesa Verde in winter. Down one of Sullivan's unnamed roads at dusk. Even the grocery store seemed, with Miranda by his side, a potential adventure of glorious proportions. In the Mexican aisle the sands of Baja would come to mind. Steaks would bring on visions of joint barbecues.

"How should I know?" Audrey was annoyed. "I mean why not just call Sully and find out everything you need to know? He, his cell phone, and his cigar are never more than one-sixteenth of an inch apart these days."

Billy did not respond well to the suggestion and shook his head. He could not chase her. After going off himself without warning? "So, you never got any messages on my machine from Miranda or any hang-ups?"

Audrey sighed, undoubtedly affronted by Billy's interrogations. "I wrote all the messages down and called everyone back." She stood up and retrieved the message pad. "Well, except for Sharon Mystery. 'Miranda has your taco pie in her freezer.' That was the only message that wasn't business-related. No hang-ups."

So, Miranda had never heard the message on his machine. Before Audrey had a chance to cross-examine him, he hit the outgoing message button. "You've reached Try a Little Tenderness. I'll be away until the third week in April. Audrey Fromm, who is filling orders, will be answering messages or can be reached at 865-8121. Happy spring to you . . . And if by some miracle this is you, Miranda, I want you to know I'm going to leave you alone from now on. For the record, I would *like* to understand you and to accept you, but you've got to meet me a fraction of the way. P.S., your dogs come to visit me all the time when you're not looking." Bee-ee-eep.

He looked at Audrey sheepishly. "While I was away, I changed my mind about leaving her alone. Since I've gotten back, I've changed my mind again, only it's unclear exactly how. If she had heard that message, she might have concluded something that I've since modified. I needed to know if that was the case."

Audrey smiled and reached into a large, well-organized canvas tote for a bag of *pepitas,* roasted pumpkin seeds, into which she plunged a small but sturdy hand. "So Sullivan's thrown a ratchet into the proceedings. Which means you're worried about his chasing her, which would explain why not only do you not want to leave her alone but why you probably want to go running after her except for that you can't. Sounds like you've made some progress in your personal life, Billy."

With a cheek full of seeds, Audrey continued to grind and talk. "All I know about her is she studies blow-in garbage and loves those dogs to death. She even put one on her lap one evening, on the rocking chair. Wayne. It was cute. I bet she sees right through Sullivan. Actually, what's with him? He was plenty rude to me last time I saw him, at that book-signing—"

"Oh, you went to that?"

She nodded. "The place was jammed, I mean to the gills. Janklow ran out of copies of Sung's latest book, and these college girls were having him sign their *shoulders!* Anyway, Sully didn't even acknowledge me, the jerk."

"For strange reasons having to do with younger women, Sullivan Novo is afraid he'll turn into someone just like Carson Sung."

Audrey burst into laughter, sending out a plume of pumpkin seed bits. She covered her mouth. "Huh?"

"He says he wants someone to call him on all his bull-shit. Of course, a second later he's traipsing off with the youngest thing in the room."

As a local food purveyor and sometimes caterer, Audrey had worked on location with Sullivan many times, planning the fare or just hauling it in. She had seen him in action. "The pitfalls of vulnerability." She shrugged. "I'm shocked and amazed he could hit a wall of any kind."

"Yeah." Billy stood up. "Well, enough about the pitfalls of boring, predictable men. I have a check for you as well as a little present in the form of a case of your favorite burgundy. With love from my mom and dad for making their son's visit a reality. How's life on D½ Road?"

Audrey's smile crept toward her earlobes. "Not bad. Mignonette takes care of things while I'm gone."

Billy halted the beer bottle halfway to his lips. A live-in after all these years of discretion?

"My new parrot, a nearly extinct type called a Buffon's Macaw. Rescued by the Durango Humane Society from cruel owners and gifted to me by the head of aforesaid organization."

Billy heard the sound of a new girlfriend. Though Cortez was not the easiest place for nonconformist sexual orientations, Audrey seemed to have had a far easier time connecting than Billy ever had, and far fewer complexes. She never seemed to lack for relationships.

"Listen," Audrey said. "You want me to call Sullivan? I mean just to find out what Miranda's actually doing there? Sullivan knows not to bullshit me, and now you've got me curious." She pulled a file out of her bag and began to work the dirt from her fingernails.

Billy shook his head and told her it wasn't that big a deal and that he'd see Miranda when he saw her.

Audrey wasn't buying it. "It sounds like a huge deal to me, Bill. I mean, she might have thought I was an ex-girlfriend of yours or something. All of a sudden charming Billy is gone and some stranger pulls in and takes over his life." She touched the file tip, like an epee, to his chest. "Or is that what you were after?"

"Well . . . you were an ex-girlfriend." It was the first time he'd mentioned the episode in almost five years.

Audrey gave him a droll look. "Congratulations," she said. "For finally bringing it up. *Now* I'm willing to consider the possibility that transformation is in the air. Well, maybe not for Sullivan, but for you." Back went the file and out came a wide-toothed hairbrush, which she ran through her curls, wincing at the knots.

"I never brought it up because it's still embarrassing. Every time I think about it, I'm either a brutish walking wienie of testosterone or a harmless little man even a lesbian could humor."

She slowed her strokes with the brush. "Billy. You know I've liked men, too, right?"

Billy waited for her to resume brushing. "No. I didn't."

"Well, yeah. I'm not repulsed by men or anything, just picky. That's why Sullivan keeps on trying. You *know* I'm not his type; but conquest for some people is everything."

Both relief and betrayal were vying for control of Billy's speech centers. "Why didn't you tell me this before?"

"To make what point, exactly? I figured it was your job to ignore trashy gossip, get to know me, and eventually to figure out that if I slept with you, I wanted to. Occasionally an attractive man comes along. You weren't really interested in me though."

"I spent hours asking myself if I hadn't set myself up for noninvolvement. Which has been a pattern of mine, a habit I'd like to try to break."

"Well, try a little harder," Audrey said, giving him a hug as she rose to take her leave. "Thanks for the wine. In case I'm trying to impress someone, will it work?"

"Guaranteed. When do I meet Mignonette?" They both knew he wasn't talking about the macaw.

Audrey laughed, didn't answer, and handed him two Saran-wrapped bones for the dogs. "A way to a woman's heart is through her pets. They're all yours now, Billy!"

After Billy had unloaded his duffel, three cases of wine, and two rare orchid plants that had slumped a bit in transport, he gave the Oscars a Ping-Pong ball and watched them push it around for a couple minutes. Then he returned to the greenhouse, opened the hatch to the sub-basement, and lowered himself into the tomato room.

The great secret of his success, which he had told no one, consisted of the daily playing and alternating of Mozart and a Theta-wave-inducing tape Elena had procured in early experimenting with meditation and self-hypnosis. He didn't know how it all worked—the music and the droning and humming (or even if it really did)—but he wasn't about to tempt fate. He started with the Theta tape (which had never done anything for Billy except put him quickly to sleep) and admitted feeling that he was, in fact, reuniting his tomatoes with their preferred vibration. After checking on each and every plant, he plucked the ripest Brandywine he could find—the most burgundy of the heirloom varieties—and took it with him upstairs and to the house.

Back in the kitchen, his stomach growled.

Vegetables, pancakes, or noodles? Not exactly inspiring fare. But Sharon had gone to the trouble of bringing taco pie (was inexorable cheer cooked into the dish?) and all it entailed was a trip to Miranda's freezer, which could hardly be considered a transgression given his new responsibility to the dogs.

Once inside the house, he could further check on the plants and reclaim the rosemary topiary he'd given Miranda, the one that she had hacked from a soccer-ball-sized bush to a small grapefruit. Sickened by topiaries now, he would take this particular one back, trim it nearly to the stalk, and let it recuperate among the other greenhouse herbs. He would leave the recently liberated Dolores for Miranda, in its place.

After locating a certain special bottle of wine, he set it into an empty crate along with Dolores and the single perfect tomato, and headed over.

In the gathering dusk outside, his orange tulips positively glowed. Lined up in rows close to the house they gave the impression of votives on stems, carrot-bright torches waving in the wind to his neighbor, a greeting from his house to hers.

Pulling clippers from his back pocket, he snipped sixteen of them, then on his way over tried to compose a note to go with them. That was when he realized that the tulips weren't the real gift, the single tomato was. Tomayto. Tomah-to. He actually knew an old song he could allude to, a song that would give him a chance to use one of the great relationship lyrics of all time. His grandmother still liked to hum the tune whenever his mother and father were arguing.

"Let's call the calling off off," he would write, leaving out the quotation marks completely. It wouldn't be lost on Miranda: It was perfect.

15

Miranda stopped to fill up at a gas station in Moab, Utah, the mountain-biking mecca of the Southwest and only twenty minutes from her final destination. A scant two hours from her house, and she had arrived in another world.

Her mint green Scout was an instant anachronism here among the plethora of metallic-toned sport utility vehicles, bicycles strapped to them in every possible configuration—up front, on the top, in the back, and sticking out of windows like carcasses after the hunt.

Wandering the aisles of Gas-n-Go, typically the place to go for Mounds bars, jerky, and sixty-four-ounce sodas, Miranda found instead a vast array of energy bars, vitamin drinks, gels, and an entire section of cellophaned patties, one of which she squeezed in order to see if the dense aggregate of seeds, nuts, and meal would actually give way beneath her fingers. It did, but only slightly.

Now she thought maybe in the relative scale of things she was a Bugles and Coke girl, after all. These people who treated their bodies like their vehicles—finely tuned machines in constant need of fuel—mystified her. They came from places like Aspen and Telluride, but they still mystified her. Had she left civilization that long ago and gone that far away?

Inexplicably, near the phone booth outside, a small vending machine offered toffee peanuts for twenty-five cents, and as Miranda stood there cracking them between her teeth, she eyed her new surroundings with increased interest. The seclusion of Otnip, especially with her only neighbor absent, had truly made a shut-in of her. Of course, everyone—Vivianne, Lydia, Aunt Raye—had been telling her this for months. Even the real shut-ins had insinuated as much.

It was the smell of exhaust that eventually drove Miranda back to her vehicle and onto the main drag, a brightly lit mile-long strip of motels, souvenir shops, diners, and cycleries. In addition to mountain biking, Moab boasted gateway status to several national parks, and the Japanese and European tourists, drawn to the American moonscape like filings to a magnet, arrived daily by the busload, particularly in the spring, before the summer heat purged the place of all but the most driven and leathery of athletes.

About halfway through town, she noted a good-sized crowd was gathered outside an older brick building, and, curiosity piqued, she parked her car and moseyed over. Well, why not? She was grateful to Sullivan for giving her a reason to drive, and grateful to Moab for providing her with a pit stop. So, she would be a bit tardy; she would call him after she had taken her time and meandered a little.

"What's going on?" Miranda asked the last woman in line, who stood reading the *New York Times* in a sleeveless denim shirt, a half dozen shell bangles calling attention to the pages being flipped.

"Carson Sung." She gave Miranda's orange flower-power scarf a quick glance before settling on her face. "He's reading tonight. I didn't think people waited on line like this in the West. Especially for someone so—literary."

It's true, the line was impressive, at least forty people so far. But the nerve. "Oh, sure we do." Miranda feigned a yawn as she contemplated what the West meant to this woman. The union of casualness and illiteracy? "I mean he's practically a celebrity now that they're about to make *Sky* into a movie. He was in *People* magazine a couple weeks ago."

The woman gave her a troubled look, as if sarcasm were a dead language this far into the dummy zone.

What luck, though: In all the fuss with Billy being hauled off to the Cortez jail, she had forgotten about the reading back home. Carson Sung! She had reread nearly all of his books in the past year, starting with *Wicked Sky*—her favorite—the story of a ranching couple, a blistering winter on the range, and the sudden arrival of a traveler at their door. Sung had made life seem like a state of blind, snow-bound half expectancy given definition only by sexual desire. "Samuel Beckett on Ecstasy," said one reviewer's quote on the jacket. Miranda had loved that.

Just as she craned her neck, tiptoeing for a glimpse of the man, the line began to move forward, and, thrilled now at her opportune timing, she progressed with it.

An hour later—and given how movingly he'd read from the book—she found herself purchasing another copy of

Wicked Sky. Having him autograph anything else would have seemed miserably inappropriate. When her turn came, Miranda handed Sung her book, told him her name, then smiled as he took a long look at her, presumably pausing to think of something new to write or to look as if he were. With massive shoulders hunched, he scribbled, renegade locks of gray hair falling over his brow. His full lips met in a wavy line, a line that seemed to suggest life's vicissitudes, all laid out. Staring at the now fleshy cut of his cheekbone and jaw, she thought he must have once been handsome to a fault. Absently, she peered at the words as he wrote them: *To Miranda, whose eyes speak unspeakable volumes.* The date, written 22 April 00, was scrawled beneath, then *Sung.*

To her utter astonishment, having just completed the flourish on the g of his name, he had looked at her with his deep-set eyes and asked her if she had plans for dinner. Other fans, fresh books poised in hand, listened in disbelief as Miranda declined, mumbling something about having to keep an appointment at a remote location.

"Miles to go before you sleep, then?" He had managed to find and secure one of her hands in his. "Pity." His grip was firm and straightforward enough to make her wonder whether she might not have bettered herself by dining with such a heap of man and mind as this.

But having rebuffed him, she had no choice but to flaunt it, and swung herself through the door, jean jacket aflame with residual burning stares of the patrons. Flashing on Vivianne, she thought a cape might have been just the thing to take the dramatic moment to a higher level; but then a moment later she was just another tourist receiving petroglyph-therapy from every shop window she passed. Spirals, tall men with spears, herds of deer, lizards, and horned humans. Not a single cape.

Hunger panging for the first time, she ducked into an overcrowded brewpub, sat at the bar, and ordered a small Greek pizza and whatever beer the bartender recommended. Then she flipped to the part in *Wicked Sky* where Ishmael, the traveler, seduces the wife. Kneeling before her wheelchair like a supplicant, he unbuttons her blouse, reaches in and removes the pale breasts and suckles them, thereby reawakening the faculties in her that had become numb in the face of the husband's selflessness and pity. Moaning, she touches the spot where his lips and her breasts meet, eager to feel his tongue on her fingers . . .

Miranda's face and neck had flushed a deep pink. Her own nipples, beneath the nylon and spandex of a tight camisole, stood erect, just as they had when she had read the passage last winter. Then, too, it had been Billy's mouth upon her, his tongue tending to every one of her urgent needs . . .

Consumed by this insight into the literary-turned-romance-novel fount of her own desire, she was oblivious to Sung's having arrived with a smattering of fans, most of them too young to order beer with their pizza. Oblivious, that is, until she felt a hand touch her shoulder, at which point she slammed the book shut and looked up.

"Ms. Blue, it looks as though we were simply destined to meet again." He planted his bulk on the stool next to hers and ordered a lager, fans receding into the woodwork as if hidden.

"Don't be embarrassed," he said, noting her glow and

probably thinking her shy. "I merely happened in, and here I find you. What fools do not find fate tantalizing?"

"I'm not embarrassed," she corrected him, struggling with his syntax. "Alcohol of any kind makes me flush." His sidling up and quick familiarity reminded her of—Sullivan! "Listen," she excused herself, "I have to make a call. Feel free to have a piece of this. Please, I'll be right back. Don't go away."

Sullivan, who had expected her for dinner, was swift with his justice: a lecture on the rudeness of not keeping in touch in an age of cell phones. "I was worried you'd gotten lost! Where are you?"

"I stopped for dinner in Moab," she explained, slightly irritated. "I mean you have to realize I don't get out that much. This is the big time. There are pizza joints here. And bookstores. You didn't seem to be the worrying type to me."

"Well, I am the worrying type, Miranda." He sighed a harsh *hh-a-a-a-a*. "You're only about twenty minutes from the shoot. Make sure you reread the directions I gave you and turn left after the two huge boulders on the right side of the road or you'll never be found again." There was pride in this threat. "She called again, you know."

"Who?"

"Ro." Sullivan laughed. "That's what she wants me to call her now."

"Listen, you're not scaring me with your inside knowledge," she lied, panic buttons flashing. "I'm coming out there not because I'm desperate but because I'm curious. I also happen to realize now how much a little diversion means every so often."

He chose to ignore her. "Tonight you could have had

arabasi soup, dolmas, bulgar pilaf, and these outrageous spicy lamb balls no one could get enough of. We're about to have baklava and coffee thick as mud. That's all I'm telling you. You might get here in time for the entertainment."

Miranda, thrilled to be eating decent pizza and drinking wheaty beer, couldn't imagine it bettered by anything, except maybe dessert. "Well, maybe you'll save me a piece of baklava. What does my house have to do with anything Turkish, by the way?"

"You'll see. Now get over here. Don't tantalize me playing *hard to get here.*"

"Touché," she said, noting the second use of the verb tantalize in so many minutes.

Back at the bar, the celebrity author was signing napkins. Someone had translated *Wicked Sky* into French and German and the Euros began handing him their national parks maps for an autograph as well.

"Okay." His hands went up in a final blessing. "Now enough of this nonsense. *Andale, por favor, mis amigos.* Get on back to your dinners." He watched Miranda pick up a slice of pizza and bring it to her mouth. "I don't suppose you're like that character in Zola's *Germinal* whose hair turned white all at once."

"No," she answered, more willing now to be given the attention others so obviously craved and further pleased to be somewhat blasé about it. "No, I'm not. But I did begin to turn white at a very young age."

"Did you." He was staring so hard, Miranda lowered her gaze. "May I ask where you're headed? I'm not in the habit of following women around, but . . . fortune favors the bold they say. *Audaces fortuna juvat.*"

It was hard to imagine a bolder man. "I'm going some-place a TV commercial's being shot, a commercial for Gatorade, you know Gatorade? An acquaintance scouts out these locations the LA people use. In the middle of nowhere." Perversely, she had reserved her worst sentence construction for an eminent wordsmith. "Evidently," she continued on, "my friend has hired Turkish caterers to do the food. I promised to be there in time for dessert."

"Mm." Sung's moan registered two octaves below middle C. "I adore the food of Asia Minor." He stood up as if ready to take his leave. "Would that you had need of an escort."

Miranda's surprisingly sharp pang of disappointment at what she thought would be Sung's leave-taking was fol-lowed by the equally surprising consideration of him as an adjunct companion. Why would he follow her, though. He was famous! Did writers chase down characters or just chase down women like other regular men did? It was not the first time Miranda had been pursued on the basis of her looks alone.

But when she reminded herself who this *was*—that this was the creator of pitiable but triumphant Rosemarion Fall—despite everything else, his stature preceded him. He might chase women, but good Lord, he understood them. Maybe he could tell her something about herself she didn't know, couldn't see. Furthermore, it might be interesting to see what Sullivan would do with a surprise guest on his hands. And later, Billy would find out that in spite of his absence, she, too, could leave Otnip and have adventures of her own.

"Maybe you'd like to join us all for baklava," Miranda said spontaneously, the caped ghost of Vivianne alighting at that moment on her shoulder like the bouncer-angel of bad choices. Mentally, she countered with information from the jacket cover of *Sky,* telling herself this man had published eleven books that had been translated into twenty-six languages, had held teaching positions, been nominated for several awards, and continued to run his ranch. Vivianne was stamping her feet and waving her un-caped arms around, flailing them in protest as Miranda continued.

"You could follow my car. It's not far from here." She grabbed the bill before Sung had a chance to pay it. "People will come to look for me if there are any delays. And I want you to know I carry flares, Mace, and an all-purpose tool." *Rifle,* she kicked herself, *I should have said rifle, for God's sake, like everyone else around here.*

Only after she had started driving, out of the town and into the deep black desert wilderness did Miranda think to ask herself if she was not setting herself up as a victim, if victimization didn't lurk in her subconscious like a latent disease. If that blow to the face hadn't been inevitable, after all.

The thought depressed her. Deep down, Miranda did not truly believe her love affairs—her dalliances, even—had been rooted in masochism. Shortsightedness, perhaps. Escapism, almost certainly. Irresponsibility, without a doubt. Maybe she had remained emotionally stuck right where she had been at the time of her parents' death. Arguing with them about college credits and her life's calling. Dating boys she was sure her father would hate just to prove he didn't have control over her. But they had been gone now for a third of her life: And how, if at all, had she grown up in the meantime? Was it possible she had still not acknowledged that they were never coming back?

From behind, Sung had begun flashing her with his brights. *Oh Geez, here we go.* No dogs. No rifle. It was payback time, for her long-lived patterns of irresponsible behavior. Miranda nevertheless slowed the car and allowed him to pull up beside her, and, terror welling, surrendered a scant inch of glass so that he could speak to her (all the while fingering the Mace she'd laid on the seat beside her).

Instead of rolling down the passenger window of his vintage Volvo—presumably his writerly and not rancherly car—he opened his door and stood looking over the roof. "I just had to tell you, I've never been down this road in all my ramblings in southeastern Utah. Not once. I'm indebted to you already. Do you smell the sandstone? Hear the bats?"

"Great, yes." She had to lift her lips to the crack at the top of the window. Her doors were locked and her foot poised on the gas pedal in case he tried anything. "We're almost there, I think. Was there anything else?"

"Well, I've been trying to divine where you're from. Not Colorado, I shouldn't think."

"Nope," Miranda said, feeling the muscles of her ankle tense in anticipation of forward momentum. "Divine again."

"I was thinking New Mexico." He pronounced it Nyew. Miranda was about to correct him when he added, "But I rather think California now. *Northern.*" This impressed her. Billy had had to guess about half a dozen states before getting it right. Of course, he'd wasted his first guess on "the state of anxiety."

"Correct," she said to Sung. "Very good. Now what do

you say we get to where we're going?" She peeled out, not a small accomplishment in her old Scout.

The encampment, for lack of more correct terminology, came into view just as the crescent of a new moon began rising over a distant cliff band. Miranda parked where rows of rental Jeeps and vans had been tidily positioned for the night. Now that she was safe, she felt Sung, completely benign again, might just be the perfect party-crashing cohort.

"Sounds like Middle Eastern dancing," Sung said, as if it were a normal thing to be identifying, like the call of a coyote. Or the sound of bats.

As they approached the center of activity, he continued to articulate, narrating each of her thoughts for her. "This is quite something . . . Look at all these incredibly fine rugs, strewn on the earth like doormats!"

Miranda spotted Sullivan sitting off to the side on a hassock, cigar in mouth, phone attached to ear, watching a veil-clad and midriff-baring woman on a makeshift stage. When he finally noticed Miranda approaching with Sung, his mouth dropped open far enough to cause the cigar to drop.

"Maybe he recognized you," Miranda said, just as the dancer discharged multiple veils to the floor.

 16

Billy, who had been napping on Miranda's bed for the last hour, awakened to the sound of the phone ringing. For a moment, so natural was his feeling that he had already moved in, he thought the call might be for him.

Tenancy had been earned in the last twenty-four hours through his careful tending of both plants and dogs. In addition, the night before he had completed his first uninterrupted meal at her kitchen table: taco pie, served on a disc of milky, mint green plastic reminiscent of hospital dinnerware. He had consumed the well-executed casserole staring from her window into his and feeling very much in the shadows of women. Sharon. Audrey. Miranda. His mother. His grandmother. It had felt good.

After dinner he had gone home for the night, but not before convincing the puzzled dogs to accompany him. It was Audrey's dog bones that had done most of the persuading and all the tiring out, but eventually the dogs had conked out on his couch.

He, too, had remained at her house in spirit. He could

still smell her pillows and the clothes and robe that hung on the back of the bedroom door, and remembered opening her jars of cream and snapping the cap off the shampoo for a whiff of—apricots. The kitchen smelled of linoleum and coffee and the living room of old LPs. And in a flood of soft sensations, Billy remembered how much he had liked living with a woman and how natural it had seemed. Perhaps Begay had been right that women could make a heavy world light and a light world lighter still, that women reconnected men to the beauty of everyday things. He had promised himself that the next day he would lie on her bed, just to see what it felt like.

The next morning, he had taken the dogs, eager for air, out for a long walk toward Rocky Torez's place.

"Hey!" said Rocky, a man who never stopped tinkering with things both in the house and outside. He had been working on sealing six more beehive boxes. "What's goin' on, Billy Steadman? Ain't these Miranda's hounds?" The dogs had run to Rocky's side at once.

"Yup," Billy had said, admiring Rocky's skill with tools and projects and wondering why he had lived alone all these years. Maybe someday Billy would work up the nerve to ask him. "She's out of town for a day or two."

Rocky resumed stirring what looked like hot beeswax and brushed it on the wood, the light smell of honey sweet in Billy's nose.

"Saw her go by. Wondered why the dogs weren't with her."

If he was waiting for an answer, Billy wasn't about to give it.

"You know my brother, Bud?" Rocky had continued, undaunted.

"You know I know your brother, Bud, Rocky, he helped me install my fish tank. We spent two days together. I did a terrarium project with his juniors one year. His middle name's Alejandro and he lost the tip of a finger his first semester of teaching shop. We know each other. Now what about him?"

"He met Miranda at MinuteBurger a few days ago. He said she ate like she hadn't eaten in three days."

The minute he'd said it, Billy could picture it and felt like a starved man himself. "That's how everyone eats at MinuteBurger." He tried to modulate the defensiveness. "It's the nature of the beast. I've seen your brother put away a small pile of hamburgers himself, a regular Wimpy—"

"All I'm saying is: he liked her. A lot. So if you have any designs in that direction . . ."

"Yeah?"

"I would get in there, boyo. People have been underestimating Bud his whole life, just like they've underestimated me. With me, it's I'm picky. The last woman to knock my socks off was Miranda's sister. You know, she knows more about bees than your average apiarist. Something else about her, can't put my finger on it. Anyway, I'd keep an eye on Bud. Of course, you don't go to MinuteBurger these days."

"No."

"Personally, I think it's overrated. Bud swears by the Beefalo and says what's his name—"

"Travis."

"Travis down there at"—he bent down to stir the wax again—"MinuteBurger is a genius. You know they're doing a maple shake now."

"No, I didn't know. Listen, I've got to be going, Rocky." Billy always felt that the more time he spent around the man, the more like him he became, his brain rolling in weird loops ending in twangs. He was jealous Rocky had met Miranda's sister and jealous that Bud had gotten a seat next to Miranda for dinner, and he didn't want to hear about it anymore.

"Maple," Rocky had repeated, glancing over his shoulder as Billy had started hoofing it back over the lumpy earth, climbing fences where he needed to and squeezing through lengths of barbed wire as the dogs slunk under. Suddenly overcome with the delayed fatigue of the long drive, he had had to take off his flannel shirt just to feel the sharp chill of the morning air against his bare arms.

When he finally arrived at Miranda's with the dogs, he had removed his shoes and headed toward the bed he'd been dreaming about. Wayne, probably confused by a switch in the most sacred of spots, had started to whine. Of the two, Wayne was the sensitive one, the one prone to sitting on laps.

"It's okay, Mr. Wayne," Billy had mumbled low, barely able to keep his eyes open. "She'll be home soon." Then he'd dozed off, clutching one of her pillows to his chest. It had felt resistant, as if someone had taken care to fluff it regularly, and before drifting off, he had heard his own heart beating against the stuff of wings.

Of course the phone wasn't for him.

As he reached for it, reason coming back through sleep, he considered the possibilities: It might be Miranda, or her sister, or her friend Lydia, any of whom he would want to talk to. It might be some other family member, an ex-lover, or someone else from her secret past. All interesting.

But it was an older voice, a man's, someone who hardly let Billy finish his "Respect for Your Elders" greeting. *"I believe a leaf of grass is no less—"* the voice roared before stopping short. There was a pause. "This isn't Miranda," he said, more to himself than to Billy. "I must have misdialed. Seem to be doing a lot of that lately. I should be whittlin' more to keep my fingers nimble."

"You dialed Miranda's house," Billy reassured him, wondering now what manner of client would begin a phone conversation in full declamation.

"I did?" The man was too polite to say *Then who are you?* but that's what was implied.

"I'm her neighbor. I, uh, just happened to be near the phone."

"Is Miranda there? You can tell her it's Greg Vogt. I'm one of her clients. You must be the hydro-farmer."

Billy plopped down at Miranda's desk. "Yeah," he said, thinking that at least his telescope did not broadcast images of Miranda to the rest of the world, where, on the other hand, she and a headset were all that was needed to disseminate the particulars of his life. "That would be me."

"Tomatoes, huh, the kind people box each other over. That's what Miranda said. Well, it's nice to meet you. If omission were any indication of your status in Miranda's life lately—*am I on speakerphone?*"

"Yes," Billy confessed, "but Miranda's not here at the moment. I don't know how to work this headset thing she wears, so—"

Gregory was silent.

"She took off for a few days," Billy explained, surprised that he was having to tell her clients she was gone. If anything, she seemed overly responsible. How had Sullivan enticed her to drop everything and go?

"But she just called me!" Greg Vogt countered.

"She did?"

"Indeed she did. I read my Whitman to her as usual—" He stopped. "Come to think on it, I asked her why it sounded as if she were in a wind tunnel, and she replied she wasn't on her regular phone. I guess it wasn't her regular headquarters either—"

Billy should have known: Sullivan had set her up with a cell phone, that's what had happened. Only she hadn't expected anyone to call *her* at home. No, I guess she was coming to you live from somewhere in southeastern Utah. I'm amazed she didn't tell you that."

"Well, she's proud of her professionalism, you know. And does a real good job of it, if you want my opinion."

Billy paused, thinking this might be an opportunity to ask a question or two. He glanced around her desk and noticed that indeed her index cards were gone as well as her three-inch-thick DayTimer. Dolores had filled up the empty space nicely.

"It's a very sweet line of work," Billy agreed. "Does she ever talk about herself? I mean, if she's mentioned me and my profession, she must be pretty—forthright—about her life." "Forthright" sounded like the kind of word he should use with this man.

The old guy laughed, then coughed something deep, raspy and raw. It sounded tubercular, and Billy imagined blood in a white handkerchief. "Are you okay, Mr. Vogt?"

"Call me Greg or Gregory, please," he stammered, then cleared his throat. "Even m'damn kids do." He paused again. "You two sort of sidestep around each other, don't you?"

"What makes you say that?"

"Well"—he considered his words—"we've all tried to find out more about you than Miranda's been willing to say."

"Who's we?"

Silence, then a couple sniffs. "Dammit all," he finally uttered. "I knew things would just start slippin' out. Not that it matters—now that Ro called your friend Sullivan and all."

It was Billy's turn to sputter and spin his wheels and to curse himself for having ever left Miranda alone in Otnip after imposing an introduction to Sullivan on her. "Back up," he said, invoking calm by standing up from the desk and pacing the floor, dogs eyeing him suspiciously as he did so. Wayne started to whine again, and Billy began to stroke his flews absently in order to calm him. "Who's Ro—and how does she know Sullivan?"

"Ro is another one of Miranda clients. A real card, and a bloodhound with her nose to the ground as far as Miranda's concerned. Well, for that matter, so's Evalina . . ."

Billy listened with increasing interest as Gregory filled him in on the three elders communicating, Rochelle's having called the police and gotten the name of his greenhouse, their calling his number and getting the recorded message, calling Audrey, calling Sullivan. Finally, he stopped and said, "Say do you mind if I ask you a question?"

"I think you should! Just so that someone else doesn't get the last word in on what appears to be my life story. Did this Ro manage to call my mother as well, or my brother Bobby? And what did the guys at the station have to say about me, anything? Do you all know about my dead wife yet?" He regretted it the minute he said it. "I mean this sort of feels like trespassing. And Miranda? She's not going to like this one bit."

Greg Vogt sighed and proceeded carefully. "No. And I'm a little ashamed, to tell you the truth. It's just, well—*Miranda*. We're all so fond of her, the care she gives us old fogies. She single-handedly changed my daily life, did you know that?"

Susceptible to this particular notion, Billy was quiet.

"She got me reading Walt Whitman," the old man declared. "I spout it out, she listens . . ." He huffed in frustration. "It's just we all felt as if Miranda were missing something or hiding something or not getting her due. And she's given us so much in a brief amount of time—we wanted to pay her back."

"I understand what you're saying. But like you just said, she runs a business and considers herself a professional. She keeps her accounts separate, right? What's going to happen when she finds out you're in collusion? Isn't it going to make her feel as though she's failed as a caregiver—that instead of laying out a balm of companionship and rendering professional services, she's portrayed herself as someone in need of an emotional rescue?"

"You may have hit a certain nail on the head there." There was resignation in his voice. "But the girls—Evalina and Rochelle—knew of each other before they got in touch. Miranda had mentioned each to the other, you see, certainly conjecturing that the two might get along."

"But not necessarily wanting *her* to be the focus of their attention."

"No, probably not."

Billy sighed. "You better give me the numbers of each of these women. I need to talk to them." He had to protect Miranda, now, protect her from—everything.

Gregory made Billy promise not to be too hard on the girls. "You know, I mentioned early on to Miranda that I might be interested in talking to you about your tomato operation."

"You did? Why?"

"Oh, I've been interested in this stuff for years and years. I keep up on things by reading *High Times*. I bet you know it."

Billy suppressed a grin. "Sure I know it. Good call."

"Which is why—until we talked to Rodney LeFevre—I thought you'd been hauled off for growing *cannabis*."

Gee-zus. Privacy did not exist. "Yeah, well, I've been known to lead people on in that regard. Miranda said a long time ago she didn't want to have anything to do with me because of it."

"Did you believe her?"

"I forced myself to want to believe her. She stayed safely at arm's length that way."

"So you don't grow marijuana?"

"Nope. Well, one little female plant I root-clipped into a Bonsai some years ago."

"Does she know you're completely legitimate?"

"Now she does. But there's other stuff going on."

"Like what?"

"I don't know." Billy was irritated by the persistence,

mostly because the man cared enough to ask the important questions. "And at this point I'm going to say maybe you should ask *her.*" It was time to be honest. Billy pulled off a swift meditation breath, then continued, "For the record, I'm in love with the woman. I'm not really sure why I'm telling you this. I guess now that I've told my mother, I figure the whole world might as well know. Yeah, well, so . . ." He paused. ". . . I'm crazy about her."

There was a long silence. "I trust your voice, your manner of speech, young man, and you've just touched me deeply. Now, I'll bid you adieu."

Billy went through all the kitchen cabinets after hanging up with Gregory to see what he could scrounge up. It was obvious he would be making a few calls and needed some liquid refreshment, maybe a cookie or two. It was above her tea selection that he noted the largest array of over-the-counter pain relievers he had ever seen: aspirin, ibuprofen, naproxin, acetaminophen, homeopathics, herbal formulas, and ointments, too. He stared at the bottles, boxes, and tubes, all nearly full, wondering what she was trying, unsuccessfully from the looks of it, to treat. Cramps during her period? Lots of headaches? Backaches? He did not like it. Might he ask Mr. Vogt's two associates if Miranda had ever mentioned chronic pain? He did not have the chance to find out before the phone rang again.

"Respect for Your Elders," he said, already sounding more professional than the last time. "William speaking," he added, rooting himself firmly again at the desk. He needed to see if you got cramped from the lay of the curious plastic chair. Maybe her complaints were workplace related.

There was a pause. "Is this the Respect for Your Elders, the companionship service?" She sounded worried.

"Yes," he said. "It is. Who's this?"

"Well, this is Saint Mary's Hospital in Grand Junction calling in regards to one of your patients—or clients I guess is what you'd call him."

Billy wondered how many patients of Miranda's were in the hospital and was overcome with tenderness—for her, for them, for people taking care of other people everywhere on earth. He had taken care of fish and plants in the last eight years. Miranda was taking care of human souls. He was thus unable to tell anyone Miranda was absent, that she wasn't at her place of business. "Yes?" he said again.

"Well, we're very sorry to inform you," the woman proceeded, "that Rochambeau 'Keeper' Dix passed away yesterday morning at 8:24. We wanted you all to know that per Keeper's request and given the absence of family, there will be no memorial service but donations are being accepted to his favorite charity in lieu of flowers."

"Okay," Billy swallowed hard, hating the vocabulary of death. "Which charity—we'll be sure and send something."

"Well, that's just the thing, Mr.—"

"Steadman."

"Mr. Steadman, that's just the thing. It was Respect for Your Elders that was named as the charity of Keeper's choice."

"This—" he stammered, "this isn't a charity, it's a business." It was all wrong answering Miranda's phone.

She continued on, oblivious, as if being coached. "Keeper's lawyer will be contacting you regarding a special

221

fund created by tax-deductible donations to pay for calls to other severely injured firefighters. Keeper left two envelopes here, which we've sent to you via US Express Mail: one marked Respect for Your Elders, and one marked Miranda Blue. Is she available?"

Uncomfortable, Billy nevertheless had to struggle to keep up the pretense. "She's out for the rest of the day."

"Well, how far is—Otnip—from Grand Junction?"

"Only about two hours away. Close to Pigeon."

"Oh, yes, Pigeon, that's right. Why you're just right around the corner! What a shame you never met Keeper."

"We can't necessarily meet our clients, Ms.—"

"Davore. Nini Davore. No of course not."

"Nevertheless, death makes it clear to us just how much we would have liked to—" Billy, meaning the words even though he knew he sounded like a mortician, had no choice but to keep on talking. "In terms of these donations—well, I really don't know what to say."

"You people helped Keep—," Nini's voice cracked for the first time. "Forty-two years old, the lamb. He—" She stopped, unable to go on.

"It's okay," Billy said softly, wondering about this man his own age. "I understand." What had Miranda done for him? Poetry? What would she be saying to this woman now? "We'll await the call from the attorney. It will be an honor to provide comfort to other firefighters."

"Yes." She seemed bolstered. "His memory will live on."

"It certainly will."

After hanging up Billy stared glumly out the window toward his house. Earlier bright skies had clouded over, and it had begun to rain softly, as if the earth itself needed comfort, a small drink of water brought tenderly to the soil's parched lips. He wondered if it were raining in Moab.

Could he call and give Miranda this news over the phone? It seemed wrong. Hurtful. But if she picked up the mail on her way home, she would get the information in a roundabout way, nothing having prepared her for it. He decided to go to the post office later that afternoon and intercept the envelopes so that he could break the news gently to her before handing over the paperwork.

For no particular reason, he returned to the tea closet and began pulling out all the medications, fingering the aspirin bottle as if it were a lamp with a genie inside. He took two aspirin, as if willing himself closer to Miranda, returned to her desk, asked himself again whether he should page her, fiddled with the headset until he'd figured it out, then dialed not Sullivan's cell number, but the number for Rochelle Meyer.

17

Sullivan was in awe of the man, that much was obvious to Miranda. After offering them Turkish coffee, baklava, and seats by the stage, they simply sat watching the dancers and listening to the music.

Finally, during a short break for the pouring of raki (a Turkish anisette served with water), Sullivan offered Sung a Cuban cigar and admitted while clipping it that he'd read all his works at least twice. Well, listened.

"An audio fan, are you?"

Miranda had a vague sense that this twist of fate had more to do with bringing Sung to Sullivan than Sung to her or her to Sullivan; but then fate was something that always seemed clearer as it happened to other people.

"Is it your estimation"—Sung puffed, then scratched his chin crusty with baklava honey—"that Everest Goldberg can be bettered? Magnificent resonance. He's stayed with me all these years, too."

"Your own voice is better; but he's pretty damn good." Sullivan abruptly shifted gears and looked at Miranda. "So.

You two met in Moab? Just happened to connect and drive out together?"

"At the book signing," Miranda explained. "But I was just an excuse to ditch those groupies that flutter around him like moths to a flame."

"Some faces," Sung proffered in his own defense, "launch a thousand Volvos. It was obvious this woman needed an escort."

Miranda reddened. "I'm surprised you didn't meet him in Cortez, Sullivan."

"Too crowded." He extended a lighter to Sung's cigar. "Lots of moths. Don't you ever tire of the fawning?"

Miranda could not contain an eruption of laughter.

In a flurry of puffs and smoke, Sung answered. "I've been told *Sky* is now on the syllabus at several colleges. Freshman English, that sort of thing. As I see it, smitten by Ishmael, female students are simply transferring their feelings. Tired old stuff. Would you suggest I complain, Mr. Novo? I should add, the public relations people love it—an author with a fan club, that sort of thing."

"Who plays Rosemarion Fall?" Miranda was almost afraid to ask.

"There's been some difficulty casting her." He stared hard at Miranda.

"Yes, I would think so." Every time Miranda tried to picture a face for the woman, she saw her own, even if she knew perfectly well every other woman did, too.

"They narrowed down the location yet?"

"Ah, yes, the location question from the scout. No. Not as of yet. They want the back two hundred acres of my ranch. But I don't like the idea one bit."

"No, don't do that, for God's sake, *please*. They'll ruin it! That whole section off 467LN will never be the same. Let me think about it," Sullivan relit the omnipresent stub for the fourth or fifth time, then glanced at his watch just as Miranda yawned. He picked up a megaphone. "Thanks everyone. The lovely and talented Ziir, Amira, and Hasna will be back tomorrow. Breakfast will be served from eight to nine," he continued. "No lateness will be tolerated unless you're the director, related by blood to the director, or have a note from the director."

About three dozen people rose slowly from their chairs and began shuffling to their tents for the night. Miranda followed Sullivan and Sung to her quarters, a roomy tent set up for a single person. Several exquisite rugs were strewn across the floor. Sumptuous, jewel-toned fabrics had been draped from the ceiling in billows. Even Sung wheezed in delight.

"What does any of this have to do with my house?" She stared longingly at the cot, the candlestick, and the copy of *Tales from One Thousand and One Nights*.

Almost distracted, he answered: "Your wood floors scream out for coverings, Miranda. And it doesn't get any better than this."

Sung had stooped to finger the cinnamon rug. "Where did these fine things come from? This is an Usak medallion!"

"From the rug guy in Telluride." Sullivan sat on the cot. "Rugs acquire value with wear, see. So, it being off-season, I was able to convince him to let me borrow a truckful. He's here, if you want to know anything about rugs. Or about hashish, I imagine."

Sung stood up. "This is outright seduction," he said, turning to Miranda. "I can see why you come visiting."

"Actually it's my first time," Miranda said. "And I'm not easily seduced." She pea-shot a look at Sullivan. "Tomorrow we talk."

"I like the sound of that." Sullivan grinned, then motioned for Sung to follow him to his own tent, which, he said, always came with a spare cot.

The next morning, when Miranda stumbled out for coffee at 8:58, Sung was already deep in conversation with Sullivan. She managed to sneak a cup of what tasted like good American coffee without being seen by either of them and sat down at an empty table, whereupon a lanky, thinlipped woman wearing a Gatorade sweatshirt informed her the entire table was reserved for the director's morning meeting and could she please find another.

"Oh," she said, noticing the woman's new red, white, and blue cowboy boots, and stood up. "Sullivan didn't tell me—"

Sullivan showed up precisely at the moment his name was uttered. "What's the problem? Miranda, this is one of the PAs, Cahill Henry. She'll be showing you where the food is—"

"The food is put away, Novo, you know we're trying to keep to a sched—"

"The director's conferencing with the talent, Cahill—at a different table. Just chill out, baby. Loosen your ponytail."

"I prefer not to be addressed in such a manner."

"I prefer that you not be *dressed* in such a manner." He looked at her feet. "You need to wear tennis shoes to keep up with this director; believe me, I've worked with Warren before. Come with me, Miranda. We need to talk anyway."

Miranda, letting herself be led away, had never been around these kinds of people, even in Aspen. "What's a PA?"

"Oh, production assistant. Today we have to organize our talent—five guys and a girl and their titanium-framed bicycles—which means make them up, coach them on the scenes, and have them ride the terrain that's been specifically picked out for the commercial. The director's a good guy, basically, but you'll never actually hear him speak. That would be the first assistant director's job, to translate every one of the director's needs into executable commands. The PAs are nine for this particular shoot: Cahill's the bitchy pain in the ass who has put herself in charge. There are, in addition, two other director's assistants, whom you'll hear quite frequently telling people what to do. Also on hand: ad agency, production company, Gatorade folk, and assorted stragglers like the rug guy, the caterers, and the drivers of the big vans. Forty-one people plus you two."

Miranda followed Sullivan into the food tent, where four people were already preparing lunch. "It'll take all day to convoy to and from the location and do half the shoot, and these lovely and talented Turks will be seeing to our feasting needs." He smiled at the older woman caterer, who had on a peasant dirndl and Gatorade baseball cap. "Don't forget all the Evian." He took her rough hand in his, then brought it to his lips, causing her to blush.

Miranda was given a plate of something deliciously eggy and a soft bun, garnished with white cheese and tomatoes.

Plate in hand, she followed Sullivan to his tent per his request.

"I have to make calls," she said. "I don't think I can drive out with you."

"You can make calls from my car *and* be there for the action," he said. "Listen, Miranda, before the big guy comes looking for us . . ."

Sung was the big guy now. "Yeah?"

"I want to—to thank you—for stopping at that bookstore in Moab. It's all so—curious."

She took a large bite of soft bun and felt it fill her mouth pleasantly. "Frankly," the words were muffled from dough, "I don't know why he's here. Maybe writers do weird shit. When they're not authors with groupies, they're just lonely people like the rest of us." She swallowed, thinking of what she had just said, how she might have never said such a thing even twelve hours ago. "Beats me. It occurred to me he could be a perv; but from my end, I just wanted to slam-dunk a little something unexpected into your hoop. I had no idea he was such a god. Where is he, anyway? I have a yen to transfer my feelings."

Sullivan smiled at her. "The director snagged him and is grilling him about the movie. No one else here has ever even heard of him! Anyway, he was looking for you but I need to talk to you first. You look like his wife, Miranda. He told me that last night."

"Jesus, his dead wife? The one Rosemarion was based on?"

Sullivan nodded. "He just took it as a sign. We'll get back to that, but first I have to talk to you about Billy."

Miranda looked off into the distance. It was too early in

the morning for surprises and far too early for all this honesty. On the other hand, isn't this what she'd recently wished upon herself? Looking squarely at Sullivan, she waited.

"Miranda, Billy was married years ago."

There it was, he was married. Had he run off? Was his phone number unlisted because the ex was from back where his parents lived and wouldn't be able to track him down this way? Had he had an affair with the woman on the refrigerator? "Billy was married years ago," she repeated.

"He should have told you this. And his wife, Elena—"

Miranda took a scalding gulp of coffee, waiting for it to burn her throat and clear her brain.

"Was very beautiful. I introduced them to each other, as a matter of fact. I did that wonderful, awful thing."

Very beautiful. This was mentioned for one reason alone. "Because—she broke his heart. Didn't she?"

"Well, yes." Sullivan, in old jeans and a black tee shirt, threw on a Gatorade-emblazoned denim jacket. "She did."

"And he never got over it." She said the words as if it were a tired story, a made-for-TV movie, a thirty-second commercial for antidepressants. It was all so obvious now.

"Well, I'm not sure he could. Grief varies from person to person. Elena had leukemia, and she died almost nine years ago."

Miranda's head jolted up. Sullivan was looking her directly in the eye.

"Don't panic," he said, coming around behind her and massaging her neck with what Miranda sensed at once to be experienced fingers. They were warm and strong. "Don't panic. It was a long time ago. He got over it, in his own way. He never really had any interest in anyone until . . . *you*."

She couldn't think of anything. "Shit," she finally felt her mouth move. "Shit, shit, *shit*."

"No," he kept massaging, as if he somehow knew that she feared her own tension, its buildup, its effects. "It's fine. Why should you have known—wouldn't that have just made you pity him or act unnatural?"

"It's all unnatural anyway." She breathed deep. "What was she like?" The vague but permeating power of ghosts.

The massaging stopped. "Warm and funny—*alive*. Adored Billy, spoiled him rotten. When she died, he got so involved in his own withdrawal—well, even though the rest of us were suffering, no one's grief could compare to Billy's. I mean I understood, but I loved her, too."

Billy was a widower. Miranda was an orphan. There were words for people who lost a spouse or both parents, but what about words for the rest of humanity, someone who had lost a friend, someone who had lost a child, someone who had lost one parent instead of two? A barbaric language had gypped these people, not given them a category of their own.

Carson Sung strode over then, looking fresh from a good night's sleep. He wore a silk scarf around his neck.

"Ah, there you are," he said to the two of them, then looked at Miranda's plate. "I've extricated myself from that tedious director. Are the buns not wonderful?"

She nodded.

"Have I interrupted?"

"No, no," Sullivan said. "We're just getting ready to head out."

A strident voice had just begun to announce the departure of the convoy of trucks, vans, and Jeeps to the location.

"The woman has very little grace or sense of hospitality," Sullivan said, raising the megaphone to his lips. "Lunch," he announced, "today will consist of dolmas, pastirma sandwiches, red lentil soup, and filled pastries, and tea will be served during the whole shoot by our lovely dancing trio. It's time to go—we'll see you there shortly."

Sullivan handed Miranda his cell phone, her cue to fetch index cards and appointment book from her car. Ten minutes later, she was in the backseat of a Cadillac flying top down through the warm desert air at the tail end of a ten-vehicle convoy. She was feeling sorry for Billy, sorry for Sung, sorry for Sullivan, and sorry for herself, though she did not know precisely why. At the moment, all of them seemed to need and deserve—compassion.

Phone in hand, she knew she could not delay the beginning of her workday, in spite of a compromised sense of privacy and a general sense of vulnerability. She made the first call to Agatha Colgate, who had recently gone from the New Testament to the Old and from being quizzed to quizzing Miranda. Miranda was nervous at having to fudge her way through without a Bible.

They were discussing the Book of Ruth, which Miranda had read, but not well except to note, coincidentally, that the action had begun in the biblical Moab.

"Boaz," she answered Agatha's first question, and then added, "I don't live that far from Moab, Utah. Isn't that something? . . . No . . . I don't know, what do *you* think? . . . Of course I read it . . . Ruth's mother was named . . ." She paused. The two men in front had ceased their quiet chatting.

"Naomi," Sung said quickly, his deep voice almost inaudible at a whisper.

"Naomi," Miranda repeated. "No, I didn't just look it up. No, I'm on a different phone, that's all . . . Her great grandson? . . ."

"King David," Sung hissed, turning around to face Miranda.

"King David," she echoed, smiling at Sung who seemed thrilled to be of service. "Interesting thing about this particular book? . . . Well . . ."

"Written in a female voice," Sung, now completely at her disposal, was obviously in his element, "and concerns the autonomy of two immigrant women as well as the relationship between a strong mother and daughter."

"I'm here," Miranda assured Agatha, carefully rephrasing what Sung had said, wondering if he knew as much on every subject. "I was struck by the autonomy of Ruth and Naomi," she said. "Working the marriage thing with Boaz, taking control of their lives like that. You were, too?" She winked at Sung, who was nodding.

"Do you want background on the time of the rule of Judges?" he further queried. Miranda shook her head. She could hardly become a biblical scholar overnight. After she had hung up, she punched Sung in the shoulder. "Boy, you came in handy. How did you know so much about the Book of Ruth?"

He ignored her question and stared at her box of index cards. "So, this is what you do?"

She nodded. "Most of the time I have my materials right

at hand. It's not just the Bible, or I'd be in trouble. Easier stuff, mainly. And I've never gone on the road with Respect for Your Elders before. They can't know I'm not at home—it would seem unprofessional."

Sullivan laughed. "One of these characters called *me* up yesterday to do a little nosing around about *her* Miranda," he told Sung. "She wanted to let me know that she thought Miranda was a woman on the run from something. Holing up in Otnip. And in love with Billy, her only neighbor—my best friend."

Miranda, furious with the indiscretion, willed herself not to overreact. She could feel Sung watching her as she fumbled with the buttons on the phone, trying to make the next connection to Gregory, who would simply recite and sit there and listen and not be interrupted. But Gregory suddenly wanted to talk weather: What was it doing out there in Otnip? She assumed Otnip's weather was the same as Moab's and started describing the warmth and the clouds out West. So what if Rochelle thought she was in love with Billy?

"Storm coming in," Sung observed quietly, like a golf commentator. "Cumulonimbus clouds. Almost mamma-tocumulus in appearance. Desert bounty."

"Maybe a storm coming in. Lots of those thunderhead type clouds forming," she said, only half-there. "How is it where you are? Uh-huh . . . uh-huh. What are you reading today?" She covered up the mouthpiece. "He reads Whitman," she whispered proudly, carving the words into the air with her mouth. Gregory was lamenting that there was just too much to choose from. "Well, how about you just crack open the volume and read whatever's in front of you . . ." A small tribute to John Franco Costa, one which now made her smile.

Once he'd begun, Miranda handed the phone to Sung, who began listening with increasing interest. " 'Crossing Brooklyn Ferry,' " he mouthed, nodding, listening intently for the next couple minutes before handing the phone back to Miranda quickly, like a hot potato.

"See," she said to Gregory. "There's more than one way to skin a cat. . . . No, I'm on a different phone than usual." The car had come to a halt just as Gregory fortuitously announced he'd forgotten to use his inhaler and needed to excuse himself. "I'll call you tomorrow," she said. "For more of 'Crossing Brooklyn Ferry.' " He seemed surprised she knew the poem's title and she had to answer it had been in one of her high school poetry anthologies.

"Impressive, huh?" Miranda said to Sung, who nodded as he took her hand to help her out of the car.

"Beautiful reader. I'd forgotten the poem: How things flood back, sometimes."

Sullivan had raised his lips to the megaphone. "And, Rochelle wanted me to tell you that they found out from Audrey that Billy was due back last night. *They* being she and her friends, Gregory and Evalina. That they all think you need company, Miranda Blue."

Miranda grabbed the megaphone from his hand just as she felt her eye twinge. It had been three weeks nearly, and the last headache she'd gotten had been in this man's presence. Why? Vaguely she felt the answer must lie with him or his messages, and bringing the megaphone up to her mouth, she wondered how to make words out of her feelings.

"Que sera, sera," was the first thing to come out, her voice strong and melodic, the pleasure of singing immediate. "Whatever will be, will be." The amplification made everything so—real! She continued on, remembering Doris Day's smile as well as Majesta's directives on proper phrasing. "The future's not ours to see . . ." Sung joined in like a bassoon, *"Que sera, sera!"*

Miranda managed, between clients, the phone, the megaphone, and the distraction of shooting an actual commercial, to ward off the headache until the late afternoon, when, with Sung dragged off again by the director and Sullivan pelting her with personal questions, it manifested at last. In the back of the Jeep she lay, crippled, Sullivan's coat wrapped around her head while she tried to breathe, tried to breathe and focus on nothing at all.

18

It was raining hard by the time Billy arrived at the Otnip post office, a small building reminiscent of a New England clam shack. Dripping wet, he flung open the door just as the first clap of thunder sounded.

The place was empty except for Vicki Schuster, who stood on the top rung of a stepstool carefully removing a prodigious assortment of Easter decorations from the walls. He smiled at her tight Wranglers and the shearling scuffs on her feet.

Vicki glanced over her shoulder, grinned widely, and immediately began her descent. "Look who's back!" She took a bag from his hands and started brushing water from his jacket sleeves before yanking at them. "Take this thing off, you'll catch your death." She glanced quickly at her feet. "Lord, I wasn't expecting company. No one ever comes in at this hour."

Last year at Easter Billy had done his own decorating in Miranda's yard. Sneaked over in the morning with six bags of jelly beans for her lawn, and a basket for her door. This year, he had not been home to observe the holiday or to observe her observing it: This would not go unnoticed, he was sure of it.

"How's my favorite postmistress?" He opened the brown bag and pulled out a six-pack. "A little-known, top-notch back-East microbrew. For you, darlin'."

Vicki brewed her own beer. "You *doll*." She beamed. "Thank you. I've heard of this but never seen it out West. Reusable bottles, too. You didn't have to."

"Yes, I did." He laughed. "Because I wanted you to be happy to see me. I know I'm a pain in the ass about picking up my mail."

She looked at him quizzically, unused to such pleas for forgiveness.

"Today I've come to pick up my own mail—and Miranda's, actually. She's away for a few days."

Vicki eyed him hard. "That's a first, isn't it?" She disappeared into the back room and returned with shoes on. "You want some popcorn? I was about to make some."

Billy thought about it. "Microwave?"

"Hell, no!" She was pointing a finger with a rubber tip at him. "What do you take me for?"

"I sort of liked the slippers," he said, "especially now that we're about to have popcorn."

"I never wear slippers here, but at softball practice the other day some peabrain threw the bat too far and it hit me in the ankle. Idiot, didn't even make it to first. New guy. Trying to impress the women. Made a real impression on me."

Vicki lived for spring softball. "Anybody good on your team?" he asked her.

"Depends on what you mean by good." She disappeared

again into the back and reappeared holding an old-fashioned electric popcorn popper, which she held up like a trophy, then set down on the counter next to the postal scale. "If you mean any good players, yes, we do have a few of those. If you mean interesting new faces who play moderately well—"

"Meaning eligible bachelors—"

She paused for a moment, mentally reevaluating the lineup. She plugged in the popper. "No. Sort of made me want to go back to women's league ball. But then if I went, you *know* someone would show up."

"You ever thought about dating Buddy Torez?" Billy asked, bending down and lifting the cuff of Vicki's jeans. What looked like cowboy boots from the front turned out to be slip-ons without backs. Bruise hardly did the thing justice: it was a puffy greenish yellow swelling the size of a hockey puck. "Wow," the word escaped.

"Yeah." Her voice was flat. "I'm surprised I even let you near my ankle without flinching. Not nearly as tender as it was. Almost slapped the doc who took a look at it."

Billy stood up, recalling how Miranda had started when he'd reached toward her eye at that last breakfast.

"In terms of Buddy Torez." She pulled at the collar of her white shirt, straightening it. "That would be hard. Because I used to date Rocky."

"You dated *Rocky?*" That surprised Billy. Not because it was hard to imagine the two of them, but because he had never seen any degree of affection—or aversion—between them.

"Yes, that's what I said. I used to date Rocky Torez. V.S plus R.T. Sort of."

"Sorry it didn't work out. I was recently thinking how much Rocky needed company."

Vicki was behind the counter pouring oil into the Teflon of the popper and adding kernels all at the same time. "No need to be sorry. And in case you hadn't noticed, Bill, everyone out here seems to need company. I can never quite figure out whether lonely people move to these parts or whether the lay of the land makes us all into lonely people. Then on top of that we're proud of it, like it's something to be proud of." She sniffed as if to call the matter to a close. "No, I liked Rocky fine—but there wasn't any chemistry between us. Can't force nature."

"So maybe you'd have beakers and Bunsen burners with Buddy."

Vicki smiled, her eyes shiny with secrets. Billy studied her plucked eyebrows and dirty blond hair all piled up into a complicated heap, then squeezed into a large rhinestone clip, and marveled at the beauty of women, each one the proverbial snowflake. It had something to do with the efforts they made, their vulnerabilities. It was all magnificent in a tiny, cheerfully bright way. Brave, that was the word.

"What are you smiling at?" he asked. "As if I just said something that went over my own head."

"Buddy Torez was last seen having a bite to eat with your Ms. Blue at MinuteBurger. Is it a coincidence you're trying to pair him off with me, or am I overestimating the swiftness of tittle-tattle here on the range?"

First there was one pop, and then four, and then all the kernels in the popper burst out of their shells at once like a loud chorus clapping vigorously at Vicki's insight.

Billy, however, used the racket as an excuse to look

mildly shocked for a moment, then said, "Buddy is handy, generous, pretty sharp, and great with kids. And he doesn't have Rocky's weird combination of backwoods brain and big words."

"I never said I didn't like Buddy. It's just I don't want to hurt Rocky's feelings—in a place like this, you know. It would almost seem like spite or something."

"Oh, Rocky." Billy pictured him, literally minding his own beeswax. "Rocky's pining for Miranda's sister. It might as well be for Rita Hayworth, but can't tell him that."

"Miranda's sister? She just move here, too?"

Billy shook his head. "She's only been here once, when Miranda bought the house. I never met her, but she got Rocky all fired up, I guess. Insect specialist."

Vicki thought about this as she unplugged the popper and tipped it upside down. The top became a bowl. "I never said I didn't like Buddy," was all she said as she shook a little butter flavoring and a little salt onto the pile of popped corn.

Only after listening to the rain for a spell and indulging in talk of inconsequential things was mention made of the neighborhood again. "So . . . what's the deal with her, any-way?" Vicki maneuvered her tongue at a corn kernel stuck between a gold cap and a canine tooth. "I'm coming straight out and askin'."

"What do you mean?"

"Don't you play innocent with ol' Vick. What's the woman all about? The living alone, the hair, the eyes—Audrey said they hardly said two words to each other. Meanwhile, Travis over at MinuteBurger was the one told me she'd come in. It was the first time he'd ever met her. Said he liked her!"

"What else did Audrey say?" Billy was thinking of Travis at MinuteBurger though, and Buddy Torez cozying up to her as if she were just an ordinary woman. Then he thought maybe that was what she needed: ordinary companionship. Maybe these regular guys, with their quick assessments of the basic needs of women, would supplant him. Maybe chemistry was nothing more than a handy excuse when things didn't work out.

"Uh-uh, no you don't. You don't answer a question with a question. Unless," she conjectured, "you're desperate for information."

"Well," he said, "maybe I am."

She smiled wide. "Maybe you are, then. Audrey said she felt sorta bad not explaining to her why she was there—did you know Audrey has a new girlfriend? She also asked me what I knew about Miranda."

"I know Audrey has a new parrot. What did you say about Miranda?"

"I said I thought she had run away from something or other and that she sort of wanted to be left alone, but not really. *And* of course that she was interested in you."

Billy faked a cough as his face reddened. It seemed so obvious now: Vicki's characterizations grew as she slid mail into the slots and people slid in and out of the door—in much the same way, in fact, that Miranda filled up her index cards, one character trait at a time. "And what makes you think she's interested in me?"

Vicki had her hands on her hips by the time he finished the sentence. "Because she tiptoes around the subject of you just like you do about her. By the way, I got something Express for her: she's supposed to sign, but since you're here . . . From Saint Mary's. In Junction. She have a sick client or something?"

Billy ignored the question. "She's actually gone on location with Sullivan for a day or two." He stared at the envelope Vicki had retrieved, the awful weight of responsibility heavy again. Under what circumstances would he tell her he had answered her phone and received the news that one of her clients had died?

Vicki's surprise at the mention of Sullivan and Miranda together began in her eyes and ended in her arms, which she dropped like heavy bombs at her side. "On location with that man? And you're worried about Buddy Torez? For the love of night, Billy!"

"Thanks, Vick—for adding that dimension of hysteria."

"Well, it's just—*Sullivan*. He's about as—I don't have to tell you what he is."

"No. You don't. I trust she'll come home a better person for having gotten out of Otnip, though." He didn't trust anything having to do with Sullivan. And he hated the whole idea of Sullivan's having nominated himself as her liberator from Otnip bondage.

"Yeah, for the first time in how long? She's never gone anywhere, probably not since she moved here!"

Billy considered this, then pretzeled his arms. "We all know too much about each other around here if a person can't even ditch her dogs and her life for two days without anyone having something to say about it."

The handful of popcorn never made it to Vicki's mouth. She put it back in the yellow plastic top and clapped her hands together as if that were the end of the whole affair— the salt, the little husks, the grease, maybe even the conversation. She stared down at her fingernails before glancing up at Billy.

"You're right, of course," she finally said, pursing her lips. "But the snooping sort of fits right into my other theories. There are not-so-mysterious forces at work."

"How's that?"

"Well, we all know what it's like out here. It's sort of like if people aren't watching you, you don't even exist. So we watch each other. Keep track. That way, someone will know if one of us *really* disappears—gets swiped by a mountain lion, chewed up in barbwire, bit by a rattler, who knows—or even goes on a little road trip *himself* for the first time in a real long while." She paused. "People here think that if two people who live squarely facing each other don't eventually give it a go, just to test the chemistry, say, that they've spit on a gift from above." Another sniff.

Before Billy had a chance to show further embarrassment, Vicki added, "Now lemme go get all the mail, yours and hers, and the slip for you to sign for the Express. Maybe you should deliver these in person. From the burn-care unit. Yuk."

As Billy walked to his car he considered Vicki's point, considered it all the way home. He further considered it while grabbing his shaving kit from where he'd left it on the kitchen table, getting back in the car, and stopping at Miranda's for the dogs before heading to Moab—from which point he would call and demand the exact coordinates from Sullivan. There was a time to make a move, even if Vicki Schuster had to be there to point it out to him.

Billy hated hospitals. Hated mysterious illnesses, was

panicked by them. He thought of Miranda and her cabinet full of pain relievers. What if she was sick? Or didn't know how sick she was? Aneurisms, blindness, brain tumors could all begin innocently enough, with eye sensitivity. Elena's leukemia had begun with bruises.

Chest tight, he rallied the dogs and hustled them into the back of the pickup where they waited, a-tremble, for any kind of forward momentum. Billy watched them swallow the air in great gulps, ears and jowls flapping like loose sails, and was reminded to take deeper breaths himself. These turned into meditation breaths, which he was able to maintain all the way to MinuteBurger where, on another moment's spur, he turned in, opting for the drive-thru. Travis looked surprised to see Billy, but not unhappy.

"You got my message then? No hard feelings, I hope."

Billy didn't know what he was talking about but, in his fragile state, didn't necessarily want to see the corners of Travis's mouth or curls of his mustache sag downward. "I'm ready to become a customer again, for one thing," he said noncommittally.

"Especially with your tomatoes gracing the bun, I expect. Do you have any with you?"

Ah, Billy thought, that was it, he had come around. Whom had he given the message to? Miranda? "As long as you know I can't give the tomatoes away, Travis. Didn't bring any with me, wanted to make sure you were serious."

"I want them less than salad-ripe," he countered quickly. "Choppable, that should count for something. They take less vine time."

Billy laughed. "So a medium-rare burger should cost less

because it takes less grill time—I'll give you the best price I can."

"If you were to stop giving away tomatoes as bribes, your prices would be more competitive."

"I hear you met my neighbor." The dogs had started pacing the back four sides of the truck and jumping up as if they were in a padded cell.

Travis was packing something up for him without ever having asked what he wanted. "Oh, I met her all right. She was eating as if there were widespread famine in Otnip. Sat at the counter, had herself a chat with—"

"Buddy Torez," Billy piped in. "People seem intent on telling me that."

"I do a maple shake now"—Travis salted the fries—"as well as your choice of milk or dark chocolate. I'd recommend the maple. Those her dogs?" He was staring toward the back of the truck.

"Yes they are. I'll try the maple."

"I've changed my sauce on the burgers, too. I'll let you tell me what you think next time I see you. This is on me, by the way. Just my little way of saying I might have been wrong about the tomatoes. Eventually I always give the customers what they want. Call me on Monday, and we'll discuss business. Didn't know you were so cozy with her dogs."

Billy took the bulging bag that was handed to him. "They like to get out of Otnip every once in a while, just like the rest of us."

Travis smiled, his mouth open enough for Billy to see the gap between his two front teeth for the first time. "You tell that neighbor of yours, she's welcome back anytime. Kind of exotic, if you ask me. I'm sure that hasn't been lost on you, though."

Billy mustered a considered, even stiffly academic, tone. " 'Exotic' is the operative word, I suppose."

In order to remain calm as he drove, Billy counted things. Eight red-tailed hawks spiraling wide. Three ravens pecking at roadkill and twelve on the wing. A single remarkable bald eagle standing, soldierlike on the side of the road, nearly four feet tall and moving only imperceptibly to make way for the truck. He returned to counting breaths until he passed a tractor bouncing along slowly enough for the driver to be reading a newspaper.

But once in Moab, his anxiety returned. He had come chasing her. Her dogs were barking at every stop sign and every carload of bikes they passed. He did not want to call Sullivan, he simply wanted to show up unannounced. What could he do?

Then it dawned on him that Sullivan would have hired at least one business in Moab to furnish something or other for the shoot. By sheer dumb luck, it turned out to be the first place he stopped, the grocery store. The manager seemed eager for anyone to move the half dozen boxes waiting for pickup and handed Billy a business card as if wanting to rid himself of it.

Billy reached someone named Cahill, to whom he gave a false name. He had treats for the talent, he said, and had stopped at Moab's grocery store where he'd seen boxes marked for the shoot. Could he be of service? He mentioned the inadequate directions Sullivan had given him, which sent the woman flying into a set of directives so precise he wondered if the commercial weren't for the US Army.

In eighteen minutes, feeling as though he had finally played by Sullivan's rules, he triumphantly rolled into camp, a thematic setup even more elaborate than the last one.

Miranda's Scout was the only vehicle parked close by, except for an old Volvo station wagon. Billy presumed camp was deserted because they were still filming somewhere; and after parking the truck and clipping the bewildered dogs onto leashes, he began scouting the premises.

Ten minutes later, after a brief conversation with the only soul to be found, a Turkish woman cooking furiously in a large white tent, she followed him outside. Waving her arm to the distance, she repeated, "Shooting! Shooting! Dinner seven o'clock!"

Although it was nearly that, there were no signs of any convoys returning, so he got back into the truck and started following tire treads in the dust, which proved easy enough. After rounding the bend of a magnificently red tower of rock the name of which Sullivan would undoubtedly know, he spotted them far off and gunned it until he reached the Jeeps, scanned greedily for familiar faces and, spotting them, hauled the dogs, still on their leashes, with him for moral support.

As he got closer, he noted things seemed to be in a state of utter confusion and disarray. A bicyclist on a stretcher was being tended to by two women, both on cell phones. When Sullivan saw Billy, his eyes got big and he glanced at Miranda and then slowly, with his hands on her shoulders, rotated her so that she could see him too. A large man in an ascot also turned to stare at Billy.

It took only a few seconds for the dogs to detect Miranda's presence, at which point Billy was catapulted forward by the gee force of desperate animals without choke chains. At a distance of fifteen feet or so, he could no longer hold on, and let the dogs go. Bounding over, they threw themselves at Miranda, licking her hands, one of which held a megaphone.

Sullivan wore a rare expression of anxiety as he watched Billy approach.

Billy didn't know why until Miranda looked at him. "Jesus, Miranda—what happened to you??" Not only were the whites of her eyes engulfed in red, her eyelashes were missing completely. Denuded of protected fringe, her orbs consisted of rings of pale ice surrounded by fiery bloodshot. He swallowed hard.

Miranda reached sloppily for her eyes, rubbed them, then stuck her tongue out at Billy. "Don't even think about saying anything. You have absolutely no idea what's going on here."

 19

A towering woman wearing the ugliest boots Billy had ever seen had meanwhile appeared, hands on her hips, at Sullivan's side.

"There's nothing you can do for a broken collarbone," she announced in a voice Billy immediately recognized. "Luckily," she spat, "the rug guy had muscle relaxants with him. Rug people are constantly straining their backs. So we gave our *talent* some Flexeril. He hasn't mentioned a lawsuit yet, Novo, but I'd like to be the first to point out that shit happens when you bring in *outside people*." She glared at Billy. "And who's he?"

"I was the one who picked up the groceries," Billy told her. "You weren't back at camp in time for dinner, so I drove out to see if anything was wrong."

"Everything's wrong," she said over her shoulder as she marched back toward the more alluring mayhem.

Sullivan finally spoke. "Clever of you, finding something to deliver. Listen, though, before you make any snap judgments—"

"Miranda won't let me speak, and you won't let me think. How reassuring." Billy glanced back at Miranda who stood gesticulating to the imposing man at her side, words gushing out in torrents from the looks of it. She had never gushed with him, she'd been stingy with her words. He had never observed her gushing with anyone. "Who's the professor—" He became instantly testy. "And why is he staring at Miranda like that?" Even as he said this he realized how blind you'd have to be not to stare at her.

Sullivan was delighted by the query. "He was a professor, Billy. Now he's just another novelist about to be raped by Hollywood. You don't recognize Carson Sung when you see him?"

Maybe it never occurred to Billy that the least likely person on Earth to be present would be, but upon closer scrutiny there was no doubt as to who the man was. "Sure enough." His tone was flat. "I bet you're going to tell me why he's here, too, and why Miranda is stoned out of her gourd."

"Did you know they teach him in college now?" He pointed at Cahill. "Look at her, tattletaling to the director. She's unbelievable! Doesn't matter, the director's courting him."

"What's Miranda doing here? What's he doing here? How did you get her out here—"

Sullivan sighed wearily. "Miranda called *me*, Billy. Weird thing is, I had just received a call from one of her clients. So, I invited her out: Okay I baited her. Did she need out of the Otnip repository of the lost and/or lonely? Does a bear shit in the freaking woods? It was the perfect opportunity to fill her in on you—and get to know her a bit."

"Which client called you?" Billy didn't want to know the other stuff. Not yet.

"Rochelle."

"Go on." Billy's own conversation with Rochelle had begun with him assuring her that Miranda was eating enough and getting enough fresh air. When she further inquired as to whether Miranda was getting enough *attention,* Billy admitted that besides the dogs, the masochist in him took regular stabs at it as well. This seemed to placate her. Evalina's first question, on the other hand, had been if Billy thought Miranda's dogs would get along with two old cats. What about him, did he like cats?

"We all get the feeling," she had abruptly shifted gears, "that Miranda needs to talk, Mr. Steadman. But given the professional nature of her duties, she can't do that with us. Oh, she hints at things. Reaches out, then recoils. Finally, it got so I suggested she call an old friend of mine, Kitty. But. You can't exactly force psychotherapy down someone's throat."

"So, you think she needs—"

"What she needs is *someone* to talk to. Why," she continued, "would she move to the shriveled-up middle of nowhere? She doesn't strike me as pioneer stock." The sound of loud purring punctuated the sentence. "Does she talk to you?"

"Not too much." He'd wished he could have answered differently. "Not about herself." But she might have if he had been more honest to begin with.

"Well," Evalina had concluded, "we're putting the ball in your court, young man. Because if I'm not mistaken, you've taken a shine to her. Do I have that right?"

"Pretty much," had been his eloquent reply.

Sullivan removed his Gatorade cap, then ran a hand through his thick hair slowly, messily, to bide his time. "Rochelle called to find out about you. I used her as further incentive to get Miranda here. But I had no idea Sung was coming: She came up with that one herself."

"He followed her here?" It was just so implausible.

"People seem to do that. The guy that endo-ed? He spent half the day trying to impress her by not dabbing on this gnarly section of slick rock. Then when she got the headache and disappeared, he was straining so hard to find her in the crowd he broke his fucking clavicle." To endo was to tip down, headfirst, on a bicycle. To dab was to touch down with a foot. Both were to be avoided at all costs, especially during filming.

Billy was staring at the line of Miranda's neck, a piece of curved marble in the soft evening sun. "What does that have to do with her getting stoned?" Sung was walking toward them.

"It's all connected. But reiterate your beef with that for me, would you please? Because the minute you say any- thing it will sound so stupid, you'll shut the hell up."

"What—was it a little experiment on her?" He couldn't stop himself.

"She was in the grip of a crippling migraine. Stuck in our Jeep—where it was impossible for her to run away like she did at her house. That's what that was about. This time, see, she had to come clean: migraine headaches."

Billy was silent.

"Sung," Sullivan said, just as the man drew near, "was the one who suggested the pot."

"Sung?" Billy repeated.

"I was." The massive man extended his hand, the extremity that held the pen that wrote the books. The grip was fierce. A famous author had followed Miranda to the filming of a Gatorade commercial. Had she slept with him, was that it? Certainly she must have had needs over the past months—and to his knowledge hadn't done anything about them, at least not with another human.

"I had no idea, however," Sung continued, examining Billy with eyes that took everything in at once, "that cyclists often train under the influence, and that we would have several varieties of marijuana at our disposal. In a messenger's bag, all labeled as if they were spices from a distant land!"

Sullivan was nodding in concurrence. "Wheelchair weed, man, totally debilitating—something called Skunk#1/Northern Lights. Anyway, she sucked in too hard and didn't cover the airhole completely on the bong. The flame shot up."

"Jesus. She could have hurt herself!"

"Ms. Blue was already in a considerable amount of pain," Sung noted. "Debilitated, from what I could see. My wife suffered from migraine headaches for years. Would that we had discovered *cannabis* far sooner." He paused briefly before detailing the function of seratonin and dopamine receptors, suspected anti-inflammatory effects of the plant, and further suspected benefits of its essential oils. "For Ms. Blue," he finally concluded, "the pain went away almost instantaneously."

Miranda, who had joined them, was blinking excessively, obviously uncomfortable. Billy, relieved that her medications had been for migraines and not an undiagnosed tumor, nevertheless puzzled at the cover-up. "I guess pot has a purpose, after all," he said to her with as little inflection as possible.

"The purpose is relaxation." Miranda pulled Sung's scarf free from his neck and wrapped the paisley yardage around her head like an oversize turban. She turned to Billy. "I met the illustrious Mr. Sung in Moab, at a book signing." She reached for her eyelids, rubbed, frowned, and began blinking quickly again. "When I close my eyes, I see turtles."

"You obviously don't know what you're doing or saying." Billy's voice was low. His only weapon was a contemptuousness he doubted Miranda had ever heard as it was startling even him. As for Sung, he knew things about women, that much was clear from his books. Had he seduced her, just as Ishmael had seduced Rosemarion Fall?

He might have embarrassed himself had Sung not politely taken his leave at that moment, hungry, he said, and eager for dinner. "The convoys are assembling," he added perfunctorily, as if he'd been convoying with ad people and Turks his whole life. "And the sun is about to bid adieu to all those who worship it. Ms. Blue, I suggest you eat something." He looked at Billy. "Can you see to that?"

"Sure." Billy shrugged. "I was about to see to that." As if he couldn't take care of Miranda, or something.

Miranda watched Sung walk off and finally turned to Billy. "What are you doing here, anyway? Last time I looked you were gone. Taco pie was delivered. Audrey fed the fish. Spring came . . . You're back now, is that it? And for extra credit you've shown up here?"

He blushed. "Why didn't you ever mention headaches? When I saw all the pain relievers in your cabinet—"

"So you were in my house." Her words were slow. "Nosing around."

Sullivan, megaphone at the mouth, was urging people to load up. Billy led Miranda by the arm toward his truck. "I'll take Miranda back." He waved at Sullivan. "The dogs would go nuts if she were in a different car!" Untrue, but Sullivan wouldn't know that. He turned back to Miranda. "I was taking care of the dogs, Miranda. Audrey passed the house sitter's baton on to me, so it was all completely legitimate."

Sullivan, smiling, waved them on, then turned to Sung with what looked like an explanation. Billy cringed at the idea of synopses, both overembellished and oversimplified.

The sun, an orange ball of fire about to disappear over the distant cliffs, had cast long and unnatural shadows, and as the Jeeps and other vehicles proceeded southward single file, the silhouettes evoked a dark city marching across the plain. Miranda's melancholy face, haloed by twilight, made Billy want to stop the truck until the world itself stopped, made motionless by the vanished sun. He wanted to begin again. But that was impossible.

"Anyway while I was inside feeding the dogs, a Mr. Vogt called and we had ourselves a chat. Then I talked to Rochelle and Evalina." *And to the hospital,* he would say once she was coherent enough to handle it.

"They've decided that I need saving. So what did you tell them about me?"

Billy's great discovery in conversing with Miranda's clients had been how little he really did know about her. "Shouldn't you be asking me what they told me about you?"

"That too." She looked pained. "The turtles are back. I thought getting stoned was like riding a bicycle. This stuff is—way different than what I smoked in high school. I need sugar. B vitamins. *Something.*"

He smiled, relaxing slightly for the first time since he'd arrived. "You smoked in high school," he repeated, then reached into the glove compartment for an unopened bag of peanut M&Ms his grandma Lewisia had given him for the road.

Eagerly, Miranda wrested the crimped plastic apart. "I believe I've already told you I am not who you think I am. Or *was* not who you thought I was."

He watched Miranda's teeth hit shell, chocolate, and nut. "What if I told you I already knew you were more than you were letting on: Would that cover it?"

"No." She stared at the second fistful of candies in her hand. "But first, before we go into that, a word from our sponsor, MinuteBurger, home of the maple shake. I have a message to deliver to you from Travis: He wants your tomatoes. So does Vicki Schuster. Have you promised any to Greg Vogt yet?"

"Miranda," he began, taking the bag from her hand. Maybe he would change his tack and tell her about her client now.

"Don't," she interrupted, "think that just because I get migraines, I'm a victim. I handle them. And now, I've got this new weapon. One you ironically can't supply me with because you're not the you I thought you were, either." She grabbed the bag back.

"True: The only pot plant in my possession became a Bonsai long ago. It's sitting comfortably on your desk, as a matter of fact, a replacement for the rosemary topiary you had brutalized."

She appeared to be straining to follow the logic. "I needed rosemary, lots of it, for this one chicken dish." There was a pause. "You certainly had the run of my house in the short period I've been gone. It's almost as if you *missed* me or something." Threadbare sarcasm woven into its thin cloak made Billy's heart thump loudly, as if it were the only functioning organ in an otherwise cold and hollow body.

"Sure I did. And other people missed you, too. There were calls while you were away."

Her face clouded. "Not my sister, I hope, or Lydia, or that busybody Aunt Raye—"

"Your sister didn't call," he reassured her. "But I did learn who is carrying the torch for her."

"Old news," Miranda rolled her eyes. "Rocky Torez. As it happens, she recently threatened to come out and may, in fact, show up this time. I don't think it would be good for Rocky though."

"Why not?" Billy wanted more ordinary conversations, just like this one. He'd been denied a year's worth of conversations and wanted to collect on them now, make up for lost time.

"Because my sister has been known to play with people, Billy. And she always goes for rich men."

"And what about you, Miranda, what kind of men would your sister say you go for?"

"I guess you'd have to ask her that."

"Commanding father figures who write novels?"

She stared at him and then half smiled. "You're jealous—"

"Why'd he follow you here?"

"I invited him."

"Why did you do that?"

"For an adventure, Billy. To surprise Sullivan—even though I had no idea he worshiped the man."

"What did you tempt him with?"

"What, you think I—?" Indignation was her amphetamine. "I tempted him," she whispered seductively, "with Turkish food. Not," she added, "that he's not attractive."

Camp came into view like an oasis burning bright. The evening meal had been laid out on two giant banquet tables, torches were being lit, and the director had been given the first of some tall, exotic beverage with the word *"Serefe"* to go with it.

Billy came around to open Miranda's door. "So what did your clients tell Sullivan?"

"Probably the same thing they told you. What'd they tell you?"

Billy brought his hand to her brow to remove a smudge of dirt, a movement she bore without starting. "Nothing I didn't already know. Are you hungry?" He had liked the feeling of her bone, the firmness of contact.

"Starving." She continued to rub where his hand had been. "But I need to call this one client in the hospital." Billy became very still. "We're both addicted to Victor Hugo, and I'm late already on account of all the commotion earlier. Can't let him down."

"Maybe you should get something in your stomach first, like Sung said." He would tell her. He would tell her as they ate.

"Well, maybe a quick bite to keep further headaches at bay. It smells so good!"

Billy thrilled to the eagerness in her voice, something he had not ever heard before. Yet as he sat down, he feared it might be his last dinner with this particular version of Miranda, and helpless to do anything about it, cursed a fate that had never given him his first.

 20

A small, dark Turk with shiny black eyes and a wide mustache was announcing the food at the top of his lungs as it arrived on the table. *Manti!* The tiny pasta filled with meat came first, then *dolma!* Once Miranda started eating, she could not stop. *Zeytinagli!* A vegetable and olive oil course. *Sis kofte!* Shish kebab. *Pilaki!* Cold, lemony beans. All of it was wonderful.

Billy, who had not said a word since they'd sat down to eat, appeared to be washing dinner down with copious amounts of wine. Miranda noted that the doe-eyed dancer had already refilled his glass three times. Glancing down the length of the table, however, it appeared no one else was holding back either. And so as the feast burned on in the dark desert night, Miranda relaxed, feeling happy— ridiculously happy, in fact—to be in the middle of Sullivan's marvel, this rigging of tents and torches, dancers, rugs and gauze, and delectable food. Maybe the pot had loosened her up.

Sung had his hand raised in a toast, and, lifting her own

glass, Miranda smiled, remembering his coaching on the Bible, and poetry, his discourse to one of the Turkish cooks on the spit-roasting of grouse, and the advice he'd given Lael Vanderpin (the only client she actually let him talk to) on the writing of mysteries. Lael had never heard of Sung, but she had read the works of an obscure English crime writer, Septima Krouse, which had astonished him, but not nearly as thoroughly as Sullivan's listing off his rare recordings of the very same author reading from her own works.

Now, Miranda thought about connecting Sung and Keeper Dix and wondered if Keeper knew Sung's work, his Rosemarion Fall, or Kendall Moe from *Long, Dry Cry of the Desert*. Sung could wax on about the world as metaphor, and Keeper could parry with his own fabricationist views of reality. Keeper Dix was a ready-made character waiting to be wheeled into a Sung novel: Why shouldn't they meet?

"*Yufka!*" Out came the flat bread. "*Cacik!*" A cucumber, garlic, and yogurt concoction. It occurred to Miranda then that she could call Keeper right from the dinner table, give him a sort of remote broadcast from the center of it all, and then hand him over to Sung, who seemed to need saving from that director again. Why not? She reached into her pocket and pulled out the phone Sullivan had loaned her, a miniscule thing in silver and lime green, then rose to fetch her index cards from the backseat of Sullivan's Cadillac.

Billy wiped his mouth quickly. "Where are you going?"

Miranda detected a certain swallowed panic in his voice. "Going to get Keeper's number. The guy I have to call."

"Miranda." He put his hand over hers, over the phone.

"What? I'm lucid now, recovered, I promise. You're busy drinking, anyway."

"I don't usually drink like this. You don't need his number."

The first strains of Arabic music pierced through the PA system. *"Muhammara!"* came the cry for red chili paste. "I do if I'm going to call him. What are you talking about?"

"You're not going to call him," Billy repeated, almost harshly.

"Okay, already. Why not?"

"Because he's not there. While I was at your house, I got another call. From Saint Mary's Hospital. In Grand Junction."

Miranda was momentarily silenced. "You got a call from the hospital. He's not there."

"Yes. From the hospital, yes." Billy grabbed a large bottle of Evian off the table and began swilling it as if water were wine's antidote.

"And they wanted me to call back?" Chaos was chopping at Miranda's thoughts, hacking them into sharp and irregular pieces. "Where is Keeper?"

"No, you don't have to call, they gave me the message."

"The message?" She stared at Billy as he nodded, kept on nodding, his head bobbing like it couldn't stop. A lump materialized in her throat. "How could they give you any message? I left this number on the machine. If you hadn't answered the phone, I could have gotten that message—" Her voice, increasingly louder and more shrill, caused several diners to glance over, including Sung and Sullivan, who stopped conversing. She shoved the phone, the instrument of deceit and betrayal, at Billy.

"The message would have been the same, Miranda," he said.

The world was neither contained nor calm, the fish tank had cracked, and Miranda was spilling all over the floor. "Yeah, well—messages are meant for specific people and are not supposed to be intercepted by inappropriate *other* people haphazardly in their path." Miranda rarely cried. But primed now by overdue accumulations of grief and sadness her ducts opened wide and tears the size of peas squeezed out, slowly at first, then in a continuous stream.

"I didn't mean to intercept, it just happened. I took a nap on your bed and the phone woke me up. It was Greg Vogt. Then it rang again and it was this Nini Davore at Saint Mary's." Billy grabbed another bottle of water and squeezed it until water started coming out the top. "He left you money. For a fund to be set up for other firefighters needing companionship. Your companionship."

Miranda had dropped her face into her hands to gather the accumulating wetness in some fashion. She had never even seen a picture of Keeper Dix; it had seemed too cruel a request. But she should have asked! They had created a private world with their voices, yes, but it was just a tiny sliver of him, the most fractional piece. Had he known the end was near?

"What about his possessions?" She blew her nose. "Who took his stuff? Who were his parents? Or his siblings? Or— or friends? How did he get burned, for God's sake?" *We take all these things for granted when people are alive, that eventually we will find out everything about them, in good time and completely. And then—they're gone.*

Sullivan, cigar in hand, was approaching with Sung. "What's going on here?" he said to Billy, as Miranda looked up, trying to open her eyes more than they would open.

"Oh," she felt her mouth make the words, "people die. Every second of every day. I have to get out of here."

"Who died?" Sullivan fired the question at Billy.

"A burn victim, firefighter, client of hers. I happened to be at her house when the call came in and had to tell her." He looked at Miranda. "This might not be the best time to drive . . . Let me just—let's walk to your tent, then you can decide what to do." He took off his jacket and draped it over her shoulders. There was a chill in the air.

She pulled his coat tight around her and shook her head. "I'm not staying here. Moab is fifteen minutes away. I've got the dogs, I'll get a motel room. I need—" She brought her hands to her eyes again. *"Something."* She could feel the stares of Sung and Sullivan as Billy followed her.

"Miranda, listen," Billy said. "I came here to tell you, to break the news, and then I couldn't do it right away. You were stoned, there were people around. Then I tried but—"

She opened her clear plastic overnight bag and started packing it, saying the words to herself. Pink pajamas. Yesterday's shirt. Cosmetics kit. "I don't think I'm capable of a conversation right now."

"Maybe a conversation is what you need most."

"Yeah, I need a conversation with a guy who's dead. I need to ask all those questions I never asked. But he's dead now. Where he once held a tangible place on this planet, there's a howling vacuum."

Billy was silent, and Miranda remembered he had suffered such a loss. She swallowed. "Did that woman say if

265

they were cremating him? It seems wrong to cremate a burn victim!"

He shook his head. "She just said he had no family and didn't want a funeral."

"Oh God, no family! He, he was such a—"

Billy shifted and looked down. "A what?"

Miranda sighed. "He just—he understood a lot more than he let on. And I never knew that much about him. I never asked him how—Never asked him enough questions." She yanked on the zipper of her bag, then confronted Billy. "And now I'm supposed to offer my services to others in his position? Have them die on me before they've had a chance to express themselves?"

Back outside, Billy opened the door of the Scout for her. "Your dogs are happier in the truck. I could follow you."

"Nope," she shook her head. "I'll be fine." That was a lie.

"Miranda," he said, *"please*. Let someone in."

She shook her head, then shut the door. Billy put his hand, fingers spread, on the glass, lifting them only as she shifted into first and pulled away.

But there on the dirt road, driving in the shadow of the steep black cliffs—Billy's warm fingerprints long gone—the glory of space and distance and isolation began to wither. She could not recall a Greek god of privacy, or one of solitude: These were not things people worshipped. On the contrary, isolation was punishment, and privacy, a modern invention. Nothing became interesting without contact, nothing. Contact is what Keeper had achieved with her. Miraculous contact. Still, she had not taken full advantage of it before he had been snatched away. She rolled down her window and stuck her head out, sucking in deep gasps of cold air. Then she stopped the car and retched on the side of the road.

"Your timing on the dead guy really sucked." Sullivan approached Billy and started lighting a silver Zippo over and over by running it down his leg to open the lid, then up just as fast to turn the wheel and watch it flame. The rear lights of the Scout had disappeared from view.

"It was the reason I came out here, Sully. I'm waiting ten minutes, then I'm going after her, once she's checked in somewhere." Above, the stars and moon pulsed in a sky so dense Billy swayed. He jingled the keys in his pocket.

"I told her about Elena." Sullivan was truculent.

"Thank you," Billy replied, "I figured you had." Neither of them spoke for several moments, and then Billy continued. "Did you know Sung was a widower?" He had overheard Sung say so at dinner, to someone who had been attempting polite conversation with a stranger. *Widower.* Billy had never used the word.

The flame of the lighter remained on as Sullivan spoke. "He wrote *Wicked Sky* after nearly killing himself with booze. It was about her, Billy." He flicked the lid shut. "You knew that."

Billy shook his head. "I never knew that."

"How the fuck could you not know that?" Sullivan barked, then slapped Billy upside the head, hard. "Everybody knows that, Billy. Everybody." He slapped him again, and then grabbed him by the collar and jerked him into a headlock. Billy didn't fight back at first, but then Sullivan tightened his grip suddenly as if meaning to strangle him, at which point his reflexes kicked in and he twisted, yanked himself free, and shook himself off.

"Fuck you, Sully."

Sullivan's rage might have ricocheted obliquely off Carson Sung, but Billy knew it had originated much closer to home, with Elena and with him. With things left unresolved and long patches of time obliterated and dark. Billy had not drunk himself into a stupor after Elena's death, but he might as well have, because even if he'd tended plants in exile, all the humans in his life had suffered, including Sullivan. Most of all, Sullivan.

They stared at each other. "Sung's wife died, Billy. He wrote about it. He'll talk about it if you ask him. I asked him. I could never ask you, though, could I?" He kicked the dust. "You know, after Elena died, I lost everything. I lost her and you, and I lost you two together: You were my personal standard for the right kind of couple. I lost faith in endurance and recovery—how can you love without endurance and recovery? Just now, though, when you walked Miranda to her car—"

Billy interrupted, "I couldn't get through to her."

"She needs you." Sullivan pulled out a fresh cigar and ran it under his nose. "And you owe me."

"How do I owe you?"

"You owe me because every second, the world teeters perilously close to annihilation and is saved only—and every second—by the commitment to love and be loved." It didn't sound like Sullivan, but then after wine and multiple shots of raki, his tongue might not have quite been his own, either.

"This man quotes me just as I quote my Roman heroes." Sung approached with a tiny cup of coffee, which he handed to Billy. "You're heading out, I presume?"

Billy didn't say anything but stood there like a dog in a moment of deep, empty thought. Then he nodded.

"*Primum vivere, deinde philosophari.* Live first, talk later. Miss Blue's clients are going to keep on dying, I'd wager my life on it. I hope you have the resources to comfort her after what I'm assuming was her first casualty."

Billy took the coffee and tipped it up, the sweet, acrid mud coating his teeth. He wanted advice now—from living writers, from dead Romans, from friends. He wanted all the advice he'd refused in the last ten years, and he wanted people rooting for him again. "I might. Any other words of wisdom?"

Sung crossed his arms like massive knotted sausages. "*Dente lupus, cornu taurus petit,*" he said finally, giving Billy the once over. "Horace."

Tijuana Spanish and high school French were Billy's only tutors. "The horns of the bull are nothing compared to the teeth of the wolf."

"Not half-bad, but incorrect. To each his own weapons. Use what you have—the wolf his teeth, the bull his horns—to win a battle."

Billy was nine minutes down the road back to Moab when the phone in his pocket rang. It was the phone Miranda had shoved at him like a dirty weapon she no longer wished to touch. He answered and the tiny mouthpiece exploded with a commanding female voice wanting to know who he was. He said his name as bugs smashed onto his windshield by the thousands.

Identifying herself as Vivianne Blue, she then said, "Are you the neighbor Miranda's lied about until just the other day?"

269

"Maybe." So she had kept him under wraps, too. "What did she say?"

"Well, the party line had been that you were one-legged, had lots of cats, and lived reclusively. I figured she only left out toothless to be polite."

Billy smiled. "I've been showering your sister with attention ever since she moved in. She would identify it not as attentiveness, however, but as torture."

"Under duress she admitted that she'd possibly been in the wrong rebuffing you all this time. She then alluded to your good looks and wittiness. Is she in the vicinity? Where is the vicinity, by the way?"

Billy's heart was beating hard. Good looks and wittiness he considered ample ammunition with which to win not only a small battle but a war. Weapons! "Well, she's on her way toward Moab right now. We were on location for this TV commercial."

"You got her out of Otnip? Now I'm impressed. Albeit, I already knew she wasn't in Otnip because that's where I am."

"You're in Otnip?"

"I'm in Otnip! At her house! I thought I'd come to cheer her up, but it sounds as though you're taking care of business in that department."

Billy heard crooning in the background, voices from a bygone era, and had a great urge to be at Miranda's house with her, listening to her sing along with one of those corny, curly-headed blonds. "Not exactly. Miranda just found out—I had to break the news, in fact—that one of her clients died. She bolted. I'm in pursuit." Billy heard Vivianne heave a sigh.

"That was bound to happen eventually, seeing as how

she's never openly acknowledged the connection. Setting herself up with these old folks, knowing they would die. Forcing herself to deal with people who are themselves trying to cope with imminent death. Do you see?"

Billy did not see. "No. Not really."

There was a pause. "No, of course she never told you that either. That our parents died in an awful wreck twelve years ago when she was twenty. In our bizarre Blue fashion we were closer than most families. Miranda never cried or did what people are supposed to do. Get numb. Deny. Break down. Accept. Move on. Read the literature of survival. She wouldn't take anything from the house except their record collection. I took the whole lot, thinking someday she would change her mind. Hasn't happened as of yet."

"Is that when the migraines started?" Billy couldn't decide whether he had stopped at *Get numb* or *Deny*. Dashiell Hammett and Raymond Chandler had provided him with his literature of survival.

"Migraines—what migraines?"

Miranda had not even confided in her closest living relation! "She gets these crippling headaches. She had one on location before I got there."

There was a long, thoughtful pause. "I had no idea. For all intents and purposes, when she moved to Otnip she vanished from the face of the Earth and took all her problems with her."

"It's not that remote," Billy countered.

"It's a virtual disappearing act. My purpose in coming here was, in part, to disappear myself—and I must say, driving here in the dark was like driving blind to the ends of the Earth. And I've been here before!"

"Did you fly into Cortez?"

"I did. Rented a car there, drove to Mesa Verde, discussed raven flight and ambulation with a park docent—then wended my way to the magic bean zone, past the clouds and just down the road from the giant's house."

"Why did you want to disappear?" A question he had never been able to ask Miranda was effortlessly redirected at her sister.

"Why else?" A high-pitched trill functioned as a laugh. "Man problems."

"Does it run in the family?" There had never been resources on Miranda before—no one this close with whom to talk, let alone interview. Greedily, Billy took advantage.

"Probably in every family. Man problems. Woman problems. Although Miranda's house is remarkably cozy, she came here to go on a man fast, revamp her diet. I must tell you my baby sister has spent a dozen years going out with the polar opposite of our deceased father. Rebels, mechanics, drug dealers, musicians. I've spent the same amount of time looking for his twin. Scientists, obsessives, neatniks, autodidacts. Each thinking, of course, the other was the one helplessly executing the fated cliché. Now why can't I say that to her? I should send her a telegram to that effect; she's always been partial to notes."

Billy smiled. He liked this family—these women, their voices, and their brains—and wanted them all to be together in Miranda's house for an entire meal where no one ran away from the table. Five courses including a salad of nothing but fresh herbs. A rich dessert. Strong coffee, then cognac. "Even not having known your father, I bet I fall squarely in neither category."

"Nothing's impossible," she replied, that familiar cynicism asimmer on the back burner. "I guess I'll see for myself—"

"Tomorrow," Billy completed the sentence. "We'll be by just as soon as we get home." Use of the first-person plural did not seem to faze Vivianne. To Billy, though, they were brave, new words, and as he drove into Moab, he fiddled with his chances of keeping the world balanced on the impossible fulcrum of love. His weapon was his wit; all he had to do was use it.

 **21**

The only motel flashing a Vacancy sign in Moab that night was the newest one on the strip, a Southwestern edifice decked out like a giant bedspread in teal and terra-cotta; and after reluctantly parting with $124, Miranda lay staring at the twenty-five-inch television, blue glow illuminating every contour of her troubled face. She did not move except occasionally to raise the remote like a zombie, then lay it back down again.

Television, it turned out, was not comforting at all. A commercial for tires. Breath mints. Lite beer. Colombian coffee. Someday, people would see a commercial for Gatorade Guava and get thirsty watching bicyclists panting in the desert. She switched to HBO and stared blankly at movie credits while trying to remember her very first conversation with Keeper, but for the life of her she could not come up with it. She reached for a tissue just as the tears began to flow again, flow from a deep well whose origin seemed to lie both at the back of her brain and the pit of her stomach. Her sobs prompted Wayne to hop down from his bed and up onto hers.

"Thank you, Wayne," she sniffled and, lowering her head to the pillow, yanked the seventy-pound dog up so that he was parallel to her. Around his warm body she draped an arm. Two minutes later she was asleep.

A series of sharp raps jerked her upright about half an hour later. Trembling, she looked around the room for something to grab: a plastic ice bucket, the remote, a suitcase shelf, and a Bible were her only weapons. Wayne, fully awake, growled low and crept, tail down, toward the door, but before either of them could do anything else, the knock repeated itself, this time a bit more softly.

Whoever it was wasn't going away.

Miranda stood up and tiptoed over, Wayne following her until his nose reached the door where he sniffed at the crack. He gave one wag of his tail.

Okay, she took a deep breath: It was probably either the manager, busting her for keeping dogs, or some lost and drunken athlete knocking on doors until he found the room he and his friends were sharing.

Miranda put her face up to the crack in the door without opening it. "I am sight-challenged," she pitched her voice as low as it would go, "have a dog, and carry a gun." That would cover all her bases.

"And I am relationship-challenged and carry my heart on my sleeve. This preview of coming confessions is only good for thirty seconds, however, unless you open the door."

Billy. Miranda's legs, rubbery with relief, were about to give out. "Are you alone?" She made a monumental effort not to miss a beat.

"I've been alone for eight years. I'm still alone. But I

don't want to be alone anymore. Seventeen seconds."
Wayne had started to wag and sniff in earnest, whereupon
Art, finally awake, dragged himself over and sat down du-
tifully next to his brother.

"Are you aware that following me could be construed as
an act of desperation? That your pursuit of me could be
seen as nothing more than a weakness for convenience?
Your only neighbor is an easy target, I daresay." His laugh
was low and sexy. Miranda had never heard that kind of
velvet in his voice. *You're supposed to be mourning a client
here.*

"The convenience factor does interest me," he replied.
"Although others have preferred calling it Fate. As far as
your being an easy target, Miranda—" He stopped.

She put her ear to the door, then plastered it like a suc-
tion cup to the metal. Maybe her time had run out. She
knew he was capable of making an exit, he'd done it before, that time she had missed out on coffee in bed.

She swung the door as far as the chain would allow. "Let
me see your heart on your sleeve," she challenged. "Then
I'll know it's you."

He slipped his arm as far as it could go, through the
crack.

"I don't see anything," she said. The dogs had begun
their full-flank wagging as they licked Billy's fingers.

"Well," he said, "of course not. *What is essential is invisible
to the eye*, Miranda. *It is only with the heart that one can see
rightly.* Or, in the case of hound dogs, the nose."

"So then, correct me if I'm wrong, but if your heart is on
your sleeve, you should be able to see rightly inside this
room. Tell me what you see."

Obediently, he twisted his hand and pointed up to the chain on the door. "My heart sees chains, Miranda. Unchain my heart."

"You'll have to remove your heart for me to do that."

"Can I trust you?" He opened his palm, questioning.

"No, of course not," she said. "But what choice do you have?"

He retracted the arm. The dogs whined; it was the first sound they'd made. "SShhh!" Miranda hissed as she undid the chain and opened the door about a foot. "My most loyal companions were about to blow the whistle on me. They've never done that before."

Billy came in noiselessly, bent down to stroke them, then turned around and rebolted the door. "Your perspective is off. The dogs were excited. They could not contain themselves." He made his way to the sink to wash off the slobber. "They were in fact taking a stand against containment, and restraint, and holding back. Would you not agree that eventually this stand must be taken?"

"Maybe," she said, wondering how her hands smelled, and quickly checking for teeth scum. Did she have Dumpster breath from the quick nap? "It would be interesting— for experimental purposes—to agree with something you've said."

"Especially that particular thing. Which brings us to my presence here. But you've certainly had time to conjecture why I've come."

On TV, a petite but buxom woman had chosen that moment to disrobe, peeling off not only her shirt and pants but her black bra. As the flesh flopped out voluptuously, Miranda felt everything in the world come undone with it.

She pressed her lips together, hoping the inevitable sounds of lovemaking would at least be muffled. Weren't some people mute in bed, for God's sake? Evidently not on cable.

"No idea, really," she said from the sink alcove, washing her face, back toward the screen. Motels were made for tawdry sex. The two beds taking up 85 percent of the room. The whole ice bucket phenomenon, refrigerator stocked with minis. The hot tub outside. Soft porn on the television. It was overwhelming, brutish, even—as if subtlety was a thing long lost to the past.

"Can I speak freely in front of the dogs?" Billy took off his jacket, the one she had worn earlier. Letters in track and lacrosse.

Miranda could smell the leather. "I didn't actually turn *on* this show," she muttered. "I fell asleep . . ."

Billy laughed. "I like it, Miranda. It's basic. It shows what people do when they're attracted to each other. Of course, what you don't know about the characters could fill a book."

She crossed her arms and stared down. There was a small hole at the fourth toe of her left sock. "Really," she said.

"Sure," he nodded. "For instance, she may look wanton, but the fact is she hasn't had love and affection—not to mention biblical *knowledge*—for some time."

Miranda glanced up and looked Billy in the eye for the first time. He reached up and wiped the right side of her face—still wet—with his shirtsleeve.

"And how do you know that?" She ran one wet hand through her hair trying to coax a hairdo out of it. "I mean about her?" *You're addicted to banter, Miranda. Clients die, and you continue to banter. You not only need love and affection but professional help.*

"Because I've seen this movie, and I've seen the prequel."

"Oh, the prequel. So you know why she's cut herself off, then?" *You're addicted to indirect methods of communication, preferably strewn with the debris of sarcasm.*

"That specific issue was unfortunately never addressed."

Miranda uncrossed her arms. "It was addressed in the sequel—which came after the prequel. She'd made some bad choices in the past, you see."

Billy stared at the screen impassively for several moments before turning it off with a quick click of the remote. "Miranda," he began. "Complicated neighbor of mine. I napped on your bed yesterday, and was overcome with desire. Years' worth. Today, when I showed up on location and Sullivan had gotten to spend some time with you, and Sung had followed you, I was jealous and resentful. But now that I'm here—"

"It's *too* complicated, right?" She should have known it would never work out. He was just being honest for saying so. She hated him. She wouldn't tell him she looked like Sung's wife: What good would that do now?

Billy stood up and approached her, reached toward her neck, and fingered the string of glass beads she wore, repositioning the clasp so that it was at the back of her neck. "Listen, I haven't been straightforward either. I should have told you about being a widower, and not growing weed. About Audrey, and about visiting my family—which I did on the spur of the moment having realized after that little breakfast party at your house that the people who matter in life *matter*. Then tonight I should have told you about your client right away. I should be telling you now that your sister called the cell phone, which happened to be with me in the car. That I know about your parents' death, that you chose Otnip to exorcise men from your life. That Vivianne didn't know about the migraines."

Miranda's face fell. All sentences collapsed onto the last one. "No one knew about the migraines." Her character profile was as pockmarked as they came.

"But why?" he asked her. "Why didn't you tell anyone?"

"You're asking *me* why I've kept things to myself?"

"Extreme hypocrisy. But yeah—I'm asking you. Did you start getting them out here? Maybe it's radon—there was a scare in Otnip some years ago. We could have tests done—"

"It's not radon. First of all, there's enough ventilation in the house to line-dry Levi's. No, I know what initiated the headaches." She took a deep breath and held it in.

"Well, what?"

She stared straight ahead, and breathed out. "I got hit in the face, Billy." She dropped her shoulders. "Hard. Hard enough to break my nose." More words pressed against her lips, straining to be free. "Hard enough to turn my face black-and-blue. Hard enough to scare the shit out of me for letting myself get into that position. I never told anyone. The headaches started shortly after that." She couldn't look at him. She waited.

Finally, he broke the silence. "Tell me who hit you. Why would anyone hit you?"

A tone not of pity but of bewilderment. She considered her answer. "Remember that man fast?" She glanced at him quickly. "Well, it was precipitated by a particularly poisonous man meal. My then-boyfriend."

This was it—he would never think of her the same way again. How could he be attracted to a victim, someone who had not only let such a thing happen but then run away?

"You had a boyfriend who hit you." The monotone of disbelief and his instantaneous recategorization of her.

She cringed. "It's distasteful, I know—I never told anyone, that's how embarrassing it was. They'd never see me the same, just like you won't. I've already changed in your eyes—I've got baggage!"

Keeper's last words came back in a flood, then. His tone, his exhausting himself to make a point. *We've all got baggage!* She tried to make herself believe it, believe that he had said these words for a reason, that his short stay in her life had had meaning and purpose, that he had been fated to meet her and she him. She had complained to Keeper that Billy was the one with the baggage: had the projection been as obvious to Keeper as it was to her now?

"People don't necessarily want to see you at your weakest," she said. "Or know what eats away at you, or what you're hiding, or how you're hurting, or how convoluted it all is."

"Miranda," Billy began, rolling up his sleeves, "what attracts people to each other isn't just about strengths, it's about vulnerabilities. The term 'baggage' is popular, but truly stupid. As if we could just let the baggage go—throw it overboard. Or decide to travel light. Check it, lose it, repack it, whatever. I just can't see the accumulation of experience in life as baggage." He stopped. "You're the same exact person. Impudent. Sarcastic. Stubborn. Except that some things make a little more sense now." He paused. "Was the fucking asshole drunk?"

He sat down next to her on the bed and, with both hands, grabbed her left foot and began massaging it. He pulled at the hole so that her toe wouldn't poke through.

She shook her head. "No. He had full and complete use of his small brain and mediocre motor skills." Billy's gentle pressure to the lower phalanges seemed to be having the effect of Phenobarbital. "I told him I'd been cheating on him."

"And he flew into a rage."

Very strong hands. From weeding, pruning, and squeezing hose nozzles. "Not exactly. He didn't do that until I told him that his replacement was an entomologist, and I'd contracted herpes. *Then* he flew into a rage. He believed me, for one thing. He feared for the life of his medium-sized organ."

This elicited a tiny smile. "So, were you lying? What about—your cheating, your lover's love of insects, or those nasty little blisters?"

"All three."

He stopped massaging until Miranda continued on.

"I needed an easy out. This particular boyfriend never paid any attention to me anyway. And at some point I lost track of what I was doing in the oh-so-wrong cast of the oh-so-wrong movie." Majesta had not liked Keith and reveled in counting the ways. *He'll never understand anything about you, I don't care how much you like riding on the back of that motorbike*. Her diminutive word for Harley. Now, *Billy* and Majesta talking and laughing, Miranda could picture that.

Billy had grabbed the other foot, and Miranda felt his thumb in that soft spot right below the ball of the foot. Was this a Vulcan trick? Calm enveloped her.

"So . . . exactly how much attention did you need?"

"Well," she began, loath to admit to more than one need at a time but drunk enough on massage not to want to stop. "I needed a birthday present, actually. A puny little gift, something to indicate brainwave activity in a boyfriend. He couldn't make the call from his stupid bachelor party to say Happy Birthday? It pissed me off, the selfish fuck! I like birthdays! They've always been very important in my family!" The pressure on her sole had released something angry. Art hopped on the bed, while Wayne, apprehensive, lay down to wait out the storm.

"See, Viv spoiled me rotten. At age seven, *Denizens of Pond Life* was the theme of my party. At thirteen, *Winged Beings in the Gothic Period*. There were others, too."

"Otnip must be a real letdown come September 29." Billy pulled off one sock at a time, laid her feet out, and stared at them, not touching.

"What, did my sister read you the entire file?" Never before had Miranda thought of her feet as lonely; now they seemed to represent and speak for every other part of her body. Her toes crimped involuntarily.

"Evalina told me." Billy kept staring at her feet. "Right before she lectured me on every person's need for companionship. You'd have to agree with her there, wouldn't you?"

She shrugged. "Sure," she said carefully. "I would, at this juncture, have to concur that companionship is an essential component of a happy life. *The* essential component, perhaps. Of course, the right kind of companionship is critical." She shifted, tucking her feet under her primly. "And—things must not be rushed."

"Don't worry," he said, "this isn't my ploy for staying the night. For one thing, your dogs require an entire bed for themselves."

"You're going home?" The words came out faster than they should have. Well, what had she expected—for him to stay?

"Abandon you here?" Nothing had been lost on Billy, who appeared to be gloating. "Leave you just after discovering a bit of what makes you tick? No, babe: I got the room right next door for the night."

Her heart was beating. "Really. Even before you knew the real me."

He ignored her and continued on. "It was the closest possible re-creation of our home environment. This way, you can sleep peacefully while knowing old Billy is right next door, tossing and turning. Burning with desire for you, just like at home. With just one difference."

"Uh-huh." *Burning with desire.* "Why don't you tell the audience?"

He smiled. "Not so fast . . . Billy knows he may not go one step further in the attention-giving scenario until the *audience* indicates—either by unmistakable gesture or actual touch—aforementioned eagerness to proceed."

She considered how utterly extraordinary it was the two of them could resort to banter at a time like this. Billy had not changed and neither had she and it was nothing short of miraculous.

"Go back to that part about my sister," she said, wondering how small a gesture would satisfy the requirement to which he had alluded. A friendly punch in the arm? Brushing the hair away from his eyes? "What else did she say?"

"Oh, nothing much. Except that she's at your house." He didn't give her time to react. "Where she's been relaxing to your parents' records after having tired herself out at Mesa Verde debating raven factoids with a ranger. She did mention her need to disappear—and how successfully Otnip seemed to have erased you from your past life. She seemed thrilled that an old, one-legged cat lover like me would have such a youthful voice and said she looked forward to meeting me. I told her it would be soon. Very soon."

"Hmph." At some point, your life collapses on you in a heap—even if you have done your best to keep the compartments separated and stacked gingerly on top of each other. Surely, some law of physics is to blame, something involving space, density, and eventualities where actions stack upon each other creating a gravitational force field, the weight and power of which eventually sink a person to the ground zero of life. "Well. We'll need time at breakfast together. I need to fill you in on Vivianne before you meet her."

"Indeed we *will* need time together," Billy answered quickly. "But don't think the reference in the first-person plural counts as having batted the eagerness ball back to me. The sense of touch was specifically noted as a requirement."

"Or"—Miranda pretended not to hear him—"I could go straight home and call clients."

"Tomorrow's Saturday. You don't call them on Saturday."

She had lost track of the days. Sullivan's Turkish delights had scrambled the space-time continuum. "Sometimes I call people on the weekend." Keeper had been the only one. "Mostly, I do other things."

Billy stood staring at her. "I know what you do on Saturdays, Miranda." He unchained the door. Before letting himself out he raised his hand toward her face, and then dropped it. He was outside. "Good night. I'm next door if you need me. Do the chain."

Her pulse was throbbing everywhere, in her throat, her chest, her temples, her wrists. All she knew was that she wanted to grab that tentative hand, and gently force it back to her face. Slowly, she reconnected the chain. Then, from behind the safety of the bolted door and before having a chance to edit the impulse, she reached through the opening. He quickly moved toward her, narrowing the gap until not more than six inches separated them.

Timidly, she reached for the lapel of his coat and fingered it, at which point he put his own hand over hers, moved her palm to his mouth, and kissed it, in the hollow. Good thing for the chain. Good thing for the barrier. She was a puddle, nearly gone.

"Breakfast is a very important meal." She cleared her throat of the moan about to escape from it, but did not retract her hand. "I'm usually famished in the morning."

"You'll have to be careful now, Miranda," he said. "By your lovely—if achingly subtle—gesture, you've just satisfied certain requirements for matriculation in this relationship. And thrown in a bonus verbal tease. You know what a man does with such things?"

"Unh-uh." She forced herself to withdraw her hand, which he grabbed just as it was about to become hers again. He kissed the fingertips, then quickly slipped his tongue around the gold ring on her little finger.

"He becomes just like a dog. Are you ready for that?"

"Um," she said, finally easing her hand away, face red. "Maybe. As you know, I like dogs."

Once the door was closed, Miranda took a moment to regulate her ragged breaths, then fetched the spare blanket and lay on top of the bed unmoving and still fully clothed. She could feel Billy's presence just as she could feel it on 47X. Here nothing separated them but chalky drywall splinted by two-by-four studs. There nothing had truly separated them but a yellow line down a sixteen-foot-wide road.

How could she have put pajamas on? With her clothes on, sleep itself was a vigil—a vigil for morning or mourning or whatever else that tomorrow might bring.

 22

Miranda was staring so intently at the spectacle in her yard she ran into Rocky Torez's vehicle—an old Chevy Suburban splotched with patches of primer, the fog lights of which had smiley-face covers. It was parked in her driveway behind a shiny red rental, a compact.

Equally preoccupied, Billy slammed on his brakes, missing the pileup by a fraction of an inch. The dogs lurched and thudded into the sides of his truck.

Vivianne and Rocky were seated at Miranda's Formica kitchen table, which had been moved outside from her living room. They appeared to be drinking coffee and eating biscuits amidst the rest of the living room furniture—couch, armchair, and coffee table (upon which Billy's tulips had been placed). Underneath all of it lay a midsized Persian rug, the color and quality of which told Billy that someone from Moab had already been by to visit. Rocky had just handed Vivianne—a willowy creature wearing a black cardigan that came to her ankles—the creamer.

Miranda removed herself slowly from the car and stood contemplating her home life, on display before her like a floor model. The dogs did not wait for the lowering of the tailgate but bounded out to inspect the new arrangement, and Billy fell in behind.

"So this is the famous cat-collecting peg leg." Vivianne extended her hand and Billy took it, remarking on the family resemblance in the brow and hill and dale of the cheeks. She had dark eyes, however, and what he considered overly voluptuous lips. Though lissome, she was entirely without the otherworldliness of her sister.

"You know, many a man has gone off the deep end—at least temporarily—for Miranda . . ." A tiny gold scarab lay in the hollow of her neck. On her feet were beaded slippers in red, which seemed somehow to have generated the rug beneath them.

"No," he said, "I didn't know. But I can imagine."

". . . Most of them, in my opinion, hopelessly defective in one way or another—" She continued to scrutinize Billy.

"Viv," Miranda interrupted, stomping her foot before staring good and hard at the rug.

Vivianne held up her hand without having yet looked at Miranda. "She had to move to Nowheresville just to get away from the pesterers and creeps, not to mention the equally unworthy men in whom she actually showed an interest. Now, an *author* has been added to the roster—" She paused long enough to bring the biscuit in her hand to her mouth. "But my first impression of you is one of . . . normalcy almost. Are things actually progressing?"

Billy was about to protest his normalcy when Vivianne turned to Miranda, presumably to greet and indulge her.

The teasing expression she wore, however, was quickly
supplanted by one of alarm. *"What* has happened to your
eyelashes?" It was Billy to whom she turned.

"Don't look at him!" Miranda shot back. Rocky was
frozen in rapt attention. "I singed them off. Smoking pot.
Which I was doing in a desperate attempt at relief from
head and eye pain."

Vivianne kept staring as if taking it all in, then at the
word "pain," slowly pulled Miranda into her arms and
sighed. "Why didn't you tell me? How long has this
headache thing been going on? Look at those poor reptil-
ian eyes now."

Miranda was giving Billy a look that said, *Don't.* He noted
she was not resisting her sister's embrace, but in fact
seemed to be returning it eagerly. Fascinated, Billy mentally wrapped her arms around him now that he'd been
supplied with a mock-up.

"They started after I moved here," Miranda began. "It
could be radon, which Billy says is common enough—and
easy to test for."

"Radon—" Vivianne repeated as if Miranda had said
green kryptonite.

"In that house?" Rocky was shaking his head.

Billy manufactured an attack of acute hunger. "Can I
have one of those biscuits? They look really good."

"Rocky made them." Vivianne pulled herself away
from Miranda and stood holding her at arm's length, as if
things would become clearer that way. "I went over to
say hello, what have you, and he happened to be making
biscuits. By the way"—Vivianne lightly touched Billy's
shoulder—"speaking of sublime food, that was the only

maroon tomato I've ever eaten. Charming note, but transcendent tomato."

"Heirloom tomatoes," Rocky said, shaking his head. "He don't tell anyone his secret, though."

"No, I doesn't," Billy spit back, sick of Rocky's redneck fakery. Rocky liked to make people think one thing, then uppercut them with science or math or mechanics. He knew the name of every indigenous grass, every invasive weed, every shrub, tree, bird, mammal, and fish in the Four Corners as well as history, archeology, tribal customs, and how wet the summer would be. Meanwhile, he liked to say *he don't* and talk in slow circles.

Miranda sat down and looked at Billy, then at her sister. "You ate a tomato that was for me?"

"Billy has plenty more," Rocky said. "He just has to be convinced to part with them."

"If you play your cards right"—Billy lowered his voice—"you'll be making salsa with them, and sauces. Broiling them, stuffing them, everything you can possibly imagine." He dug his hands in his pockets. "The note was just a quotation from a song—about *calling the calling off off.*"

Blushing, Miranda nevertheless managed to turn, all business, to Vivianne. "Did anyone call?"

"Actually, Mimi, you did get several calls."

"Mimi," Billy repeated, the door to her private world opening before him and beckoning him to float in.

"Yes, if you ever want to make her melt, call her Mimi. That's what pop called her, and Grandpa Billy, a man she worshiped—also a gardener, I just thought of that. Anyway, you had a call from someone named Janklow who says your book is in and taking up too much space, so could you come get it as soon as possible. Then you had a call from a Dr. Fujima who said you didn't call and he was worried about you. I asked him, being a doctor—an orthopedist, but who cares—what people took for migraines these days and he said he had no idea you had migraines but he would prescribe something called something-or-other and it would be at the pharmacy in Cortez. And then he gave me the name of a specialist in Denver and said he'd make a few calls. Wouldn't hurt to have some tests, he said. Wouldn't hurt for her to get to Denver every once in a while, either, I said."

"Vivianne!" Miranda flopped down on the couch and cradled a biscuit in one hand like a snowball about to be launched. "I'm supposed to be a *professional!*"

"He was happy to help."

"That's not the point."

"I don't know," Billy piped in. He had split a biscuit, and drizzled some honey marked Blue Wing on it. He began speaking with his mouth full. "You can still be the professional *and* let your people be experts: If you ignored that you'd sort of be insulting them." He swallowed. "Not allowing them to express themselves. I'd be happy to drive you to Denver." He picked up the jar of amber-colored honey. "This is incredible—what is it?"

"You don't have the patent on secrets, Steadman."

"Thank you, Mr. Steadman"—Vivianne sat on the couch beside her sister—"for your excellent rebuttal. Miranda has yet to acknowledge symbiosis in her line of work—"

"I'm afraid to ask who else called," Miranda interjected. "It's obvious Sullivan has been by to lend us a rug in need of tromping on and to fill you in on—everything, no doubt."

Vivianne took a sip of coffee and looked around. "As a matter of fact, yes, this rug was delivered in a most hideously sublime vehicle by a rather rakish man who was, in fact, the one to suggest a proper, Victorian picnic. Actually helped move the furniture. The rug is compliments of him and this Carson Sung author-person. One of whom is not shy of funds."

"Carson Sung?" Rocky's eyes bulged. "You're kidding!" Of course Rocky had read Sung, probably every last essay and poem, just like Sully. Probably memorized sections and didn't have to look up words like "oppugnant," "bloaviated," and "edacious." Billy gloated.

Vivianne looked irritated. "Personally, I've never heard of him. Who is he?"

"Local author." Rocky couldn't get over it. "Genius. I have all his books if you'd like to read one."

Miranda laughed. "You're the one who sent me *Wicked Sky*, Viv. It was in the box of steamy novels."

"It was?" For a brief moment Vivianne looked irritated, then shrugged it off, as if any ignorance of a subject on her part served only one purpose, that being to devalue it completely. "Mr. Vogt," she resumed her synopsis, "was the last to call."

Miranda's smile faded. "*Geez.* They have me surrounded."

"He's a great guy." Billy brought a small piece of biscuit too close to her mouth for her to be able to refuse. "Taste this honey."

"He's also the spokesperson for the triumvirate of seniors

obsessed with helping me live a happier life. What did he say?" The honey was truly unlike any she had ever tasted. "Mmm."

"Well, he *wanted* to send a fax," Vivianne began explaining.

"I can't believe you know Carson Sung." Rocky dug his hands in his pockets.

"Me neither, Rocky." Miranda smacked her lips. "It was all sort of random." She turned to Vivianne. "Well, what did Gregory want to send me? I don't have a fax."

"In point of fact," Vivianne trilled, "You do, Mimi! Coincidentally, that was what I chose as a housewarming present, given your love of dispatching written communications and your obvious current lack of inspiration. Brand-new and in the box. Though I respect your wanting to stay away from televisions and computers—being on the soul-searching mission you claim to have embarked upon and which I suspect you will find disappointing just as others have before you—everyone has a fax machine these days. Even Mr. Vogt. People can fax you articles, missives, drawings, short billets-doux." She glanced at Billy, who bowed obligingly at the reference. "It's odd you've never made use of one."

"Gregory has a fax? You're kidding. He struck me as sort of a Luddite."

"Not kidding. About any of it."

Rocky had started clearing the dishes. Miranda noted he wasn't wearing his signature overalls but cement gray Carhartt work pants and a white snap-button shirt. "She's not joking," he maintained. "I installed it. Top-of-the-line, and it works fine." He rocked on his heels for a moment. "Was Sung anything like Ishmael?"

Miranda considered this. "No, more like the narrator." She smiled. "As in third-person omniscient. If he ever comes over, I'll introduce you." Rocky, stunned, seemed unable to process the thought.

Vivianne was applying lipstick from a wand applicator she had retrieved from her sweater pocket. Opalescent mocha. "Anyway, when this Mr. Vogt found out you were still gone, he couldn't contain his disappointment. He had a poem that he wanted to read to you. I told him you had a fax, and why didn't he fax it. He said he could do that, but then paused. *I sort of wanted to read it to her,* he finally said. So I suggested he just leave a long recording. He ended up doing both." She paused, gazing up to watch a raven fly by and land on top of a fence post. She pointed the lipstick wand at it. "Raven brains are the most highly encephalized of any bird on Earth."

Billy raised his eyebrows.

"They have big brains," Rocky uttered like an acolyte to the high priestess. "Lots of neurons. Indicating social complexity and behavioral flexibility. They're not that predictable. That seems to be an indicator of intelligence."

"Which is why," Vivianne concluded, as if she'd set up her straight man and crow-prop in advance, "I chose the raven for Mimi's logo, so she could remember to flex her unpredictability from time to time."

The wind, which had been relatively quiet since they'd arrived, came up now, gently at first, ruffling the corners of the lace tablecloth. It held both a faint promise of the dry summer days that would follow and the far-off smell of heavy rain.

Billy breathed in deep. He wanted to know about the

poem, about Grandpa Billy, Miranda's parents, her proclivity to notes, and what book was taking up space in Janklow's Bookshop. "Seems to me she did that in moving to Otnip," he said to Vivianne. "An unexpected land of cream and honey, ravens, rugs, Victorian picnics, and smart people like Rocky."

Vivianne flashed a smile. "Well, despite your sarcastic tone, I will say that occasionally she does surprise me. As for Otnip, it has even borne a surprise for *me*."

"I feel a discourse coming on." Miranda had watched the raven fly away and disappear behind Billy's greenhouse. "You should know Viv believes what separates us from our troglodyte ancestors is our ability to make connections in life. To correlate or not to correlate, that is always the question." The wind, kicking up harder, blew dust in her eyes, which she rubbed gently. Those lucky enough not to have lost their eyelashes seemed to be screening out particulate matter without even knowing it.

"Miranda gets nervous when I make connections, see the bigger picture."

Billy contained his urge to smile. "Please go on regarding Miranda's nervousness."

"Please don't." Miranda frowned at Billy. "Just continue on predictably correlating, Viv, and go on with your surprise."

"Yes, please continue," Billy agreed. The crow corroborated his opinion by cawing three times.

Vivianne, removing strands of windblown hair from her mouth, seemed delighted to have gained an additional audience member in the bird. "Well," she began, "Rocky was giving me a tour of his beehives, you see, which prompted me to ask if he'd ever tried hiving *Bombus terrestris*—the common bumblebee . . ."

Miranda groaned. "Here we go," she said.

"—a small creature I've been somewhat infatuated with since I was young. Miranda knows."

"Because bumblebees defy the laws of physics," Billy suggested.

Rocky grunted, a combination of laughter and scorn.

"Well, what?" Billy shot him a look.

Miranda didn't like Rocky making Billy feel like a fool, especially not on her property. Her loyalty, which she had not really identified as such until this moment, veered sharply in Billy's direction.

"Tell them," Vivianne's tone was triumphant. "Just tell them what you told me."

Rocky stopped clearing the dishes and looked off toward his house. "The bumblebee has never defied the laws of physics," he said with Vivianne bobbing her head, practically mouthing along. "But only recently—in the last month, actually—has a physicist been able to illustrate exactly how they fly."

"They inflate themselves with air like blowfish," Miranda ventured, "and then move forward with tiny propeller-like wings. The dirigibles of the lower atmosphere."

Billy laughed, but Rocky ignored the comment. "It's called Unsteady Viscous Fluid Dynamics. It accounts for rapid wing oscillations in the way conventional aerodynamics never could. Bumblebees create—with their front and back wings doing different things—their own vortices of wind, which then provide them with the lift they need. Computers have been crucial in capturing just how it works."

Miranda was silent. She tried to imagine the labor involved in the creation of the minivortices. It sounded like bumblebees had to work really, really hard.

"So," Billy concluded, "the mystery is gone. Bumblebees do not defy science in lazily getting from flower to flower. Science and furiously demanding work propel them along. I find that sort of—depressing. Or bittersweet."

Me too! Miranda didn't say.

"No, not depressing, that's just it!" Vivianne had her arms up, showing them all the creation of the world anew. "Their purpose is to challenge science, to *look* like they defy reason. That's their purpose."

"They also pollinate flowers," Rocky humbly pointed out, staring at his fingernails now. "There would be no flowers without them."

Vivianne ignored him. "The point is: There is beauty in explication, and there is beauty in mystery. Occasionally, when the two collide, we must acknowledge, and celebrate!"

Billy noted that the raven had landed again. Same post. The wind ruffled its feathers, but it did not move. A couple of napkins wafted from the table. The plastic vase holding the tulips was about to topple, but he quickly reached over and grabbed it. "That's your anecdote, huh?" he said to Vivianne.

Vivianne smiled. "I've been thinking about bumblebees my whole life—and here I missed this fresh piece of scientific news. Then I make a last-minute excursion to a pinprick even on a local map—and in a beautiful moment of serendipity, I learn something germane. Yes, quite anecdotal. And useful for tormenting Ivo."

The name was too close to Igor for Billy not to conjure up a loyal lab assistant at her side. "Who's Ivo?"

"Her worthless boyfriend," Rocky offered.

"Who spoils her rotten," Miranda added.

"My current beau," Vivianne amended. "Who is flying us to Sweden for a week so he can study microlepidoptera. I've agreed to tag along for further research into Swedish faeries, the Älvor. To torment him, I may delve into water sprites, perhaps the most erotic of all male mythical creatures, and wingless at that." She beamed at Rocky, whose look was one of a suitor next in line.

Miranda fired Billy a disgusted look that said, *See how she tortures people?* Not that she wanted Vivianne going off to Sweden right away: Wasn't it already the next day there? "How long can you stay?" She supposed she had done an equal or greater amount of torturing right here with Billy.

"Leaving tomorrow, Cortez to Stockholm. Five connections."

"That seems a bit *short*." Billy disapproved: The last thing Miranda needed just then was to feel abandoned.

"It is far too short," Vivianne agreed. "Squeezed into the agenda at the last minute." She approached Miranda and stood squarely in front of her. "I came to make sure you were in good hands, and it looks to me"—she nodded toward Billy—"as if you might be. Anecdotes aside, this touching down on Otnip soil was meant as a small gesture to let you know I'm here for you—maybe not physically but in spirit. Whenever you want to talk about Mom and Dad or Grandpa Billy or a client—I'm here. I came to tell you so in person, just so you'd know. Okay?"

Miranda's eyes filled again, and she had to look up to contain the pooling water.

"Listen," Vivianne saved her, "Rocky promised me some of that honey, and I forgot to take him up on it. We'll fetch it. But I think we should all have dinner together, don't you?" No one objected, and she began folding up the lace tablecloth. Rocky picked up two corners to help, then started to whistle; it was something complicated and baroque.

Billy, meanwhile, threw sticks for the dogs and wondered whether to go home or stay with Miranda. If he left, it would feel like desertion; but if he stayed, he might be intruding. Vivianne and Rocky loaded into the Suburban, and Billy listened to the roar of what he knew to be a tinkered-with and perfectly tuned Porsche engine.

"Maybe you could help me get this stuff back inside." Miranda came up to Billy. "I'm desperate to see that rug on my floor!" The salmon-colored field showcased an intricate floral design in sap green, sienna, and bits of brilliant red. "Can you believe this thing?"

"Quite something. And just for being *you*." They spent ten minutes moving Miranda back inside, after which Billy crossed his arms. "I suppose you're through with me now that you have no further use of a strong back?"

Miranda had found his note, read it, cracked a smile, and was eyeing the envelope from St. Mary's on the top of the pile of mail he had left for her. He watched as she picked it up. She didn't open it but plopped herself on the couch.

"Why don't you make your index finger as useful as your strong back and play that message. You need to hear Gregory recite. You like poetry, don't you, with a name like that?"

"Poetry is my middle name." He observed how she had placed herself on the couch, as if half waiting for someone to sit down next to her. He pressed the message button, and, before thinking any more about it, sat so close to her the only thing to do with his arm was to reach it around her.

"Miranda," the deeply raspy voice began before she had a chance to react to his arm. "I spoke with your sister, who said I might do this. The girls agree with me I found the perfect poem for you—for us all, really. Whitman yet again. Forgive my voice, I've had a bit of a chest cold. Don't worry, I'm taking care of it." He cleared the wet phlegm from his throat, spit, and began.

"*A noiseless patient spider.*" The words were slow and deliberate. "*I mark'd where on a little promontory it stood isolated.*" He emphasized the last word and Miranda tensed. Billy pulled her closer, then, with his other hand, took the envelope from her and laid it on the couch. One thing at a time.

"*Mark'd how to explore the vacant vast surrounding.*" Miranda focused on the feel of Billy's warm hand on her right bicep and his arm around her neck. She breathed and dropped her shoulders.

"*It launch'd forth filament, filament, filament, out of itself,/ Ever unreeling them, ever tirelessly speeding them. And you O my soul where you stand . . . Surrounded, detached, in measureless oceans of space,/ Ceaselessly musing, venturing, throwing, seeking the spheres to connect them.*" He coughed once, a cough triggered by his need for amplified volume and intensity.

"*Till the bridge you will need be form'd*"—he sighed—" *'till the ductile anchor hold.*" He moaned sweetly. "*Till the gossamer thread you fling—catch somewhere, O, my soul.*"

In the silence that followed a gossamer thread arced and attached somewhere, the delicate echo of an image.

"It's a beaut'," Gregory finally said, "isn't it, Miranda? *The gossamer thread you fling catch somewhere.* My, my, *my.* The poet manages to peal out truth on occasion—and the rest of us poor devils are blessed if we hear at all. Well, I read that six or seven times, and you know what I did? I called each one of m' damn kids. Then I called the girls and read it to them. I think I might write about it for that old-people magazine. Fling my own thread out, feeble as it might be." He managed to wheeze out a laugh.

"Anyway, listen to me babble. Call me on Monday and we'll resume with *Song of Myself.* And Miranda, thank you, m'dear, for all the flinging you have already done."

A beep signaled the end of the message. Billy extracted his arm from around her, took her hand, and placed it over his heart. He was thinking about spiders flinging their threads and bumblebees managing to heave their swerving bodies from flower to flower. Of ravens, cawing their big brains out, as if we could understand. The world of nature surrounded him, Miranda was next to him.

"It's just an ordinary heart," he said, pressing her palm close to its quickening beat. "Scarred a bit like most people's. It buzzes and wobbles like a bumblebee. It flings things out, not often, but with faith—"

Miranda looked at him, wishing he would just keep on talking. During breakfast she had noticed a languorous timbre in his voice—a slow, Southern sort of quality. Had it always been there or had his vocal cords relaxed in the last twenty-four hours? "What exactly are you saying?" A stupid question, meant to keep him talking and in that same tone of voice.

"What I'm saying," he slowly but eagerly obliged, "is that we have a little time on our hands before Vivianne and Rocky come back. I need to check on my tomatoes and pick a few things for dinner; you could read your mail. Then, what I guess I'm saying is I hope to come back, put my wares on your counter, and sit with you again while you tell me what this guy was like, the one who died. Everything you can remember, everything that's in the packet, every impression—everything, Miranda. So we can remember him. So we can start remembering people again. We'll listen to the wind and think about birds and bees and spiders. Then we'll open the exceptional bottle of wine my mom wanted you to have."

"Your mom"—Miranda swallowed—"knows about me?"

Billy nodded. "Well, knows about your effect on me. Speaking of intoxication, we'll have dinner slightly drunk—which will allow us to risk catching each other's eye every so often. You know what we'll be thinking, though, right?"

"Uh-uh."

"Sure you do. We'll be thinking of being alone again. Of being alone *together*."

Miranda's solar plexus ached. Emotions were being born, and they came into the world kicking and screaming and gasping for breath.

"You must have some thoughts about all this—" He removed her hand from his heart and began twisting the ring on her little finger. "Tell me"—he shrugged—"a little of what you're feeling."

He was waiting. Not for the right answer, and not with the kind of expectation Miranda hated. Just waiting. "What am I feeling?" She didn't think before answering. "Sadness." The word popped up like a bubble from the bottom of the sink. She looked at Billy. "But not the black and wretched kind. A tugging, heavy, sweet sadness. A paperweight. Ripe fruit in a velvet bag." She paused. "If I were Vivianne, I'd highlight the connection to your theory of baggage. We accumulate. We weigh more."

He squeezed her hand, a small gesture that nevertheless had the effect of liberating further imagery from its original metaphor: the heavy weight of blankets in bed, she said, the weight of a fine story, of an opulent rug, the weight of someone's life and limb bearing down on her, the glorious weight of things staying put rather than spinning off the face of the Earth. Wasn't that sadness, she asked him, in a way—

Billy didn't let her finish, he sank her into the couch and lay on top, and then grabbed her hair in his fingers. "Listen," he whispered, moving hands and thumbs to her cheeks, "sadness is the deep root of happiness, Miranda. Don't you think?" Levering his full bodyweight into her, he drew a featherweight finger down her neck.

She felt him wedge his hand between their hearts, where it paused for a moment before finding her nipple and rubbing over it again and again. Breath moist, he brought his mouth down and kissed her—lips, mouth, tongue, tender, fierce. She tasted honey and felt its golden warm liquidity in her veins and sighed, swelled inside—was just about to surrender her soul when she felt herself being swept upright, off the couch and to a standing position. Like a puppet pulled up from its heap on the floor.

Billy laughed, dropped her hand, and then eyed her up and down. "Mm-mm-*mm*, woman. I want to undress you. Kiss every micromillimeter of you. I've waited a long time . . . But I'm not going to do it, not until you're ready, so ready you'll beg me. You'd beg, wouldn't you, Miranda?"

She shook her head, meaning to state categorically that she would never beg to rub herself all over someone—even if this image had completely sabotaged her neurocircuitry. "I'd do something even harder than that."

"You've got my interest now." Billy crossed his arms. "What would you do?"

Miranda could still feel his hands on her face and blushed again. She thought her whole body must be blushing. He was winning another round, she was flailing. "I'd ask you *nicely*—"

"Really." Billy stroked his chin in one clean movement. "Hard to imagine. What would you ask for? How would you say it?"

She willed herself to be clever in a time of need, to rise to the occasion—then gave up. "I'd say, 'You know what you were doing just a second ago, Billy?' "

"And I'd say, 'No, Miranda, I don't recall exactly. Which part?' "

"And I'd say, 'Don't play dumb, that part about my lips and throat and my—' " She paused, laying her hand on her own chest as if to suggest other body parts she might want included in round two. He waited for her to speak further. "Well," she took another tack. "Remember when Rosemarion Fall . . ."

"Gets it on with the stranger?" Billy was smiling his head

off, now, eager to oblige. "Yeah. I remember, Miranda. Vividly. I've read it several times."

Probably not as many as I have, Miranda thought. "Well, I—"

"Your impulses are dead-on," Billy interrupted again with a very familiar kiss on the cheek, his hand having managed, in the blink of an eye, to find the back of her neck and to caress it. "Dead-on and *fully* synchronized with mine. Now, if you'll excuse me, I'm needed in the greenhouse," he said. "Soon to return." He removed a pack of Juicy Fruit from his back pocket, took out two pieces, and unwrapped one, which he handed to Miranda. "Sublimate, baby," he advised. "I'm sure you've become an expert, just like me. Remember, what doesn't kill it only makes it stronger—"

Miranda, still trying to fathom the union of tenderness, ardor, and cunning in a single man—and in the only man in her visual range—followed him out the door and watched the dogs tag along across the road as naturally as if they'd done it for years. She watched Billy cross the yellow line, knowing he would not turn around. His tulips waved, though, when the wind came up.

Then the same wind blasted hard, and cottonwood branches thwapped against the roof. Out of the corner of her eye, Miranda saw tumbleweeds roll down the empty highway toward Rocky's place. For the first time, she wished even fiercer gusts would come screaming in from out of nowhere, red dust devils from the desert swirling at her feet. She wanted trash to fly and birds to waft sideways past her, dry squalls to lash and beckon and blow because that was what happened in Otnip, in their little corner of the world.

Her fever cooled by the native wind, Miranda finally turned and walked back to her house. She fetched the envelope from St. Mary's, took it to her desk, where she sat down, and held it in her hands like an unopened gift. Then, slowly, she bent up the prongs of the brad, lifted the brown flap, and saw the corners of a photo there, clipped to the top of a pile of papers. She peered in. He looked like his voice, and he was smiling.